Tournament of the Divine

Book Two

Written by William T. Kearney

Illustrated by Banana Takemura

Edited and Formatted by Andres Perez and Zach Cole

Title Design by James Biggie

Special Thanks to:

Matt Dennion, Ryan George Collins (The Omni Viewer), Davis Madole (TitanGoji), Daniel Sipiora, and Chloe Cooper for their help promoting the series.

A huge thank you to Ace Marrok for helping with the cover layout.

Cover design copyright 2020 William Kearney.

Art by Banana Takemura. Used with permission.

ISBN 978-1-7360625-0-0

PROLOGUE: REMEMBER THIS?

My name is Sun Wukong! The Handsome Monkey King! The Victorious Fighting Buddha! The Grand Sage Equal to Heaven! Most importantly, I'm… lost…

I don't know where I am right now. There's a large tree in front of me under a dark, cloudy sky. This tree is really big, actually. Because of the size, I swear it could be part of the Divine Tree. It isn't all divine and mighty, though.

Oh boy! I have such an urge to climb it! Mr. Knight would probably say I'm acting like a kid, but I can't help myself! Besides, I can use the view from up there to see where I am!

I leap onto the tree. My fingers and toes dig into the wood, locking myself onto the tree. Looking at them, it's weird how small my hands seem compared to this tree.

"Hey Sun!"

I know that voice. Mr. Knight! I'm so happy he's here! I was worried about where he was! I really haven't let him out of my sight since that horse thing attacked him. I think Mr. Knight called it a Knuckle-Vee? It was some sort of Celtic monster.

I turn around to see him, but I'm blown away at the fact that Mr. Knight is taller than me. Normally I am taller than him, but now he looks as tall as the tree. I have to glance up at him. He's not only taller, he's gigantic!

The giant-sized Mr. Knight stares up to the cloudy skies. "I don't want you staying out too long, Sun. It seems like the weather is going to get nasty soon."

Mr. Knight is such a worrywart with me! Sure, I've always loved that, but still, he's right. Plus, he doesn't need to be out in the mess that is coming.

"Shut up, human! I'm the Great Sage Equal to Heaven! I don't need your concern!"

Did that just leave my mouth?

I can feel my arms cross themselves, and my cheeks puff out like I'm pouting. Why am I doing this? I can't control my body for some reason.

Am I possessed? I can't be possessed! I'm the Great Victorious Fighting Monkey King! Nothing can be strong enough, or dumb enough, to try to possess me!

But then why can't I control myself, and why would I act like this towards Mr. Knight, especially when he is caring about me? That's not like me at all! At least, not anymore.

Mr. Knight chuckles as he begins to rub my head. "And, remind me, how much power does that title hold again?"

Oh, I love it when Mr. Knight pats my head! Even if he is teasing me! I can't control my body, but I can still feel my cheeks burning red as he does so! My tail is putting up such a fight not to wag.

My arms begin to wave around over my head. "S-stop mocking me!"

Why did I yell at Mr. Knight like that? I can't believe I just did that! And what's wrong with my voice? It sounds different. It sounds whinier.

Even though I can't control what I say or do, I apparently can control what I see. I focus on my own body. My arms and legs are stumpy, and my odd human breasts are missing too. That's not too much of a loss. They made me feel off-balance as I grew up. But Mr. Knight does like them for some reason…

So, Mr. Knight isn't a giant, I shrunk. I'm a kid again! Gah! I don't like being a kid! This makes it the third time I have to go through it again! But how am I a kid again?

"I'm going to do as I wish, human! So, as my servant, you will let me do so!"

2

S-servant?! I haven't called him that since…I was a kid. I'm starting to think I'm not going through a third childhood.

"I'm your caretaker, Sun. Not your servant," Mr. Knight says in a more scolding tone.

Mr. Knight never talked to me like that. Except for…wait…if I'm a kid again, then what about Mr. Knight?

I gaze toward Mr. Knight's legs. My eyes, the only thing I'm able to control, open widely at the surprise. He doesn't have his cane; he doesn't need it. Not yet…

This is… the first regret in my reborn life.

"Same thing! Now if you excuse me, I am going to enjoy myself. You can do whatever it is you do," my child self speaks in a rude way, shooing him away.

I forgot how much of a brat I was! I don't like hearing myself talk to Mr. Knight like this, even if it is a younger me. Still, even though I talked to him like this, I still had the same feelings for Mr. Knight as I do now. Well, not as strong, I guess.

Even with my stumpy arms and legs, I easily climb up the massive tree. The thunder explodes in the sky as lightning flashes above the tree. This should have been the first sign that something bad was going to happen. The skies are pitch black and the wind begins to pick up as I climb higher.

I can hear Mr. Knight yell through the loud winds. "Sun! We should go back inside!" I can hardly hear him, but I can still easily make out what he said. I just ignore him.

The thunder explodes above us again, but this time, rain begins to fall heavily on top of us.

Why can't I control my body? Why can't I stop this? Why do I have to relive it again?

This is it. This is when the lighting strikes the tree. I can't take my eyes away from the dark, stormy sky. I'm forced to watch.

I can see something through the clouds, but it's not lighting. It's huge and seems like it's made of stone. No, it looks like a giant fist falling from the sky. The lighting from the storm sparks on it as it falls closer to me.

What is happening? This is a different memory. A memory from an old life. Why do I need to relive this one too? Is it because both were caused by my arrogance?

The fist falls closer to me. My body won't move. It's frozen as it grips tightly on the tree.

I might not be able to control my body, but tears begin pouring from my eyes, down my cheek.

I can't turn away… I want to though…

"Sun!" I hear Mr. Knight yell at me. Through the roars of the wind, thunder, and rain, I can hear his voice easily.

I begin to panic. Too much is going on. I glance back and forth, up and down. I saw Mr. Knight again during this, but he was not wearing his normal clothes. He wore a familiar gown. The robes of a Buddhist monk, Xuanzang.

I feel the grip of arms wrapping around my small body, pulling me off the tree. Leading us to fall.

The fist is right above us, the ground below. Both coming closer, the world goes white…. Nothing around me. Not even my body.

But I do see something… a hand, reaching out towards me. It is not the fist, it is full of kindness and warmth as it comes closer…

"You're alright now…" I hear Mr. Knight's voice… with another, familiar voice... echoing along…

"Huh!" I open my eyes from the white void. Waking up after hearing his calming voice.

The first thing I see is the rusty ceiling of Mr. Knight's rolling house. I sit up and begin to check around. I'm back in the metal, rusty house on wheels I now call home.

4

I'm in my pajamas, my body is tall, and I have this ridiculous cleavage again! Looking behind me, I see Mr. Knight. Sleeping on the couch right next to my bed, like always.

I guess it was a dream, or more like a nightmare. I guess what happened to Mr. Knight and that monster must have gotten to me. Almost losing him had brought up some bad memories.

The sun isn't even up yet. Must still be late. I should try to get some more sleep. Besides, soon I won't have to worry about anything like that happening ever again. So, I should just toss those thoughts out of my head.

I flip over on my stomach and happily nuzzle onto Mr. Knight's upside-down head. Knowing that once the sky shines this morning, I am one step closer to never feeling distressed ever again!

I won't let my arrogance ruin anything else in my life…

I'll fight for him…

I always will…

CHAPTER ONE: CHECKING UP ON A GOD

Another weird dream? It's been happening a lot lately, ever since the Nuckelavee attack a couple of weeks ago.

I'm still a bit tired and I haven't even opened my eyes yet. I woke up to Sun wrapped around me in the middle of the night. Took me a while to pry her off me.

I want to sleep a bit more, but I'm too distracted by some sort of scratching sound. I can also hear Sun humming. What's happening?

I open my eyes, waking up to the morning ahead of me. Though I don't have my glasses, I can easily make out the first thing I see: Sun, in her pajamas, sweeping the floor with a broom.

Not sure what I enjoy more, seeing her in her revealing pajamas, or the fact she is cleaning up the RV for once. Sun helps me with the heavy lifting, but she tends to do her best at avoiding cleaning up with me.

Sun sees me waking up. "Morning, Mr. Knight!" she happily greets me.

NAMES: SUN WUKONG, MONKEY KING, VICTORIOUS FIGHTING BUDDHA, GREAT SAGE EQUAL TO HEAVEN. FACTION: BUDDHIST.

GODHOOD: DEMIGOD, ANIMAL. HUMAN NATIONALITY: CHINESE.

I begin to sit up from the couch I was sleeping on, yawning loudly. "What are you doing, Sun?"

"Well, I couldn't sleep so I figured I'd get the house cleaned. Since Hermes is coming to check up on us, it seemed like the best thing to do!" Sun says happily.

"I don't think Hermes cares about how the house looks," I reassure her. The first time Hermes was here, the house was as big a mess as it always has been, and he still gave me the okay on being a caretaker. "I'm sure he'll be more focused on how you're doing,"

"Still, I figured I'd get the whole place cleaned for you! I have been sort of a slob on you," Sun nervously chuckles. I'm glad she's aware of this about her.

As I gaze at Sun's smiling face, I let out another loud yawn into the air.

Sun inspects me with in concern. "Are you all right?"

I begin to rub my eyes as I finish my yawn. "Yeah, yeah, I'm fine. Just had a weird dream…"

"You too?"

"Huh?"

"Oh, nothing, Mr. Knight!" She utters, obviously trying to change the conversation. "But what happened in your dream?"

I reach for my glasses, laying on the shelf under the window. "Well I… I don't remember…" I tell her while I put on my glasses.

It's been like this for as long as I could remember. I have a weird dream, I wake up, and I don't remember a thing about it. I'm not even sure if it's the same dream or not.

"Y-you're not having nightmares about that thing, right?" She inquires with concern.

I guess she's talking about what happened three weeks ago with the Nuckelavee. I still feel unaffected by what I saw. It feels like I didn't even see all that horror in person. It felt more like I watched a horror movie.

"No, no, Sun. It was a weird dream. Not a nightmare."

The dreams are nothing to really panic about. I have them occasionally. It's kind of a random thing for me. Although, they have been more frequent since the Nuckelavee. I don't know, maybe Sun has a right to feel uneasy.

From outside I can hear something wet hitting the R.V., taking my mind off whatever I was thinking about.

"Sun, what was that?"

"I'm washing the house outside!"

"What?"

She points to the door with a smile on her face. I raise an eyebrow to her as she mentions this and passes me my cane.

Since the Nuckelavee destroyed my cane, Sun crafted me a makeshift one until I get the money to replace it. A long metal pipe with two tennis balls on both sides. It's sure as hell not perfect but it does the job. It's also a nice gesture.

That reminds me, when Hermes gets here, I should see if I am able to replace my God Slayer or not. Not sure how often I will be attacked by an Unfollowed, but it's better to play it safe.

With my cane in my hand, I make my way outside. As I open the door, I look to the side of the R.V. seeing Sun there, with a bucket of soapy water and a sponge.

She waves happily to me. "Hi, Mr. Knight!"

"Hey, Mr. Knight!" I hear in a familiar voice above the R.V. I walk out a little further so I can see the top of the motor home. Low and behold, Sun is also up there, mopping the top of the home for some reason.

She's been using her copying power a lot recently. A few nights ago, I played cards with all three of them. Just regular poker, no stripping involved. Well, there was nudity, but that's Sun being Sun. It was a weird night, to say the least.

What is harder than living with one sexy tomboy? Three of them, and two of them are soaking wet in their pajamas, which is a short yellow tank top and high up jean shorts.

"Both of you inside the house, now!" I yell at the doubles.

They stare at each other in confusion as to why I am upset. They shrug to each other as the one on the ceiling leaps down to the ground with her mop in tow. I walk up to the two, seeing them both soaking wet, as I thought. I try to avoid staring as the three of us walk inside.

The doubles stand back next to the original, or at least who I think is the original, as they stare at me in confusion. "I told you, I don't want you wearing that outside the house."

"But you never specified which me!" The three of them declare all together. Each one giving me a victorious look on their face, thinking they have won this battle.

"Don't play that crap!"

As I scold Sun, I can hear knocking at the door.

"That must be Hermes! Can at least one of you get changed?"

I can hear Sun and her doubles sniffing loudly. "That doesn't smell like Hermes..." I hear one say as they begin to whisper. I swear they sound a bit panicked.

"I'm coming! Just give Sun a second, she's not decent-"

As I open the door, I'm met with a sight I was sure I'd never see in person again.

Susanoo, the Shinto Sky God, stands on the other side with a ditsy smirk.

NAMES: SUSANOO-NO-MIKOTO, GOD OF THE SUMMER STORM. FACTION: SHINTO.

GODHOOD: SKY. HUMAN NATIONALITY: JAPANESE.

"Then I guess I came at the right time! Right?" Susanoo speaks in a joking manner.

She still smells like smoke and alcohol, and she still moves like she's been drinking. Even as she stands, her body wobbles in place, and her cheeks are red from drinking.

"How did you find our house?"

Of all the people I'd expect to knock on my door, Susanoo was not one of them. Mostly because we didn't tell her where we lived. Sun specifically demanded we never tell her.

"I told ya this last time, I was- Oh wait! I forgot ya were dead when I explained that." She makes it sound like that was just a mild distraction.

"Wow… Thanks for your concern…"

She continues to talk while ignoring my comment. "Well, as a Sky God I'm able to use the air around me to track down my prey, and I'm hoping to eat some monkey tonight!" She proclaims happily to me while I mentally groan, disappointed at her joke. She pushes past me as she walks right in. "Sun Wukong, my love! Prepare to spread your-" Susanoo halts what she is saying as her jaw drops at the sight of the three Sun's in their pajamas.

The three watch on in fear at Susanoo. "C-crap it *is* her!" They shout in unison.

I fear for what's to come next in this scene. "Aaaahhhh!" I hear screamed behind me. I turn to see Susanoo's Caretaker, Momoko peaking her head inside. Like the last time I met her, she still seems incredibly timid. "W-What were you doing in here?!"

I turn back and forth at her and the three Suns, realizing why she is acting like this. "*Oh*! No! No! It's not what it looks like! That's what Sun sleeps in!"

"T-Then why are there three of her, and why are two of them wet?!" Momoko nervously asks a question I'm not sure if I can answer without making the situation worst.

"… I-I don't know what to tell you…." I respond in defeat., knowing this nervous wreck of a girl has me in a checkmate.

"I'll tell ya why he has 'em like this…." Susanoo states in a serious tone. She turns to me. "You're wanting to make a Disgraced Goddess's dream come true!" She says happily. Even she is referring to herself as a disgrace. She bows her head at me. "Thank you! Thank you!" She's sounding as if she is nearing tears.

She raises her head back up and stares at the three with a perverted smirk. The three Suns gaze back at her in fear.

"Sun, turn back into one and get changed in the bathroom!" I tell her, hoping to avoid having my home as the base of Susanoo's personal harem and avoid having Sun as said harem.

"G-good idea, Mr. Knight!" The three remark. In a cloud of smoke, the three revert into one. She quickly picks up her normal clothes and rushes to the bathroom to change. Forcibly shutting the door behind her.

"What?! Aaawwww!" Susanoo whines. She glances back at me. "I thought you were cool! I woulda let ya watch!" She proclaims in defeat. I never thought a Shinto god would be this…. kinky?

"Why are you two even here? Didn't you guys leave a few weeks ago to finish the tryouts?"

Though her body shakes in fear, Momoko forces on a happy face. "Y-yes! S-Susanoo is just one victory away from getting into the Royale…"

"Really? That's great! Congratulations-"

I reach my arm out to pat Momoko on the back before she cuts me off.

The Shrine priestess raises her Kendo stick at me. "Aaaahhh!"

Shit! I forgot she doesn't like to be touched! I brace myself for what is to come next. Only to hear Momoko begin to inhale and exhale heavily. "C-calm down…. Y-you can do this…." She slowly begins to lower her kendo stick to the side and begins to relax.

Well, more so than before. She bows her head in apology to me. "S-sorry…. I-I'm getting better! I-I only hit ninety-nine percent of the people who touch me now!"

Should I be happy that I'm the one percent here?

I look at her as she continues to shake in fear for some reason. "Uh…. Would you like to come in?" I query.

The young priestess stares at me for a moment and peaks her head further in. "S-Susanoo…" She loudly whispers.

I turn to where Susanoo was standing before I focused on Momoko. But she is not there.

By the bathroom door, Susanoo's on the floor, trying to peek in under the gap between the floor and the door. After hearing Momoko, she raises her head up and turns back toward us in a bored expression.

"Wha?"

"I-is *it* hiding in here?" Momoko loudly whispers.

Susanoo raises an eye brow to her Caretaker. "Is the giant multi-headed dragon in this crappy little car-house thing? No, it's not Momo…." She sarcastically informs as she continues to try to spy on Sun.

Hearing it's okay, Momoko begins to walk inside. She timidly glances around as she enters, like an animal in unfamiliar territory.

Multi-headed dragon? There are a lot of those in different mythologies, but only one comes to mind if Susanoo was involved. The one that was involved with the most important story of her.

"Are you talking about Orochi?"

"Yeah, Momo has been shakin' in her panties about that since I started to live with her…"

"W-well you came back, right?"

"I keep tellin' ya, ya got nothing to worry about…."

Every mythology has some sort of serpent, but I haven't heard about any of them being reborn like the other gods. Maybe they're considered Unfollowed and had to be taken in by the Enforcers, like what Nemesis did to the Nuckelavee. Or they could appear completely different now, being reborn as half-human like the others.

Still…

"Not to scare Ms. Hirata more here, but are you sure? I mean, I recently had to deal with a skinless centaur, I don't want to be troubled by thoughts of a dragon-"

Sun swings the bathroom door open, changed into her normal clothing. The door hits the peeping Susanoo in the face.

"Ow! Son of a whore!" Susanoo shouts as she grips her face.

Sun glances over at me and Momoko, with an intrigued expression on her face. "What's this about a dragon?"

Instead of answering her, I point down to the injured Susanoo. Sun looks down at the Shinto god in an uninterested gaze.

"Oh… Sorry…" Sun says, not at all sounding like she means it.

"Sun, be nice!"

Sun crosses her arms and puts on a pouty face. "I said I was sorry, didn't I?" She responds in a snarky tone.

13

Susanoo, standing back up, rubs her head as she observes Sun with a frown on her face. "I'll forgive ya Bouncy Monkey…. All I ask is a kiss on my bruised head…. Or you can sit on my face, one of the two!"

"Mr. Knight, is that dirty?"

"Yes…"

My annoyed expression goes away instantly as Momoko's wooden sword flies past me. Twirling in the air. Sun backs away quickly, only for the sword to strike Susanoo in the head.

"Ow!" The Storm Goddess shouts as she falls back from the hit. Her straw hat bounces off. "Damn it Momo! I just got hit in the face by a door!"

Me and Sun are shocked about the force that went into that throw. Momoko runs past me towards Susanoo and picks up her kendo sword.

"I-I'm sorry Susanoo! B-but I told you, you have to behave!" Momoko raises her sword and begins to swing it on Susanoo rapidly. "Y-you represent our shrine! T-take it seriously!" She shouts, with a surprisingly angry expression on her face.

My and Sun's eyes widen as we watch the Young Caretaker beating her goddess with a wooden sword. Not because it is a horrible sight. It's more for Susanoo's reaction.

Susanoo curls up into a ball. "Ha ha ha-ow! Ha ha ha- ow, fuck ow- ha!" She laughs happily at the abuse.

Sun and I glance at each other, lost for words. I don't think this is abuse. I think it's only a weird spat they normally go through. The odd thing is, I can easily believe that with these two.

The sound of knocking at the door causes this whole gag to end as we all turn our head toward the entrance.

I look to see a familiar face: my old friend, Ell.

"Hey, knock-knock!" She announces, peeking her head in and waving. "I'm not interrupting, am I?" She asks in confusion at what is happening. Her eyes pointed toward Momoko who still has her kendo sword raised above Susanoo. "Oh my, this seems fun! Do I get a swing?"

"I'll give you a swing…" I hear Sun mumble. I elbow her in response. "Ow!"

I give Ell a smile. "Ell, your back in town?"

Sun sarcastically raises her arms in excitement. "Yay…."

Ell walks over and wraps her arms around my neck. Pulling me close to embrace her. I can see Sun growing angrier by the second as she glares at us.

"I came to check up on you! I was so worried when I heard what happened! So worried, I brought you a gift…." She walks back to the door and reaches her hand outside. She pulls in someone I've seen a lot in the Gods' Wrath tournaments and who I remember a little bit of from the Nuckelavee incident.

A young person, can't tell if they're male or female, two messy pigtails, a robe-like outfit with long sleeves covering their arms, and most notably, two shut eyes with markings down the cheek.

"Loki?" I shout in surprise as Ell Pulls him…her…Loki by the cheek.

NAMES: LOKI, THE LIESMITH, THE TANGLER, DADDY LONG LEGS. FACTION: ASGARD

GODHOOD: TRICKSTER. HUMAN NATIONALITY: GERMAN.

"Ow! Ow! Ow!" The Trickster cries out.

"Now…. Say it…." Ell threatens in a sinister-sounding voice that does not match her complacent expression.

"Ow! Okay! I'm sorry, darling! I'm sorry I got you attacked and killed by the skinless horse! But we had fun, right?"

"No, not really…" I respond.

"That's it?" I hear Sun yell. "Just an apology? You know the hell you put us through?" she states in resentment. "What are you going to say about this, Mr. Knight?"

Can't say I disagree with Sun's response. I mean it is because of Loki, what happened… well, happened. But at the same time, he brought me back, and it was my own fault for even being there.

Plus, there is something I realize about all of this as I look at Ell with disappointment on my face. "That's all I can ask for, isn't it?"

"I'm afraid so…" Ell says with a hint of disappointment in her voice, still gripping onto Loki's cheek.

Tricksters have been pulling these sorts of horrible pranks on people since they were reborn. They had no regrets and never apologized for them. Granted, I haven't heard of an incident as horrible as what Loki did.

I sigh as I reach my hand out for Loki to shake. "I guess that's alright. In fact, maybe I should thank you for bringing me back…"

He seems revolted at the sight of this gesture. "D-don't thank me! That ruins it!" He shouts at me, making me jump back a step. "If you're not pissed, then I didn't do anything fun, darling!"

Sun walks past me and flips him around to confront him. Giving Loki the same furious snarl she gave the Nuckelavee. "Don't talk to Mr. Knight like that!"

Loki laughs in her face. Sun responds by pushing him back. "Ohohoh! Now that's what I am talking about! Ohohoh!"

As I watch Sun turn away from Loki in ill humor, Ell hugs me again.

"I'm sorry I wasn't here for you earlier. I only recently found out what happened. This idiot decided to keep it a secret from me. I only found out after he decided to run his mouth to Ares. He didn't tell on him, Loki's just a loud talker," she says calmly as she continues to hold me.

"It's alright. I was more worried about you."

"Tck…" I hear Sun clicking her tongue next to me in anger.

"Oh my, why would that be?"

I point to the Trickster as I explain. "Well, Loki sort of caused multiple deaths and pissed off Nemesis."

"Ah, yes! Wasn't that great? Ohohoh!"

"Oh that! We only got a little hand-written warning from Hermes. Asking Loki not to do it again."

"That's it?" Me and Sun ask. I speak more in confusion; she is certainly angrier about the subject.

Ell shrugs her shoulders. "Oh yes! Not the first time I was given one of these notes. Of course, they will not do a thing about it."

"What do you mean?"

Ell leans in closer to my face. Looking into my eyes with her smug grin. "You see, Loki has a sort of diplomatic immunity, I guess you could call it. First off, he can't be captured for long. Eventually, he escapes."

"It's true! I'm a slippery little thing! Ohohohoh!

"And being Odin's blood brother not only means Odin, nor any other Asgardian, is forbidden to kill him. No faction of god is permitted to 'permanently' kill Loki."

"What? No faction is allowed?"

"Allow me to explain, my dear Mistress!" Loki snaps his fingers. The whole R.V. turns black as the lights go out. We all gasp at how dark it is. There's not even any natural lighting. Only a spotlight shines around Loki, who is now holding a microphone. I'm guessing he's using his Trickster magic to set the tone.

"You see, darlings, one Monarch's deal is all the Monarchs problems!" He quickly raises his body with his arms in the air. "Despite never getting along in the old days, they still made deals with one another. For land, humans, and so on. You know the plagues of Egypt that the Christian and his horsemen caused? That was him collecting his half of a deal with the Egyptian ruler of the time!" Loki chuckles into the microphone. "If one Monarch agreed to that deal, then all of them had to. If one wanted to take over a bit of another's domain and that Monarch was fine with it, then no other faction was allowed near that turf anymore. But these deals were not exclusively between Monarchs..." A wide grin forms on his face.

"So, when you became Odin's blood brother, you become all of the Monarchs' blood brother?"

The lighting returns to normal as Loki glances towards me. "Hm? I guess that's a way to put it. A better way is sort of a two-for-one deal, but more! Ohohoho!"

"I bet your Monarch was really happy with that deal…." Sun mutters.

"He was up to the point he realized I was quite the little bastard! Ohohoh!" Loki leaps up and down as he laughs. "Though to be fair, I am forbidden from harming any of the Monarchs or Odin's children because of this, so it's not as if the All Father got nothing in return.

That is true, in myth Loki and Odin were forbidden from harming one another after the blood pact. Whenever Loki did try to harm Odin, he normally got others to do the dirty work.

"So, he is simply allowed to go out and do more 'jokes' like this with no punishment?!" Sun yells at Ell. "I thought you said you like Mr. Knight, how could you let this thing go unpunished!"

Ell looks at Sun in a serious tone. "Trust me, I would love to see Loki get what he deserves for this. In fact, when I first heard of what he did, I wanted to choke the life out of his little impish neck…"

"Wouldn't be the first time! Ohohoh!"

Ell turns away from Loki in annoyance. "But if the Norse faction could not hold him or even the whole of the New Pantheon, what makes you think I, a simple human, can?"

"Grr…" Sun grits her teeth and clenches hand into a fist. She avoids eye contact with Ell, unsure of how to respond to her.

Ell has shown a protective side for me, but I'm pretty sure it's because she sees herself as the only person allowed to torture me. Then again, I've never been killed before, so she could be genuinely upset, which is surprising of Ell.

As I try to reach out to pat Sun's shoulder, to calm her down, Susanoo walks between us, drinking. She moves her bottle away from her lips to speak. "This is all-*hiccup*- dramatic, serious shit and all that, but I have one question I feel needs to be answered!" Susanoo speaks in a drunken slur. "Who this elegant princess before me is!" She says leering at Ell with the same lustful gaze she gives Sun.

"Oh, I am Elizabeth M. Fall. But those close to me call me Ell… Please, do not call me Ell…" Ell utters in a sarcastic manner, erasing all trace of that serious tone she had a moment ago.

"I'll call ya whatever you want! As long as we get to know each other from different angles!"

Ell glares at Susanoo with an annoyed expression. "You know I dress like this because I enjoy the style, right? I am not interested in women…" Her self-satisfied face returns. "I much prefer aggravating them than loving them"

"That's all very much true…"

"S-Susanoo!" Momoko shouts in a panic as she swings her kendo stick at the back of Susanoo's head.

"Ow! Ha ha! Alright, I'll try to be good!" Susanoo says as she rubs where she was hit.

"Oh, that's right! You're the famed slayer of Orochi. I've been hearing good things about you in the tryouts. I've also been hearing horrible things about you from other Shinto deities."

Sun looks at me, most likely wondering the same thing. Is Ell referring to the *dishonor* thing? Are we the only two that don't know what is going on with this sky god?

"Damn, you're cruel!" Susanoo asserts, sounding offended. "Why does that make me wet?"

Ell turns to Momoko, seeing her shake purely by being stared at. "And you must be her caretaker. Momoko Hirata, correct?"

Momoko bows her head in a panic. "H-hello!"

Ell chuckles behind her hand. "How cute! A perverted drunk with a smoking problem and a paranoid shrine priestess! Don't you two make for an adorable little duo!"

I watch the two and chuckle. "Well, they are unique...."

"Oh, Vergil?" Ell points to my patchwork cane. She seems disgusted. "What is *that*?"

"I made Mr. Knight a new cane since his old one got destroyed, thanks to *that*!" Sun yells as she points at Loki.

Loki looks on with a quizzical expression on his face. "I brought him back to life, darling! Isn't that apology enough!?"

Ell looks over to the god in her care. "Loki, what did I tell you about talking when people are annoyed with you?"

Loki begins to tap his two covered index fingers together through his long sleeves, as if he's a child being scorned by a parent. "Don't...."

"As for your cane, I will buy you a new one. So, you won't have to use that nasty eye sore much longer"

I see she still likes to throw her money at me, making me feel like the wife of a mobster in an old detective movie. Next, I feel like I should tell her she's too good to me, while I straighten up my hair.

I see Sun grinding her teeth in resentment at Ell's remark, not liking what Ell is saying about the cane she made me. I am legitimately worried she might try to hit Ell!

"You two don't seem to get along!" Susanoo speaks up. "You know what ya need?"

"You're going to mention something about a three-way with you, aren't you?" I ask, speaking in a bored tone at how predictable she is to me now.

"Ya wouldn't wanna see that?"

"Oh, of course he would!" Ell speaks up. "My dear Broken Knight has always been quite the pervert. Always the kinky one, too!" She begins to chuckle behind her hand.

I glare at her, bothered by the fact she openly said that. I shrug my shoulders and give an angry expression at her. She responds by giving me a smile and a light wave. Momoko watches me in horror, more so than before finding this out. While Susanoo doesn't seem to be surprised. Am I that obvious?

"Ohohoh!" Loki holds his gut as he begins to laugh. "Darling! She narked you out!" He continues. Ell glares back at him, forcing him to instantly seal his mouth shut.

"Don't say things like that about Mr. Knight!" Sun yells. "He is a classy guy! Sure he stares at my chest and butt a lot, but he always yells at me to get dressed!" She speaks happily as she pats my back.

"Thanks Sun…." I give her a sarcastic thumb up.

Glad she ignored the *kinky* remark. She doesn't need to hear that. Though between the two of us, Ell was far worst, and that was mainly from our bets.

"With all that out of the way, Mr. Knight, we should try to finish cleaning! Maybe everyone should leave? Particularly your school friend and the Shinto pervert," Sun says in annoyance, staring down our guests.

"W-what about me?" Momoko whimpers.

"Oh… I don't really care…" Sun nonchalantly says, ,aking the poor Priestess to nearly cry.

"Sun, don't be rude," I calmly scold her. "Ell flew back out to make sure I was alright, and Susanoo…. Why are you two here?"

"Huh? Oh, well the main reason is that the finals are being held here in this city," Susanoo uninterestedly responds.

Momoko turns toward Susanoo with a nervous look. "A-and you are going to win, right?"

Susanoo appears uninterested. "Meh…"

You think a god that walks around with a sword, and that looks like a samurai would be more into battle. Sun sure as hell has that itch.

"Oh! Then this will be exciting! Maybe I shall go. Would you like to come, Vergil?"

For the first time since they met, Sun faces Ell with a wide grin on her face. "That sounds awesome! Can we go, Mr. Knight?!"

"Oh…" Ell sounds disappointed. Sun turns back at her in confusion. "I was only offering Vergil, but if he wants to bring his little helper monkey, I guess I can't stop him…" She bats her hand at Sun. I can see Sun's hatred for her returning.

We hear knocking once again at the door. There floats Hermes watching the crowd in my little home. "Uh… Am I interrupting something?"

NAMES: HERMES, MERCURY, THE DIVINE TRICKSTER. FACTION: OLYMPUS.

GODHOOD: MESSENGER, FORMER TRICKSTER. HUMAN NATIONALITY: GREEK.

I'm happy he floated in when he did. I fully thought Sun was going to strangle Ell that time. I know my sister, Kat, almost did after the second time she met Ell. That's Ell for you, though. She likes to get under your skin. God knows she does it to me constantly with her teasing.

Hermes raises a brow, lost at the scene going on. "Huh… Are you busy?"

Loki waves at Hermes, both his arms flailing around happily. "Hello again, Olympian Trickster!"

Hermes seems shocked at the sight of Loki. "What are you doing here? I saw you and your Caretaker not too long ago!"

Ell waves calmly at Hermes. "Hello again,"

I guess I'll have to explain this to him…

After a brief explanation, Hermes began his inspection. Writing down things he took notice of.

Hermes smiles as he finishes writing. "Your god is doing well, she is healthy, and everything bought with the God Card is in use for Ms. Wukong. So good job Mr. Knight, you passed your check-up!"

"Awesome!" Sun yells joyfully as she hugs me with all her might.

"Gah!" I shout as my bones feel like they are about to shatter. Hearing my scream, Momoko ducks in fear.

I wasn't really expecting to fail this check-up. Like Hermes said, Sun is healthy and all that we used the God Card for are necessities. I'm glad this check-up isn't meant to see if I am all right. I'd probably fail from being hugged by Sun alone.

"The only concern I see is you're missing your God Slayer."

I glance down at the patchwork cane, and the spot the God Slayer would have originally been. "Uh yeah, it was sort of destroyed…. Is it possible to replace it?"

Glad he brought this up. I hardly used it before the Nuckelavee, so I tend to forget about it. It hasn't helped since I'm using the new cane.

The child-like god stares at me in a sudden shock. "Y-you had your God Slayer destroyed?"

I don't like how he's sounding about this. "Uhhh… Yes? Is that a problem?"

"It's just never happened before," Hermes says rubbing the back of his head. Makes sense, considering I may be the only person who has used theirs. "I guess I can ask the Forgers, but the King won't be happy… like always…"

Sun looks at me in curiosity. "King?"

I'm guessing he's referring to the leader of the Forgers. Though "King" seems a bit arrogant. I know, I live with one.

I point down to my cane. "And if possible, can it not be attached to the thing that is supporting me?"

Hermes crosses his arms. "You really want to piss those two off, don't you?"

"Congratulations, my Broken Knight! You passed!" Ell happily proclaims. "Yet, I am here…. Those two things do not usually go together for you." Ell gives a quiet well pleased chuckle. I respond back by simply glaring at her. As usual, she is not affected by it.

She always must bring up the fact I always lost out to her in every exam we took. I still passed them; I just didn't do as well as her.

"Oh! There is something I need to tell you!" Hermes says, sounding as though he remembered what he wants us to know. He pulls out a small piece of paper and begins to read it out loud. "Dear Sun Wukong, we thank you for dealing with the threat of the Nuckelavee. Thanks to you, humans can now freely enjoy the oceans as they did before. As a sign of our thanks, we, The New Pantheon, offer you one wish!"

"A wish from the Monarchs!?" Me, Momoko, and Sun shout together. Sun sounding less surprised than the rest of us and more excited.

"Be it move the stars to spell your name or carve your face on the side of the moon, name it and your wish shall be granted!"

The Monarchs are willing to go all out for Sun's wish. Or maybe not. These could be normal and simple demands for them. Still, with what Loki said, a deal with the Monarchs is huge. Was the Nuckelavee that much of an issue for them?

"Oh, I definitely know what I want!" Sun shouts enthusiastically. "I want to be in the Gods' Wrath tryouts!"

Everyone but me gazes over at Sun in confusion.

"Heh, is that it?" Ell chuckles. "A wish from the Monarchs and you demand something like that? Not very imaginative, are we?" her sarcastic voice talks down to Sun.

"What does that mean?" Sun yells in rage at Ell.

Loki bats his hand at Sun. "Anyone can sign up for the tournament, darling. You have to wait for next year's tryouts"

Sun viciously glares at the Trickster. "I mean I want to join the tournament now!"

"Wait, you wanna do *what*?" I gasp.

25

Sun joyfully looks at me. "Yeah! This way I don't have to wait!"

I was hoping that since she would have to wait for a whole year before being able to join the tournament, I would be able to talk her out of it, or at least she would get bored with the idea. I didn't count for the possibility of a favor from the Monarchs!

Hermes flies up to Sun with a bit of shock and panic. "I-I don't think we can do that? There isn't enough room for another fighter in the tryouts."

Hearing this, a wave of relief washes over me that I don't have to worry about this now. Poor Sun appears to be disappointed. Still, I'd rather have her like this than being torn to pieces for money.

"Quessssssssssstion!" Susanoo yells in her slurring voice. Gaining the attention of the whole room. "What if room was made?"

"What do you mean?" Hermes asks.

"Let's say, someone drops out of the tournament. Can they give their spot to the sexy Monkey King?"

"I-I guess that is possible. But who would drop out for-"

Susanoo stops Hermes in the middle of his question, not with words, but simply pointing at herself with a drunk grin on her face.

"What?" Me and Momoko exclaim at once.

What the hell is she recommending?

"Really?" Sun questions in excitement.

"Buuuuuttt…. Only if ya can beat me in…." Susanoo points at Sun with a limp wrist. Drinking from her bottle. Gulping it loudly as she keeps us waiting.

"Innnn?" Sun tries to get Susanoo to finish what she was saying.

Susanoo swallows one last gulp, and lets out a relaxed sigh from her lips. "If ya beat me in a fight, ya can take my place in the finals!"

Hermes flies in between the two. "Y-You can't fight with your divine powers outside of the arena! Humans could get hurt! Plus, what are you going to do if you kill one another?!"

A loud annoyed groan leaves from the Storm Goddess's mouth. "Fine! We fight more human-like! Only using our basic skills in a knockout fight! Fuckin' hell!"

"W-well…" Hermes stutters.

"All right! Then it's decided! I'll kick your butt and take your place in the tryouts!" Sun shouts in arrogance as she points at Susanoo.

"Wait, Sun, are you sure-" I try to speak up.

"We will do it in the backyard! Then we will fight!" Susanoo drunkenly chuckles.

"S-Susanoo, you can't-" Momoko tries to join in as she tugs on Susanoo's sleeve.

Loki begins to jump in place like an excited child. "Fight! Fight! Fight!" Loki chants. Interrupting Momoko, nearly breaking her into tears.

"Oh my, this is going to be exciting!" Ell claims as she grabs my arm. "Let's enjoy the show, my Broken Knight."

"H-hey! Don't grab Mr. Knight like that!" Sun shouts angerly, looking away from Susanoo. Ell sticks her tongue out at Sun in a childish manner.

"So, Bouncy Monkey, ya wantin' to fight or not?"

Sun stares back at Susanoo with determination on her face. "Like I said. I will beat you and I will take your place in the tournament!"

"That's the sort of determination that turns me on! Let's do this! Hahaha!" Susanoo lets out a loud tipsy laugh.

They're actually going to fight. They completely ignored me, Momoko, and Hermes... Well, at least Susanoo agreed to a knockout fight and they won't be using their godly powers, so I don't have to feel uneasy about Sun getting too hurt.... Now I only need to be concerned about Sun hurting Susanoo....

CHAPTER TWO: THE GREAT SAGE VS. THE SUMMER STORM

Outside of our home, Sun stretches her body next to me. She hums confidently as she loosens her muscles, readying for the fight.

On the opposite side, Susanoo awkwardly walks to her spot. I can hear a hiccup leave her mouth as she prepares herself. All while, Hermes, agreeing to be our referee, floats between the two, still seeming unsure about this whole idea, like I am.

"S-Sun, you don't need to do this,"

"Why are you so worried, Mr. Knight? It's not like a battle to the death. I'll be fine!"

The rules for this backyard Gods' Wrath match are simple. No divine powers, and no fatalities. Whoever knocks the other out first, or keeps them pinned for the count of ten, wins.

"Have you really fought without using your divine strength or any type of magic powers?"

Sun stares at me with annoyance in her eyes. "You make it sound like I'll need it!"

I point my finger to the wobbling Susanoo. "Almost all fighting styles from Japan originate from the Shinto gods. They taught humans how to fight without divine powers. She may not give off the vibe, but Susanoo is still a skilled fighter. I mean, she got this far in the tryouts!"

Sun looks over at Susanoo and puts on a patronizing face towards the sight of the Storm Godess. I turn to see the drunken god, trying to remove her sheathed sword's strap on her back.

"C-come on now.... Ya-*hiccup*- need to come.... Damn it.... My tits ain't helpin'," Susanoo mutters as she tries and fails to remove her sword from her back. Her straw rice farmer's hat falls off her head as she struggles. "Ah, damn it," She quietly shouts as she rubs at her head of long messy purple hair and the white cloth wrapped around her forehead. "Fuck it..."

Sun smiles in her normal overconfident expression. "Yeah, she seems like a true warrior."

Yeah, that doesn't help my cause in any way, but I still feel like we shouldn't underestimate her. Not only is Susanoo one of the children of Izanagi and Izanami, but she also killed Orochi. Plus, Sun herself even told me the Nuckelavee ran away in fear once she showed her true strength. Maybe that was just her divine powers, though.

Still, she didn't defeat Orochi with her powers. Long story short, she tricked all eight heads into different traps, got them drunk, and cut off each one. Not that amazing of a win, but still.

I pat Sun on the back. "Please don't get too cocky..."

"Yeah, yeah..." Sun says as she walks to her spot.

As I watch her head into this fight, I am reminded of something that has really been worrying me. Something that has been bothering me since I saw Sun fight the Nuckelavee.

I know I was sort of fading in and out, but it's just the Nuckelavee was willing to keep fighting Sun while it ran away from the mess that is Susanoo. Was Sun not seen as that big of a threat to it?

I guess I don't need to put too much thought into this. With this sort of fight, it won't matter. This is a test of skill, not strength. Sun has shown plenty of that in her fight. Even without her magical and superhuman abilities, her animal reflexes should give her an upper hand.

With Sun walking one way, I walk the opposite to take my seat. Before the fight, I laid out a few foldable outdoor chairs.

Sun begged for me to watch and I am not going to stand the whole time. Besides, it appears Ell, Loki and Momoko are going to stay and watch as well.

Ell pats the chair next to her. "Vergil, come sit next to me!"

"Is it safe to do that?" I joke at her request.

"My Broken Knight! You know you're always safe with me. Unless I want to play rough… which I always do," Ell chuckles. My spine shivers a little bit hearing this.

"Hey! What's going on over there!" I hear Sun yelling at us.

"Our Caretakers are planning to make love during your fight, while me and the Asian watch! Ohohohoh!" Loki gives his bombastic laugh before he goes back to drinking from a coconut shell…which I have no idea where he got from.

"Aaaah!" Momoko screams in horror as she nearly falls off her chair. Covering her eyes "Y-you want me to w-watch what?!"

"What was that?!" Sun yells out in bloody rage.

"He's joking, Sun!" I yell at her.

"I don't know, I think I overheard them talking-" Hermes tries to join in on the joke.

"Shut up, Hermes!" I shout. I never thought I would be yelling at a child to shut up, but he is a former Trickster, so of course he'd jump in.

I take a seat next to Ell, aggravated at what had happen, only to have Ell lean close to my ear. "You know, if you want to ravage me like a brute, all you have to do is simply ask." Ell chuckles teasingly. "Same rules as old times!"

This is what I meant when I said she was far kinkier than me. I really wish she'd not mention that around Sun. I slouch back into the chair. "Please don't make it worse…"

"Oh, but I love doing so…," Ell speaks in a fake sadden tone.

Sun, twirls her Jingu Bang, increasing it to its normal length. All the while, Susanoo rests her now free sheathed blade on her shoulder as she grips onto the hilt. Inhaling from her pipe, she places her straw hat back on her head.

Floating between the two, Hermes glances back and forth, bothered by all this. "Uhh… You remember the rules of no powers and no killing, right?" He nervously beseeches.

Susanoo moves the pipe from her mouth letting out the smoke from her lips, shrugging her shoulders. "Eh, as long as she doesn't go all out with her staff and I don't pull out my sword, we'll be good!"

Surprisingly, she didn't decide to make a joke out of saying "staff" and "pull out." I swore she would have said something about that. Her and her bad dad jokes.

"I won't extend my Jingu Bang any further than this!" Sun says.

"That's a pretty kinky name. It fits since I swore it was some sort of sex toy. Hahaha!" Susanoo lets out a loud drunken laugh.

That's more like it…

"Why would I bring something like that to a fight?!" Sun yells at her.

"Why wouldn't ya?"

Sun stomps her foot into the ground in malice. "This is my first real fight with another warrior in a long time. Can you please take this seriously?!"

"Nah…"

This isn't how I expected a fight between two Asian gods to start out. I guess I was expecting something more professional. Maybe something like an old Kung-fu movie. Talking about honor and such. Then again, these two are not professional.

"Ohohohohoh!" I hear Loki laughing next to me. I see him holding his gut as he laughs harder. "Already, this fight is amazing! Keep it up, darlings!"

"This is amusing to watch," Ell comments as she watches. Her eyes turn towards me, as her smug smirk follows behind. "Oh! Vergil, would you like to make this more fun?"

"No…"

"Aaawwww! Come on! I miss winning against you!" Ell lets out a fake whine.

"If you win will I be in some sort of skirt?" I question in a serious manner.

"Hmm. Maaaaybe…"

"Then no!"

Ell pouts. "Oh fine! I guess I can make do with the pictures of my previous wins."

"What pictures?"

"What about you little shrine priestess?" Ell asks Momoko in a happy voice, ignoring my question. I fear what she meant by "pictures of her previous wins".

"W-what?" Momoko speaks, nervously. As she should.

Ell points at the two gods. "I bet you my cute toy's little helper monkey will beat your drunken mess of a god."

"Toy? Wait, you're betting on Sun?"

Does this mean she is warming up to her? If so, then maybe Sun will feel the same and the two will get along!

"Well I sort of have to. I mean the timid girl won't bet against her own god, will she?"

And like that, all my hopes of the two getting along is thrown out the window….

"W-well, I-I don't have any doubt of Susanoo's skill, even fighting without divine power. B-but I don't have a ton of money to spend on such things!" Momoko tells Ell.

"Oh, I won't ask for money. How about this! If your god wins, I will donate about, I don't know, a thousand dollars to your shrine? If I win, you can pay me off in some other way." Ell lets out a sinister chuckle with a smirk to go along with it.

A thousand? Ell is going all-in with this bet. Maybe I should still feel flattered that she is putting that much on Sun to win.

"Come on Ell, leave the poor-" I stop as I see Momoko staring into a book.

Flipping through the pages quickly, her eyes reading it as fast as she can. I take a glance at the book. *Dollars to Yen Guidebook.* She's trying to figure out how much that is for her shrine.

"T-that translates to…." She quietly whispers. "108,904 yen!!!!" She shouts. I nearly fall over on to Ell in her chair.

Momoko doesn't sound like she normally does. I can hear excitement in her voice instead of fear.

"Do we have a deal?" Ell importunes.

"Uh, Ms. Hirata, perhaps you should ignore-"

Momoko's normal fear-ridden face is replace with determination. "I-I'm in!!!"

When it comes to things like this, Ell knows how to get people to play her games. She loves to throw around big bucks to tempt her prey. I fell for it many times before.

But Momoko seems a bit more excited than I thought. In fact, she seems a bit relieved at the offer, like this is something she needs.

I shrug my shoulders as she ignores my warning and shakes Ell's hand in agreement. Surprising, I thought Momoko would try to swing her Kendo stick at Ell. Maybe she has gotten better at controlling herself. Still, I fear about what Ell is going to do to this innocent young woman. The good news is Ell doesn't have the same sort of advantage she had in our games.

"Huh, Momoko, maybe you shouldn't-"

"I-I know what I am doing, Mr. Vergil!"

Unlike before when we played games or even bet who would do better in class, Ell was always in some sort of control. Whether it be in cards or in knowledge. But Sun and Susanoo are out her control. So, who knows? Maybe Momoko has a shot.

"G-go Susanoo! Please win!" Momoko cheers.

"Meh…" Susanoo swats her hand in response.

"Why didn't you hit her with your sword as soon as she thought up this plan?" I ask.

"S-she still would go through with it… P-plus she doesn't take me seriously when I do that…."

"Then why did you do it before?"

"Makes me feel better…" The scared little priestess utters in a more serious voice. Scaring me a bit.

I focus back on the battlefield. Sun on the left, pointing her staff at Susanoo as she stands opposite of her. Unlike Sun, though, Susanoo doesn't seem as battle-ready. I can see her eyes wandering around as she scratches her cheek. She's not even removing the pipe from her mouth.

Hermes floats between the two. "Are we ready to fight?"

Sun points her staff away and bows respectfully towards Susanoo. "Despite how I feel, I hope this fight is- ow!" As Sun gives her thoughts, Susanoo rushed over and smacked her sheathed blade onto the back of Sun's head. Sun leaps back away from Susanoo, rubbing the back of her head. "W-What the hell!?"

"What? You looked away!" Susanoo acts as if she did nothing wrong.

Hermes intervenes. "B-but the battle did not start yet!"

Susanoo pushes the messenger out of the way. "I agreed to fight! Didn't agree to wait though!" She announces in a snarky tone.

Sun flairs her nostrils and bares her teeth in hatred. "That was just dishonorable! Aren't you a Shinto god?!"

"Oh! It's as if I'm a Disgraced Goddess, who don't give a shit about honor…" Susanoo sarcastically replies. Removing her pipe from her lips and releasing the smoke from her mouth. "Funny thing about the whole honor deal. It's based on the dumbass idea that people fight fair. Also, ain't ya the Monkey King who fought any warrior she ran across all willy-nilly?"

"That was different!"

Well, I was not expecting that. Most often Shinto, Buddhist, and other Asian gods hold to the concept of honor dearly.

Plus, Susanoo seems to be giving off a different vibe than before. Her eyes have a more serious vibe to them. The same look she gave me when I wanted to know of the whole Disgraced Goddess thing after the Nuckelavee incident.

Hermes appears to be nervous, glancing at Susanoo. "A-all right, you can fight! Winner takes all!" He shouts as he flies back towards us, away from the fight.

Ell claps her hands together in joy. "Well, this is already exciting!"

"You know, when I agreed to watch two women fight in the backyard of a white trash trailer, I didn't have my doubts on how much fun it would be! Ohohohohoh!"

Sun angrily swings her staff at Susanoo. As the weapon comes in close contact with her, the Storm Goddess falls back. Not dodging it, she appears to have simply fallen on her back as the weapon swings over her.

"Huh?" We all speak to the act before us.

Susanoo stares straight up at the sky, releasing smoke from her pipe as Sun looks down at her in confusion.

"Hmm…" Susanoo hums as she smokes from her pipe.

"Uhh… O-oh right!" Hermes realizes. "One… Two… Three…"

We all watch on, unsure what is going on as Hermes begins the countdown. I guess, that look in her eyes was just for show.

Sun puts on a high and mighty face and rests her staff on her shoulder. "Heh. I told you, Mr. Knight!" Sun yells back to me. "She isn't much of a- Huh?" my overly proud Monkey King gazes down at her legs. There she sees Susanoo's legs locked around her left foot.

"Seven… Eigh- What?" Hermes stops the countdown as he sees what Susanoo is doing.

The drunken god removes the pipe from her mouth to speak. "Sorry, I was thinkin' of what to do after this…"

"D-do wha- Ah!"

With her legs wrapped tightly around Sun's foot, Susanoo rolls quickly, twisting on Sun's leg and throwing her to the ground.

As Sun lands on her back, Susanoo flings herself into the air, landing on top of Sun.

"You know, I was sort of picturing this scene in reverse…" Susanoo stares at Sun's bothered face as she holds down her down. Licking her own lips like a feral beast. "Not sayin' I don't mind bein' on top..."

My mouth drops at the sight of what is going on, leading Ell to push it shut for me. Momoko covers her eyes in a panicking fit. Hermes seems to be as sucked into the event as I am, maybe even more so. His eyes wide open, not wanting to turn away. While Loki laughs.

Sun's tail begins to wrap around Susanoo's hips. "G-get the hell off me!" She shouts as she uses her tail to throw Susanoo off.

Her tail was able to fling Susanoo into the air?! Not incredibly high, but still!

As she is thrown into the air, the Storm Goddess flips back onto her feet, landing surprisingly elegantly back onto the ground. "W-whoa…" Susanoo mutters as she nearly loses balance, placing her pipe back in her mouth and giving a thumbs up. Thus ruining the surprising landing she did.

Sun leaps back onto her feet and runs towards Susanoo, on all four, still gripping onto the Jingu Bang. The look on her face appears to be a mix of determination to win the fight and anger for what Susanoo did.

"H-hey!" Hermes shouts. Flying quickly towards Sun. "You used your divine strength when you threw her off!"

"B-but she was gonna-"

"It's cool!" Susanoo shouts. She eyes at Sun with a lust-fueled grin. "Let's keep going! I wanna see how much further I can get!"

I can see Sun shake in horror at her words. "I-I want to keep going to shut her up!"

Hermes franticly looks back and forth unsure what to do, but stops and lets out a loud sigh. "Fine. But whoever uses divine powers again is disqualified!" He quickly flies towards us. "Go!" He shouts as he watches with us.

Sun prepares to fight again, only to see Susanoo lowering her sword, the weapon slides out of her hand. The only thing she has a grip on is the sash she wears around her that is attached to the sheathed blade.

With a smile on her face, Susanoo swings the blade from its sash. Slamming the hilt into the side of Sun's face, blindsiding her and knocking her down.

Sun gets back up, looking at the tricky Storm Goddess with rage. Sun begins to swing her staff at Susanoo. Only to have her attacks be knocked away by Susanoo's swinging sword. When Sun's staff comes too close, Susanoo swings the blade onto the large ends of the staff.

She's not even using her sword properly. She's using it more like a chained mace, swinging it from its sash. I'm surprised the sword hasn't flown out yet from all that movement.

As the next swing comes for the Storm Goddess, Susanoo wraps her sword's sash around Sun's staff. She yanks it to the side as she leaps forward to Sun. Swiftly, Susanoo backflips with her foot out, kicking Sun in the chin and knocking her back.

"Grrh!" Sun shouts between her teeth as she is kicked. After falling to the ground, Sun lays her upper body up as she rubs her chin.

"Huh… I guess those Buddhist and Taoist gods weren't so tough if ya beat most of them." Susanoo chuckles.

Oh boy, this may not end so well. Susanoo is questioning Sun's strength and power. She tends to be really arrogant about those.

"What did you say?!" Sun shouts at her as she stands on her feet.

"Hmm… Ya know what. Are ya holding back on me? I feel like you're not givin' me your all! Look, I'm the sort of gal who loves having their ass pounded by someone at their fullest. If you're this weak without your powers, then I ain't gonna waste my time with someone going half-assed on me…" Susanoo says in disappointment. Still fitting in some lewd remarks, I see.

Man, Susanoo is going all out on Sun, verbally. She's clearly focusing on making Sun angry and unfocused… Which frankly isn't too hard…

Sun gets into another battle-ready stance. "I don't need to go all-out to beat you!"

Susanoo smirks in a cocky manner. "Well ya coulda fooled me."

Upset at what Susanoo said, Sun twirls her staff and swings it at the Storm Goddess. Susanoo dodges the attack and swings her blade and wraps it around the staff once more.

Trying to repeat her last attack, Susanoo attempts to yank the weapon to the side of her once again, but it appears Sun is ready this time. Susanoo seems to be having trouble pulling it out of Sun's grip.

"Huh?" Susanoo calmly responds to the situation. With a wide smirk on her face, Sun yanks at her staff upwards and pulls the tied sword from Susanoo's hand. The weapon is swiftly tosses behind the Monkey King "Oh!" Susanoo utters in a slight surprise as she gazes at her sword a few feet behind Sun. The Storm Goddess mockingly claps her hands in celebration of the Monkey King's tactic.

"Now I got you!" Sun shouts as she swings her staff downwards at the distracted goddess.

Susanoo moves out of the way of the attack once more and grabs hold of Sun's hand.

The Storm Goddess yanks Sun by the arm towards her. I can see something small and thin twirling between her fingers. It halts as Susanoo swiftly pokes up and down Sun's muscular appendage. In outrage Sun jerks her limb, causing her enemy to spin and fall on her face.

"Ow..."

Sun leans back up and turns to see Susanoo. "What was that supposed to do-" Sun stops her questioning as she looks at her right arm. She begins to move her shoulder, causing her arm to swing in place like a wet noodle. "W-why can't I feel my arm?!"

Me, Ell, Loki, and Hermes watch on in surprise at this news. All Susanoo did was role on Sun. What could she have done to her?

Susanoo lays in a more comfortable manner, holding her head up with her hand. "Yeah, that would be this!" She announces as she holds up her pipe.

"Your pipe-thing?"

"Oh yeah, we might be gods, but we still got pressure points. I just hit yours with my good ol' Kiseru when I rolled on you." She momentarily places the pipe back in her mouth. "Despite what humans thought, I was never much into using real weapons. So before getting my hands-on Kusanagi, this was my weapon…"

So, wait, her only means of defense for her lone wandering life, was a smoke pipe? I'm starting to think this joke of a god is more like how I imagined Susanoo would be prior to meeting her.

I can see Sun's tail reaching for the Jingu Bang as Susanoo speaks. "Hmm?" Susanoo hums as her eyes meet with Sun's sneaking tail. "Nope!" The Storm Goddess shouts as she swipes her grounded leg across the grass, trying to knock Sun off her feet again.

Though, it seems like Sun saw Susanoo's upcoming move as well as she leaps in the air to dodge the attack. As soon as she lands back on her feet, she grabs hold of her weapon in her still functioning arm.

The Great Sage raises her pole as she prepares to attack. "I'm not gonna lose, Shinto Bimbo!"

Sun swings down the Jingu Bang like a massive hammer. Despite Sun's speed, Susanoo's dodge proves quicker as she leaps out of the way.

The staff is prepared for another swing, Sun halts as all of us notice what Susanoo had obtained as she was avoiding the attack.

None of us saw her grab or even reach for it, but as we were all distracted by Sun's supposed finisher, Susanoo reacquired her weapon.

Susanoo grips the hilt and the sheath. Sun launches another assault as fast as she can. However, before she could land a hit, a loud click is heard as the Summer Storm pulls her sword from its holder.

She's shown us a bit of her power before, but this is nothing like that. Sun is blown back from an extremely powerful wind gust.

Leaves blow off all the trees behind Sun. I can see the sword living up to its name as the grass below flies from the ground it's planted in, leaving the scent of a freshly cut lawn. The R.V. behind us even begins to shake.

As if by instinct, I grab hold of Ell and Momoko and hold them close. Trying to protect them from the debris, if any.

Loki leaps in front of us and I see him pull something from his long sleeves: an umbrella. He opens it and somehow, the wind is slowing down around us, but the roar of it is still loud. So, it's clearly not stopping.

As quickly as it came, the powerful wind left with the sound of a click. Loki lowers his umbrella and I look up to see Sun still standing. Her staff is planted into the ground to support her from the wind. She's breathing heavily, trying to catch her breath.

I watch on, in shock at what had transpired before me. The only thing that pulls my eyes away from this is Ell rubbing my cheek.

"My heroic Knight in broken armor," She flirts. Yet still fits in a jab at me.

Momoko's response is exactly as you picture it. "T-touch! Touched by a man! By an American!" Her face completely red, she shouts in a more flustered tone then horror. As before, she swings her kendo stick, but due to how I'm holding her, she only swings it in front of herself, unable to hit me. She knows she can't hit me like that. It's as though she works by instinct.

"H-Hey!" Hermes shouts. "D-did you just use one of the most powerful divine weapons out here?!"

Susanoo shrugs in her normal bored manner. "Eh, it wasn't even a third of a way out!"

That was not even a third of her power? How strong is she when she draws out all of Kusanagi's power?

"We're stopping this now!" Hermes puts his foot down, metaphorically. "I proclaim Sun Wukong the winner by disqualification!"

"Ah come on, ya pint-sized hummin' bird!" Susanoo insults Hermes in an agitated manner.

"N-no…" Sun speaks up, still out of breath, points at Susanoo. "N-no…I want…to keep going…"

I get up from my chair and walk over to Sun. "Let it go, Sun. You won… That's what you wanted…"

"B-but, Mr. Knight…"

I pat her on the back. "That hit knocked the wind out of you, and your arm is paralyzed. Just take the win,"

"So, I lost?" Susanoo asks. "Ah well!" She scratches the back of her head with a relaxed smirk on her face.

She's accepting her loss and giving up her place in the tryouts so easily? What is wrong with this drunk samurai?

From behind the relaxed Storm Goddess, I see her panicky caretaker charging up from behind her, but I don't see fear in her baggy eyes. I see, what appears to be, rage.

"S-Susanoo!" She cries loudly as she prepares to swing her kendo sword.

As much strength as her little body can give out, she swings her wooden weapon at Susanoo. She repeatedly strikes her, though not on her head or back, but on her ass for some reason, spanking her as hard as possible.

"Gah!" Susanoo screams as she falls to her knees from the hit. She looks down for a moment, seeming as though she's disappointed with herself. "Harder…" My eyebrow raises from her whisper. "Harder, mommy!" She shouts happily with her ass in the air.

We all go quiet at this, unsure what to make of it. To be fair, I don't think any of us finds this surprising.

"S-Susanoo!"

The Storm Goddess turns back to her Caretaker after hearing her name. "Oops! Sorry, habit!" She chuckles.

"T-this isn't funny! How could you lose! T-this is the most irresponsible thing you've done!"

"I know... Maybe another spankin' will teach me a lesson!"

"Gah!" Momoko lets out an angry scream. Raising her wooden sword, she continues to beat on Susanoo. Not the way the sky god wanted, though.

"Ow! Ha ha- Ow!" Susanoo laughs in between her yells of pain like before. These two really have an odd relationship.

Pulling my eyes away from the odd duo, I notice Sun standing upright again, and breathing better. "So, I'm in the tryouts?" She asks.

The small Olympian poses in a thinking gesture. "I'm not entirely sure. I guess I'll have to see."

This may sound bad, but I was hoping Sun would lose. If only to push back this idea of hers for a bit longer. Especially seeing the condition Sun was in after Susanoo unleashed a small amount of her power. What will happen to her in a tournament of gods going all out to slaughter one another?

Sun puts on a look of determination towards the tiny god. "Well, if the Monarchs claim they owe me a favor, they better give it!"

A look of shock covers my face from what she had said. "Sun, did you just threaten the Monarchs?!"

Sun tilts her head at me, confused at my question. "Yeah, why?"

She honestly doesn't understand what the issue is?!

Hermes laughs happily at us. "I have to go! I'll keep you updated on their answer!" He announces as he slowly rises to the sky.

In the blink of an eye, Hermes dashes away in the air like a rocket, leaving me confused and concerned at what will come next for us.

A favor from the New Pantheon. In the last five years, no one had ever heard of, or thought of, such a thing happening.

I'd be lying if I said I'm not scared of what will happen if they find Sun's favor to be unsavory.

Though they've shown not to act this way, in every myth and religion the Monarchs would show no mercy to those that insult them, they say they aren't the same as before. I hope that's true.

"Mr. Knight?" I hear Sun, pulling me from my train of thought. "You all right?"

"Overthinking, hopefully…"

Ell walks up towards us, clapping her hands. "My, my! That was a fun little squabble, wasn't it?" She asks me in a light chuckle. Her eyes dash towards Momoko as she continues to assault Susanoo. "Oh, Ms. Hirata!"

Momoko jumps in fear at the sound of her own name, halting her assault on Susanoo.

She grips onto her kendo sword, tightly in fear. Very reasonable when Ell calls your name. "Y-yes M-Miss?"

I can see a sinister stare in Ell's eyes as she smiles at the timid priestess. "Do tell me, how are you going to pay your dues?"

Momoko stares at Ell in fear. Well, more fear than she normally shows. "W-w-what will I be doing?"

Ell pulls out a pen and a small piece of paper. "Oh, don't fret. I will figure something out." She claims as she writes on the paper. She hands it to Momoko. "Meet me here in five days. And if you don't want to come, I'll simply find you!" Ell informs Momoko nonchalantly, making her comment more horrifying.

I can see Momoko shaking in fear as she reaches for the paper. I am also worried about what she is planning. Especially if she is going to pay back Ell the same ways I had to. Poor girl…

Momoko looks at the paper in defeat, as if it is crushing her dreams. Then again, she did seem determined on Susanoo winning Ell's money she offered to her shrine. Perhaps more desperate than determined.

Loki leans close to Momoko with a wide grin on his face. She must really be upset if she's not trying to hit Loki for being that close.

"That expression on your face is absolutely fabulous, darling! Ohohohoh!" The Trickster mocks the poor little priestess.

"Waaaah!" Momoko whines loudly into the air. "S-Susanoo! Why would you do something so stupid?!"

Susanoo stands back on her feet, stretching her body. "Ya gotta be clearer, Momo."

Sun leaps on me with her functioning arm wrapped around my neck, causing my glasses to nearly fall off. "Not the win I was hoping for, but we're in, Mr. Knight! We're in the Gods' Wrath tryouts!"

I straighten out my glasses. "You heard Hermes. He has to see if the Monarchs would allow that."

"Well, they better!" She utters in a threatening manner.

"S-stop talking like that about the Monarchs!" I shout.

Sun gives a victorious laugh. "Still, I can't believe that she broke the main rule of our fight! The cowardly Shinto panicking at my attack like that! No wonder she's considered a disgraced! Right, Mr. Knight?"

With Sun pointing this out I glance over to the two. Momoko yelling at Susanoo, while the latter is nonchalantly smoking from her pipe, not focusing on anything.

I might be overthinking this and giving her too much credit, but I feel as if this was planned.

CHAPTER THREE: A BLESSING IN DISGUISE.

The three members of the New Pantheon, the Monarchs of Asgard, Hinduism and Christianity, waited in silence with their Enforcers, the four armored angels, the All Father's loyal wolves and the Hindu Avatar. Awaiting what their messenger had to say. All wondering what the monkey king would wish for.

The Norse Monarch stroked his beard. A slight sign of worry could be seen on his face. "What if she wishes for something horrible? What if she wishes to rule alongside us?"

NAMES: ODIN, GRIMIR, ONE EYE, TRUE-GUESSER, ALL FATHER. FACTION: ASGARD.

GODHOOD: MONARCH.

"Then we will simply not grant it. If her wish is selfish, then we will know if she is still the same as what the Jade Emperor had told us of," the Hindu Monarch spoke.

NAME: VISHNU, NARAYANA, HARI, LAKSHMIKANTA, MUKUNDA. FACTION: HINDU.

GODHOOD: MONARCH.

Odin halted his grooming. "What if she becomes hostile because of that?"

"Then we will deal with her before it gets too out of hand," spoke the Biblical Monarch from behind his hooded face.

NAMES: GOD, I AM, YAHWEH, CHRIST, FATHER, JOE. FACTION: CHRISTIAN.

GODHOOD: MONARCH.

The one-eyed Monarch crossed his muscular arms, still bothered by what may happen. "Still, the idea of even offering her a wish just feels wrong and dangerous."

Before the conversation could go any further, the door of the meeting room knocked loudly. Reverting the room back to its quiet state as it was moments ago.

The three Monarchs and their enforcers looked at the door with curiosity. "The answer has arrived," Vishnu spoke. "Enter!"

Hermes burst through the door, slamming it open. The loud sound caused Odin's ravens, Huginn and Muninn to bat their wings in fear. The slapping wings began to hit The All Father's face causing him to clench his eye shut and crouch his head as they did so. "S-stop it you two!" Odin yelled at his ravens. Hearing his demand, the two birds halted their flapping. "Must you burst in like that?"

Hermes bowed before the Monarchs. "I am truly sorry, but if it makes anything better, I do have what Sun Wukong wishes for."

The three Monarchs looked at each other in worry. They were told by two of the Chinese Monarchs of what Sun was like in the old days. Arrogant, selfish and even dreamed of being part of a pantheon. They feared what she would wish for, but they were ready for the worst.

Joe raised his hand in a presenting manner. "Speak…"

Hermes raised his head to look at them. A quizzical look appeared on him. "She wants to be in the finals of the Gods' Wrath Tryouts."

The three looked back at each other, lost for words.

"That's it?" asked the Hindu Monarch.

Hermes shrugged his shoulders. "That's it…"

Vishnu gave a sigh of relief. "Here I was, worrying about nothing…"

The Dashavatara patted the back of his relieved Monarch with a smile on his mute face.

NAMES: DASHAVATARA, RAMA, MATSYA, VAMANA, BALARAMA. FACTION: HINDU.

GODHOOD: AVATAR. HUMAN NATIONALITY: INDIAN.

"About nothing?!" Odin shouted as he slammed his hands on the table, causing his ravens to fly off his shoulders and his wolves to tremble in fear. "We cannot just throw someone in at the last minute! Besides, the tryouts are almost over and there is no room for her if we wanted to!"

Hermes raised his hand in the air as he was about to speak. "Well that's another thing. Susanoo dropped out. She challenged Wukong to a duel, with no divine powers, offering her spot if she lost, which she did. So now there is a free spot for her, right?"

Joe looked towards the flying Olympian. "Wukong beat Susanoo? Wait, why did Susanoo gamble away her spot in the finals?"

"Not sure, but she and her caretaker were there speaking with Wukong and her caretaker," Hermes pointed out.

"What, why?" the Christian god asked.

Hermes shrugged his small shoulders. "From what I can see, she appears to "like" the great sage."

"Like?" Joe repeated in confusion.

"I care not for the feelings of the Shinto disgrace! We cannot simply change the rules as we please!" Odin shouted. "What sort of tournament does that?!"

"Yes, but can we just take back her wish like that? I mean it is not as selfish as we feared," Vishnu asked. "I am just curious why she didn't wish to just be in the tournaments themselves, instead of just the Tryouts finals."

"Like what you said, we can simply not grant her wish. If you want, just tell her to wish for something else!" Odin swatted his hand in the air as he continued to yell in anger.

Hermes tilted his head at the conversation. "Then what about Susanoo?"

Odin slammed his fist onto the table, the slam echoing in the room. "She can either stay in the tournament or quit and let your sibling progress into the royal! But we can't just throw in any other god! Especially one of the Five, like Wukong!"

Joe with his Metatron and Michael next to him, stood from his chair. "Enough!" Joe finally spoke. "Do you not see? This is a blessing in disguise."

Vishnu and Dashavatara looked and tilted their heads at the Christin god. "Do explain, child."

Joe looked out the window as he spoke. "Why did we create the Gods' Wrath Tournament?"

"You made it to entertain the more aggressive gods, correct?" Michael asked his father.

NAMES: MICHAEL, THE ARCHANGEL, THE RED HORSEMAN OF WAR. FACTION: CHRISTIAN.

GODHOOD: WAR. HUMAN NATIONALITY: ENGLISH.

Joe turned his head to his red armored knight. "That is what the humans and the reborn gods think, yes. But it was made for a different reason." He turned back to face his fellow Pantheon members. "As a distraction."

The two wolf girls tilted their heads in confusion as they looked at the hooded god. "A dis-dis-dis…" Geri tried to pronounce the word she had just heard. As her sister Freki, clearly thought on the word.

NAMES: GERI AND FREKI. FACTION: ASGARD.

GODHOOD: DEMI-GODS, ANIMAL. HUMAN NATIONALITY: SWEDISH.

"A dist-*cough!*-raction?" spoke the sickly black armored figure from the shadows behind Joe's thrown.

NAMES: ABADDON, ANGEL OF THE PIT, THE BLACK HORSEMAN OF FAMINE AND PLAGUE. FACTION: CHRISTIAN.

GODHOOD: DROUGHT AND PLAGUE. HUMAN NATIONALITY: ITALIAN.

Vishnu stood on his feet. "We always feared if they are not distracted, they would begin to remember what had happened on that *Day*. So, we made the Gods' Wrath tournaments. Gods who were meant for fighting can face against each other, and even nonaggressive gods can be part of it in some way, such as the love gods being the presenters for the fights."

The All Father stroked his beard and nodded to what his fellow Monarchs were saying. "So, you are wanting Wukong to enter the tournament, just to keep her distracted?"

"And we will be able to keep a better eye on her then." Joe replied.

Odin sighed loudly at the idea. "I don't know. I don't just hate the idea of doing such a big change to the tournament, I've got this aching feeling we are making a mistake."

"If you truly do worry about this, remember who her first opponent is. Surly not one to be taken lightly," Vishnu said. The other two Monarchs nodded in agreement to his statement.

"Then, by the words of the New Pantheon! The Great Sage of the Buddhist factor is allowed in the finals in Susanoo place!" Joe yelled, as loudly as he could without causing damage to the building.

Hermes bowed to the three Monarchs once more. "I'll gladly tell them!"

"No!" Odin shouted. "This message involves the Gods' Wrath Tournaments! So, my messenger will be tasked for this information!"

Hermes crossed his arms, annoyed by what the one-eyed Monarch had just said. "Goody, the squirrel... I'll pass on the message then and maybe add a bit of teasing while I'm at it! Heh heh!" Hermes ended with a smile.

The small wings on his shoes flapped quickly as he flew out of the room like a speeding missile.

Odin and Vishnu looked upon the youngest of their pantheon with concern. "Are you sure this is a good idea, child?" Odin asked in a stern voice.

"In all honesty, no." Joe nodded his head. "But it's just as I said, her being in the tournament makes it easier to keep an eye on her."

The All Father stood from his throne. "Allow me to handle that," he said in a calm manner as he straightened his tie. "Huginn! Muninn!" he shouted, causing the two ravens to fly onto the table the Monarchs had before them, waiting eagerly to what their master wants. "Follow my messenger and keep an eye on the being she is meeting with!" the Asgardian said in a demanding manner. "Go!"

Quickly, the two birds flapped their wings and floated from the table. Swiftly, the birds flew from the table and out a small crack in the ceiling that matched their size perfectly.

Through the bright blue skies, the birds soared above the clouds, in search of their target.

INTERLUDE: THE MESSENGERS

The New Pantheon, possibly the grandest merger in history, made up entirely of the Monarchs of all factions of gods. Though not considered rulers anymore, they reign supreme in the modern world.

As before, despite their extreme divine powers, they run everything like a business. Like any business, there are different groups assigned with different jobs. One such group are the Messengers.

As the name suggests they are tasked with delivering messages to things such as various parties that serve the New Pantheon. However, they often visit caretakers and the gods they are assigned with.

Even though they have the same basic job, many are given certain types of messages.

Hermes, the Olympian Messenger, is one of many who check on the well-being of caretakers and how their gods have been living with them. He also delivers special packages needed to certain gods, and to prepare new gods who are ready to live with their caretakers.

In his case, he only deals with the everyday lifestyles of caretakers and their gods. Meanwhile, things such as the Gods' Wrath tournament are treated differently.

Messages relating to the Tournament of the Divine is not Hermes's job. That assignment belongs to another.

Being the one who made much of how the Gods' Wrath fights work, Odin picked his own messenger to deal with any and all-important news related to the tournaments.

Invitations, updates, and any other arrangements are the duty of one being.

"Me! The Climber of Yggdrasil! The personal Messenger to the All Father! The cutest thing with the fluffiest tail! The great, the sweet! I am-"

Back to the story…

"Hey!"

CHAPTER FOUR: THE ADORABLE ASGARDIAN

After a quick trip to the nearby grocery store, Sun and I make our way home after picking up a few things. Mostly food and cleaning supplies.

I like going to the store. It's a quick trip, and Sun knows it's pointless to ask if we can fly home.

"So why do we go to that store?" Sun questions in a pout, following me on her cloud with the groceries hanging from her staff. "The mall was so much more exciting!"

"Because it's cheaper there, and we don't get as bombarded by people who want pictures with you! Plus, it's easier on my leg."

"But that's the best part! All those people admiring how great I am! Reminds me why I'm a King! And I told you I can carry you and fly us home!"

I turn back towards her. "No!"

She sticks her tongue out at me immaturely. "Neh!"

A smile shapes on my face at her childish behavior, with a chuckle sneaking out. She pulls her tongue back and does the same. She knows I've gotten too used to this personality of hers and she loves it.

I needed that though. It's been a day since Hermes told us that the Monarchs owed Sun a favor. What did she want? She wanted to take Susanoo's place in the tryouts. I've been worried since then.

I'm worried they'll get angry at her request. I'm also worried they'd say yes to it. No matter the outcome, I'm stressed. The only thing I can hope for is they tell her no.

"Do you really want to be in the tournaments?"

"Yep!"

"And you say you're doing it for me?"

"Of course!"

"No other reason?"

"Well, I won't say I'm not excited to fight other gods again!"

My shoulders slouch as I look back at the trail in front of me. "Right…"

Sun flies closer towards me, by my side, still keeping a happy face. "Mr. Knight, I mean what I said. I want to fight for you. To get that prize money and life juice."

Life juice. That's the stuff Loki poured on me to resurrect me. Ever since then, Sun has had her mind on it, wanting to use it on me if something happens.

It's a nice gesture, but personally, I don't trust that stuff. I didn't like how I felt afterward. How I wasn't shocked by all the horrible things I saw in person that night, making it feel so common for me.

I told Sun this before, but she keeps telling me it would only be for emergencies. I doubt I'd be caught up in the same scenario I was with the Nuckelavee. Trust me, I'll make sure of that. Since then, Sun has become far more overprotective of me, making it hard to argue with her about this.

I smile again in response to what she said. "I know, Sun."

Sun chuckles happily at my words. "Huh?" Her happy chuckle stops as her attention is drawn towards the sky.

"What's wrong?"

Sun sniffs loudly. She only does that if she smells a god nearby. "Something's coming," She warns, sounding unsure.

"Hermes?"

Sun shakes her head 'no' to my answer. "I recognize his and that drunk Shinto's smell by now. This isn't one of them."

Well to be fair, I can tell Susanoo's scent by now, too, but still, who or what could it be? That's when I see it. Something falling from the sky.

From a distance, I can hear screams. As the figure falls closer, it appears more humanoid. Like the figure, the screams get closer too. Getting flashbacks of when Sun first came home.

"Gggaaaaahhhh!" We hear coming towards us. Sun and I watch on at the falling figure, no response towards it at all. The figure finally lands onto the ground, hard. "Fuck!" We hear in a child's voice, from the dust cloud that formed in front of us.

Since they said "fuck", I'm assuming they're fine. I'm also guessing this is the god Sun was sniffing out.

As the dust cloud fades, we see what it is. A red puffy tail attached to a kid. It looks almost like a squirrel's tail.

Sun and I glance at each other for a moment. I'm unsure what to tell her. Our gazes turn back to the human squirrel.

"Uh... You alright?" I ask.

"Guuh..." A groan leaves from the Squirrel. "Stupid Olympian..."

Me and Sun glance back at each other once more. "Are you-"

Before I can finish, the Squirrel Child leaps back onto their feet and poses with a smile on their face and a wag in their tail. "Ta-Da!"

It's a young girl, probably about fifteen. She has short red hair with a darker streak in the middle, bright brown eyes, little fluffy ears, a tiny horn on her forehead, and buckteeth that stick out of her mouth.

Despite all that, the most attention-drawing is the fact she's dressed in a female version of Hermes's suit. Does that mean she's a Messenger?

"Uh, who are you?"

She quickly takes on a new pose. "Me! The Climber of Yggdrasil! The personal Messenger to the All Father! The cutest thing with the fluffiest tail! The great, the sweet! I am-"

"Ah, your Ratatoskr!"

NAME: RATATOSKR. FACTION: ASGARD.

GODHOOD: MESSENGER, ANIMAL. HUMAN NATIONALITY: ICELAND.

"Stop interrupting me!" She yells, sounding mad. I think I may have hit a nerve.

I figured it out as soon as she said *Climber of Yggdrasil*. The messenger of Asgard, and like Sun and Susanoo, apparently a girl. I'm pretty much used to this now, sadly.

So far, she's making the kind of first impression you'd honestly expect from a squirrel, if that makes any sense.

Sun floats up towards the loud red-haired Squirrel. "So, are you a messenger like Hermes?"

"Like Hermes?!" Ratatoskr shouts angrily. She gives a sarcastic laugh. "I'm nothing like that dumb, scrawny, prick of an Olympian! No! I'm the personal messenger to the All Father, Odin, and part of the far better Asgardian faction! While *he* is an asshole who gives people the wrong location! Causing poor, cute, Asgardian Squirrels to fall from the sky!"

She's very proud and boastful. Sounds a bit like Sun, but possibly worse when it comes to these traits. Though, hearing what happened to her, I wouldn't put it past a former Trickster. Especially if she talks down to him in person like she's doing right now.

"Uh, so where is Hermes?"

Ratatoskr proudly places her hands on her hips, with a smile that matches her stance. "He doesn't deal with these kinds of messages because he's a dumb Olympian! I'm the personal messenger for all things related to Gods' Wrath!"

"Gods' Wrath?!" Sun and I say in unison.

She begins to investigate at her surroundings. "Yes! I'm here to tell some nobody named Vergil Knight and his god, the Monkey King, that they've been allowed to join the finals of the tryouts in place of that Shinto god!"

"We are?!" Sun and I speak in unison once more. I'm more shocked than Sun, who is happy about this news.

"Huh?" Ratatoskr turns back towards us, looking lost to what we had said. "*We are?* No, I'm searching for someone named Vergil Knight,"

I point at myself to clarify to her. "That's me."

"Oh…" She continues to look around. "Then, where's this Monkey King?"

I point at Sun. "That's her… the girl with the monkey tail and furry hands and feet…"

Sun waves happily. "Hello!"

Ratatoskr turns back to us, but the confidence she was giving off a moment ago feels as if it is slowly dissipating. Her arms and shoulders droop as her jaw drops.

"Y-you're the Monkey King?"

Sun leaps off her cloud, with her staff resting on her shoulder. Landing in front of Ratatoskr, Sun stares down at the small girl joyfully.

"Yeah! I'm so happy to hear this! Thank you! Thank you! You really made my day!"

Sun's being nice and thanking the Asgardian Squirrel, but as Sun looks down at her, Ratatoskr isn't looking up at Sun. She is instead looking straight forward with heartbreak written on her face. It sort of looks like she's staring at Sun's breasts.

"B-but the Olympian said you're a *king*…" Ratatoskr says, sounding as if she's ready to cry.

"Huh? Oh, that's only one of my many titles! You can call me Sun Wukong!" Sun introduces herself nicely. "Anyway, thank-"

"A-and you used to look like a full-on animal before being reborn?"

"Huh? Yeah. In fact, a lot of people thought I was a guy because of that! Even Mr. Knight thought tha-"

"H-how?"

"Huh?" Sun looks at her, unsure of what's wrong. I guess you can throw me on that boat, too. She's acting completely different than before. "*How* what?"

Ratatoskr looks up at Sun with tears flowing out of her eyes. "How did you get a chest like that?! Wwaaahhh!" She whines loudly.

Tears pour out of the poor Squirrel like a waterfall, making a complete one-eighty from that self-boasting cockiness she was showing off a second ago.

I remember the insecure girls in high school who compared themselves to their bustier classmates, but never would I see them burst into tears in front of the person they were jealous of.

Sun looks at her chest as Ratatoskr points at it. "My chest? I don't know, they just grew there. Honestly, they can be in the way…"

A laugh nearly left my lips as soon as she said that. I cover my mouth quickly before so.

The anguish on Ratatoskr's face only worsens by Sun's words. Her bottom lip quivers in sadness by the Monkey King's remark.

"Y-you don't even want them?" Ratatoskr whines, sounding shocked at what was just spoken to her.

"Nope, but Mr. Knight seems to like them, so I tolerate them!"

I hate how okay she is with sharing that fact about me. It's true, don't get me wrong, but still…

The Squirrel-Tailed Girl falls to her knees and cries to the sky. "Whyyyyy!!!" She screams.

I kinda understand the tears on this one. I mean with what Sun said, that's like someone complaining about their Ferrari to someone who doesn't even own a car. This was a bit funny at first, but now it's sad. I can see Sun feeling the same as I am.

I limp up to Ratatoskr. "You all right?"

She seems to be calming down after hearing me. Cleaning her eyes and nose as she sniffles. "H-how can a monkey god, reborn from an Asian woman, have a bigger chest than me?"

Can't say I haven't been curious about that myself. I guess that would be a bit disappointing to find out if you're a girl, who apparently has body issues.

Maybe I should reassure her. Try to cheer her up a bit. "Well, you're still young. You'll continue to grow!" I happily tell her.

She looks at me in surprise to what I had said. Quickly, she goes back to her sorrowful demeanor. "No, I won't! Gods are almost entirely unchanging!"

I look over to Sun. "Really?"

Sun nods 'yes' to my question. "Uh-huh,"

Well, I guess it's nice knowing Sun will always be youthful, fit, and energetic. I won't be. I'll grow old, more fragile than I am now, and wrinkled. Makes me wonder if Sun will keep that clingy nature of hers towards me when that time comes. Though, it's not like I'm attractive now, so an older me may not be an issue for her.

"It's not fair! I'm part of the mighty Asgardian faction! I'm the personal messenger to Odin! The climber of the World Tree! Don't I deserve big titties and wide hips, more than anyone?!"

Alright, this is getting silly and stupid. I was expecting the more rude Ratatoskr from myth… Well, she is still rude…

Sun apparently agrees with me as she chops Ratatoskr's head gently.

"Ow!" Ratatoskr rubs her bruised head.

Sun gazes down at her in frustration. "Look, I'm sorry you're disappointed with your reborn body, but *please* get back to the tournament!"

Tears still lay in Ratatoskr's eyes, but I believe these are more fueled by pain than sadness.

"F-first you flaunt those huge things in my face, then you abuse and demand things from me? D-don't you know who I am, you stupid monkey?!"

"Yes! You told us a couple of times already!" Sun yells at the crying girl. "You spoiled, arrogant, little-"

I chuckle a bit at Sun's response. "Remind you of someone, Sun? Particularly when they were younger?"

Sun crosses her arms, pouting at my joke. "I don't know what you're talking about!"

She's still extremely arrogant, but Sun was far worse as a kid. She never broke out into tears like Ratatoskr here, but she did throw her fits. Normally, I had to bribe her in some way to get her to stop and behave. I think I may have a solution in our groceries.

I reach into one of the bags hanging from the staff Sun is holding. Digging through all that we bought, I find what I'm searching for: a chocolate bar!

With this in hand, I crouch down a tad to be at eye level with the crying Squirrel. "If you calm down and tell us what you came here for, I'll give you this!" I raise the bar to her face.

I know, a creepy twenty-something year old bribing an underage girl with squirrel features. Trust me, when it comes to gods, it's the only way to get answers or just quiet down for a minute.

Ratatoskr looks at the candy bar for a moment. She's still not happy. "Y-you fucking dirty creep! You're offering a young girl candy! You must be either a perv or an idiot if you think this will-" She stops her foul-mouthed complaints as she sniffs it. "Almonds?"

Eagerly, me and Sun wait for Ratatoskr to finish the last bite of her candy bar. She basks in every taste she takes as her face is smeared in chocolate.

She gulps the last bit as she gives a satisfied sigh. "Yummy!" She yells in a far better mood than before as her puffy tail wags happily.

I let out a relaxed sigh as she calms down. "Are you good now?"

She whips the mess on her face onto her sleeve, before standing with her small chest out proudly. "Of course! I'm always good! What else would you expect from the personal messenger of the All Father!"

Exactly how Sun acted after I gave her bribes, as though the fit from before didn't happen.

Sun bends over to Ratatoskr's eye level. "Now, can you please get back to the tournament?"

Even though Sun's face is right in Ratatoskr's, the poor little Squirrel can't take her eyes off of Sun's chest. I can relate to that a lot of times. Though, I don't make a face as if I'm trying to hold in tears like Ratatoskr is.

"How? …" I can hear her mutter as she sadly stares at Sun's breasts. She quickly turns away in a huff. "Yeah, you are personally invited by the Monarchs, including the great All Father, to be in the finals of the tryouts in place of that Shinto god…."

The Monarchs actually agreed to this drastic change in the tryouts? Sure, they offered rewards that far surpassed Sun's wish. However, the idea that they would do something like this at the last minute…

Particularly, Odin. I heard Gods' Wrath was his brainchild. I hear he also takes great pride in it. He's always one of the Monarch's present at the big tournament events.

With a vigorous fist raised in the air, Sun's smile shines bright. "All right! We're in, Mr. Knight!"

"Huh? Oh, yay…."

"What's wrong?"

"Just concerned, Sun."

"I'll be fine, Mr. Knight!" Sun bows her head to Ratatoskr. "Thank you for bringing this good news to me!"

Ratatoskr looks at the one she was envious in surprise. Her prideful face returns quickly though. "Well, of course! I am the messenger of the All Father and the Gods' Wrath tournament! It's my job to bring great news!"

Sun stands back up. "I am sorry if I upset you."

"Upset? Me? Ha! Sure, I cried, but that was for something else! I don't cry over such petty things like that!" Ratatoskr lies through her prideful voice.

"Really?" Sun asks, unsure of if what the Squirrel speaks is the truth.

"Wellll… I did also cry a bit when I met that Shinto god you guys are replacing!" Ratatoskr wraps her large fluffy tail around herself as she shakes in a cold shiver, as if she's haunted by something. "T-those things were weapons-grade… They still haunt me…"

Agreed. I also can't stop thinking of Susanoo's breasts.

Hearing the complaints of Ratatoskr, Sun stares down at her large bust. "I honestly don't know what the big deal with these is. The only good thing about them is Mr. Knight likes looking at them,"

"You've made that *very* clear, Sun!"

"They're a *big* deal, because they're *big!*" Ratatoskr begins to cry again.

I tap my patchwork cane onto the ground, creating a mild thumping sound on the dirt road. Luckily, it's enough to get Sun's attention.

"Sun, stop talking about your breasts to the body-conscience girl, who is here to give *you* the news you've been waiting for!"

"Oh right!" Sun grips her free fist close to her in a determined stance. She crouches down to Ratatoskr, nearly scaring the squirrel with her enthusiasm. "So, I'm in?!" She speaks, with a sparkle in her eyes and a wag of her tail.

"Uh, not yet. You still have to register!" Ratatoskr says, returning to her boastful personality.

"Register? Are you asking for money?"

"She's saying you need to sign a contract, Sun."

This makes sense. It was very common for human athletes when the sports of man were still popular. It certainly was common in myth as well. Deals among gods and demons are some of the most recognizable stories. Though, ironically this sounds closer to the former of the two.

"Correct, Caretaker to the Titties!"

"Please don't call me that..."

"If that's all it is, then let's sign it now!" Sun speaks excitedly, her body fidgety with glee.

"Hold on, Sun. Let me read it over first." From both what I read in myths, and my personal experience with the contracts for becoming a caretaker, it's probably best I scan over it first. I don't want us to owe our souls or something to the New Pantheon.

"I'm not the one you're signing with! That task belongs to the leader of the Librarians!"

"Librarians?" Sun asks exactly what I'm thinking.

I've never heard of the Librarians. I guess they are another branch of gods that serve under the Monarchs. I only know of the group that made my God Slayer, the Forgers, and the Messengers. The only reason I know of them is that I was told of their roles after becoming a caretaker.

"All right, where do we go to find them?"

Ratatoskr strikes a heroic pose as a little confidence-filled grin forms on her face. "Fear not! I, the Climber of Yggdrasil will send us there!" She proclaims, reminding me more of Sun at her worst.

The small red-headed girl digs through the pockets of her dress shirt, fishing for something.

Her face exudes frustration as she tries to find what she needs. About a minute later, her eyes sparkle as she happily shows her buck teeth in a grin. It seems she has found what she was looking for.

"Ta-da!" Ratatoskr shouts in victory as she holds up a small glass bottle with what appears to be an acorn.

Sun and I stare at the bottle, Sun appearing more impressed than I am. Does that mean she knows what it is?

She sniffs the bottle loudly for a moment and looks back at me. "I think it's a piece of the Divine Tree."

"W-what?!" I nearly drop my cane out of surprise. "Are you serious?"

Like many gods, it has many names. The Tree of Life, the Tree of Knowledge, Yggdrasil, and so on and so forth. Nowadays, we know it as simply 'the Divine Tree'. Large trees appeared alongside the Monarchs five years ago, appearing around some of the world's greatest cities and former places of worship.

The New Pantheon said they are branches of the Divine Tree, even though they dwarf all of our skyscrapers! Kind of scares me on how big the actual tree is.

The Divine Tree, along with the Monarchs and reborn gods, replaced all of the greatest wonders of the world. It's also the new workspace for the Monarchs and those who serve them. And this cute, fluffy-tailed girl has a piece of it in a glass bottle, holding it in front of us.

"With this acorn, I can send us anywhere as long as I know where to go!"

Sun raises an eyebrow. "So, you don't actually *climb* it?"

Ratatoskr lets out a surprised gasp, sounding like an offended teenage girl. She stands like one as well. "Of course not! That's just a title! Why would I climb on anything?"

Pointing at her tail, Sun lets out a confused chuckle. "Aren't you a Squirrel?"

"It kind of makes sense," I join in.

"S-shut up! You're a monkey! Do you climb up trees?"

"Yeah! In fact, that's what-" Sun stopped as she looks at me. Her head turns away, but I can see her thick eyebrows lowering in shame. "Uh, never mind…"

I glance down at my cane, knowing exactly what is going through her head. I've told her not to trouble herself about that. I've moved on from the experience.

"You know how big the Divine Tree is?!" Ratatoskr yells, ignoring Sun's sorrow and continuing to rant. "It would destroy my little heart and lungs if I actually climbed it!"

Pulling back from her somber thoughts, Sun watches the whining Squirrel in frustration. "All right! You're a squirrel who can't climb! Can we just go?"

"I-I don't need to climb! Nor do I need big titties either! I-I'm fine the way I. Fucking. Am!" Tears try to sneak from her eyes once more as she brings up the topic of Sun's chest again.

So odd hearing such horrible language from such a cute and childish voice.

Her tiny body full of rage, Ratatoskr flings the bottle at the ground behind her. With the sound of glass shattering, a bright flash of light glows from the dirt below.

With the light fading, I can see the acorn sinking into the soil below. After being completely swallowed in dirt, vines explode from the ground. Bending and wrapping around each other.

Sun and I watch in awe as the little plant grows into a gateway. Like a decorative garden gate, pure white, sparkling leaves hang from small branches that stick out of the wooden doorway.

Around the base of the gate, beautiful flowers begin to grow. It's something I have never seen in this walkway, and I've been here since I was eighteen. That would be seven years now.

As amazing as this gate appears, what's *in* the doorway is certainly more mystical. A swirling blue and white vortex of some kind. Glittering sparkles dazzle from the obvious portal in the center.

"This is how I *climb* the Divine Tree!" Ratatoskr speaks proudly. Clearly, she's still upset about before.

Sun walks up and inspects the botanical doorway. "So, will it stay up forever for random people to walk through?" Sun, once again, asks exactly what's on my mind.

"Of course not! When we enter it, it will disappear. When we return, it'll reappear!" Ratatoskr informs, happy with how smart she thinks she is. "This is just a simple short cut though! Something I use to get to combatants' homes to deliver their messages faster than if I repeated how I got here in the first place! And I don't have to worry about that prick of an Olympian giving me the wrong fucking directions again!"

"If this is meant to be a short cut for you, then why did you put it here?"

"What's wrong with here?"

I kind of hate that I have to burst her bubble on this. "Well, our home is still about six minutes on foot up ahead. May not be much, but it seems like a hassle,"

"W-what?"

Sun points her staff forward, nearly flinging our groceries off the end. "Yeah, it's not that bad of a trip! Especially if you can fly! You are a flying squirrel, right?"

"No, I'm not!"

"Then why did you fall from the sky?" Sun mentions, looking upwards.

"Because that stupid Olymp- S-shut up!" Tears get stuck in the corners of Ratatoskr's eyes. "I can walk for six minutes! Not a big problem! Especially, not in the dark… when owls show up and try to attack me!" She's about to break down again.

I'm confused if she is referring to before being reborn in her current human form, or recently?

Sun rests the Jingu Bang back on her shoulder once more. She looks on at the Furry Messenger. "Ssssooooo… Can we go do this?"

Cleaning her puffy tearful eyes, Ratatoskr stares up at Sun. "Y-yeah, let's just get this over with!"

"All right!" Sun leaps gleefully.

"Uh, Sun?" I stop her little victory dance as I point out something to her. Those being the grocery bags hanging from the end of her staff. "Can we at least bring those home first?"

If I'm going to sign a contract, I'd rather come off as professional as possible. And that means not having Sun walk in looking like a cartoon homeless person with a satchel. I guess that's a bit hypocritical since this is coming from the same guy who applied to be a caretaker in a stained gray shirt.

"Aw, come on, Mr. Knight! This won't take long!"

"It will probably take longer for that than to walk back home for a second!"

Sun stands next to me, wrapping her free arm around me. Pulling me close to her. "But I'm excited! Even if we're only gonna sign a piece of paper! Come on!"

"H-hey, wait!"

Sun drags me to the mystical door. As frustrated as I am that she's not listening to me, the closer she brings me to this gate, the weirder I feel. It's not uncomfortable. In fact, it's the opposite.

Ratatoskr, with her eyes and nose clean, stands in front of us as we approach the gateway. Happily, the Asgardian Squirrel points to the vortex. "Next stop, the Sanctuary of the Librarians!"

I don't feel as concerned with this as I was a second ago. Actually, as we step through it, I feel good. Really relaxed…

CHAPTER FIVE: BOOKS OF LIFE AND SECRETS

"Oh, cold! Cold!"

The nearly bare feet of the Monkey King dance on the tile flooring. It was only about a second or so ago that the exposed toes and heels of Sun Wukong stood on the warmth of the soil-covered ground that was heated by the giant star that shared her name.

Bouncing her feet up and down trying to warm them, Sun swings not only the bags of food and such that hang on the edge of the Jingu Bang, but also her Caretaker who she still had a grip on. Strangely, he showed no complaint to taking part of that comedic waltz.

With a whistle, the yellow cloud the Monkey King used as a mount returned below her feet, lifting her off the cold tile. Her legs folded as the cloud rose, tossing her Caretaker in her lap.

With a relaxed sigh, she stared at her strangely quiet Keeper. "Sorry, Mr. Knight. I know you don't-"

Her apology was put on pause as she was met with the laxed expression on his face. "Mr. Knight?"

"Oh, Sun!" He spoke in a calm, happy gesture as he patted the head of his god. "You're such a good monkey…"

Despite being confused about how he was acting, the Monkey King took both the gesture and compliment happily as her tail waved frantically. "Th-thanks, Mr. Knight!"

He wrapped his arms around her to hug the Great Sage, causing her tail wag more. Though, this was still new to her as she's the one that usually gave him hugs, never the other way around.

"You're so awesome. You got sexy abs and your breasts feel so much softer than Ell's…"

"How do you know how soft hers are?" She maliciously questioned, which quickly turned to fury by what was just spoken. Her wagging tail even halted.

Her Caretaker rested his head on her fur covered shoulder. "I love you, Sun…"

The rage she felt quickly extinguished as her heart begins to beat rapidly. Her face became bright red and her tail swayed dangerously. "R-really?!" Her mind was full of thoughts as to what that might lead to.

"Stop ignoring me!" A voice yelled in order to gain the attention of the love-struck Monkey King and her lazed Caretaker, much to the former's annoyance.

Ratatoskr stood in front of them in a huff, tapping her foot, waiting for them to notice her.

Sun stared at her, frustrated that the little Asgardian Squirrel had to ruin the moment. "What?"

"*What*?! I brought you to the Sanctuary of the Librarians! One of the branches of gods that serve the Monarchs! You could show a little respect and bask in how amazing this place is!" she shouted with her arms out as she presented the new location they had been sent to.

The first thing they noticed was the glass window ceiling, which reached as high as the skies itself. In the center was the symbol of the New Pantheon, a giant G in gold stain glass with the different symbols of each faction circling it. All of it sparkled and dazzled from the reflection of the sunlight outside.

However, despite the glory of this sight, Sun and her calm Caretaker's attention was focused on what surrounded them. At first glance, they seemed to be walls. In actuality, they were shelves. These structures stretched as high as the walls that held up the high ceiling above.

"Thaats a lot of boooks…" the Caretaker pointed out as he examined what rested on each of the many shelves.

Books of different sizes, colors, and designs. Thousands, millions, perhaps even more than that, all squeezed into those compartments.

"Wow! Look at all these books, Mr. Knight! I bet you're loving this, right?"

"This is so cool- Oh my god, the girl with the squirrel tail is here! It's so fluffy!" His hands made a grabbing gesture.

Ratatoskr investigated the odd Caretaker in annoyance. "The hell is wrong with him?"

"M-Mr. Knight, are you alright?"

"I feel amaaaazing…" he announces as he rested his head back. "The books are cool too…"

"Wait, I heard of this happening before," Ratatoskr scratched her head as though she was trying to dig the answer out of her head. "Ah! Did he bring his God Slayer?!"

"Huh? Uh, no. That got destroyed…" Sun answered casually to the question.

"How the fu- Never mind! Anyway, the God Slayer isn't only meant for Caretakers to defend themselves. It's also meant to defend them from the side effects of certain divine powers!"

"W-what do you mean? What's happening to him?"

"It is called the Eden Effect! *My voice echoes in the massive library that is my Sanctuary*."

Sun turned, with her dazed Caretaker in her arms, towards the self-narrating voice. Glancing up at one of the colossal bookshelves, they saw a figure walking straight down it. Unaffected by gravity or physics, the individual smoothly marched down the center of the shelves that split the rows of books like a tightrope walker.

Several books floated around him, with only one placed in his hands. Each one's pages flipped rapidly, as if they were being read at top speed. Once one reached the end, it flew away, back to the top of the towering shelves, only to be replaced by another from the shelves he passed by.

Though, this wasn't the oddest thing about this man. He wore a suit with wing-like coat tails, a visible button-up undershirt, and a scarf. His short, neck-length hair shared his clothing's color. It was a bit messy in style and ruffled like a bird's feathers.

Though, what stuck out from the man the most was his face. It was completely covered by a black bird-like mask, appearing almost like a plague doctor's mask from days of old. On it were golden markings forming the outline of a mouth and a familiar shape around his eyes. They were the eyes of Ra.

Sun leaned toward the Messenger Squirrel. "Who's this weird bird guy?" she whispered.

"This is the leader of the Librarians and registrar for the tournament! His name is-"

"Names: Thoth, God of Writing and the Mystic arts, The Self Maker. Faction: Benben. Godhood: Knowledge, Muse, *I introduce myself to my guest as I multitask with my reading*."

Thoth. Sun had heard stories of that god by her Caretaker. He often lived in Benben's, the Egyptian faction, an underworld called Duat. There, he worked with the Death God Anubis.

His voice sounded monotone to Sun, and the way he spoke was as though he was reading a fable out loud to them. The thought of something being wrong with this god went through her head as she continued to observe him.

"Stop interrupting me like that, stupid bird!" Ratatoskr shouted in a fit.

The bird-like man flicked his finger upward, opening a small portal in front of him as he continued to walk. As he went through it with his books, another portal opened in front of the three. Thoth walked out of it, still surrounded by the flipping books.

"I can't be stupid. That's impossible for a Knowledge God, *I inform Ratatoskr as she whines, which she normally does when I see her. I still ponder if she is aware of how loud and distracting she often is.*"

"S-shut up!"

Tilting her head at the odd bit going on before her, the Monkey King grew more frustrated with the gag these two were pulling and not getting answers as to what was wrong with her Caretaker.

"Ha ha!" the Caretaker laughed. "These guys are as funny as that scared priestess and the big tittied samurai…"

"Can someone please tell me what's wrong with Mr. Knight?!" Sun shouted in both anger and panic. "Is he going to be alright?!"

"*I close the book in my hand. The bang of it causes an echo. With this book shut, I let go of it and wave my hand to send it and the others hovering around me back to their shelves.* He will be fine once you leave. This is common for humans when they are close to the Divine Tree, *I inform them, hoping to have surprised my guests of their whereabouts.*"

"D-Divine Tree?" the dazed Caretaker spoke, almost sounding as if the news he heard was sobering him up from whatever was happening to him.

"Mr. Knight!" the Monkey King said in a relieved voice.

Still in her arms, the Caretaker began to survey his surroundings more closely by focusing on the nearby walls. Other than what appeared to be old Egyptian illustrations of Thoth with a scroll in hand, Anubis standing next to scales, and a beast with the head of a crocodile, the body of a bear, and the legs of a hippo, he noticed the walls were being held together by branches.

In the only two corners they were able see, some of the branches stuck out with white sparkling leaves on them.

Even in his intoxicated state, the Caretaker recognized the aura the white leaves produce. They gave off the same relaxing aura that Ratatoskr's gate made.

"Of all the side effects to Divine powers, this is one of the better symptoms to be exposed to, *I try to reassure the two with this information.*"

The Caretaker understood what the Knowledge God was saying, even in his relaxed state. In fact, that must be what he was talking about, the Caretaker thought.

All the panic and concern he felt before coming here was gone. All that was left was joy and tranquility. His body felt as though he had woken up from a great sleep, far different than how he felt after having that resurrection juice poured on him. His body was so at ease he began to move his legs from the muscle-bound arms of his god.

"M-Mr. Knight, be careful!"

His legs touched the ground, but his cane did not. He let his grip go from the Monkey King who cradled him.

Without any support, he nearly fell, his worried Great Sage reaching out for him before he did. Suddenly, by instinct, he stopped himself and regained his balance. The young man stretched his legs out as he stood upright.

The Caretaker, Vergil Knight, for the first time in the long while, stood on his two feet with no issues. His left knee felt no pain, as it did before. It was as if it was never harmed.

He stepped on the newly healed leg, then the right followed. He took a few more steps. No limping, just walking.

In shock, the Great Sage dropped her staff, along with the groceries hanging from it, leading to a loud bang as the weight damaged the floor, while missing the bags.

"*I stare down at the damage floor in annoyance at what transpired...*"

Sun's eyes widen with surprise as a happiness glowed on her face. "M-Mr. Knight! You're standing without the cane!" She reached out her arms and hugged her Caretaker happily.

He let out a relaxed chuckle. "Man, this is awesome!"

The fact he did not grunt from being hugged by her did catch Sun off guard. Nearly ruining the moment, she became filled with concern.

"The Eden Effect. The Name the Christian Monarch, Jehovah… Joe… gave to this symptom. It was used for his personal Garden and all the creatures in it, to prevent them from harming one another and simply ruining his lovely garden. Thus, the Eden Effect was born, *I explain in detail the origin of this experience.*"

Still hugging him tightly, Sun looked over to Thoth. "So, does that mean Mr. Knight is healed?"

"No, *I speak, preparing to explain the matter at hand.* He is not healed. He is simply numb to pain right now. He feels no negative nerves nor emotions. He will be like this until he leaves. Then all the pain he'd normally feel will return. Perhaps he should not be walking right now, to avoid any further issues he will have once he leaves, *I advise as I point at his leg.*"

Sun's head lowered in disappointment. She hoped if his leg was healed, she could stop feeling guilty for what happened. Now, she was worried as to how much pain her Caretaker would be in when they left.

The possibility of getting a second redemption was seeming more unlikely to the saddened Monkey.

"Come on, Mr. Knight. Let's get this done-"

The depressed Monkey King stopped as she noticed that her Caretaker was no longer standing next to her. "M-Mr. Knight?"

She looked frantically for her Caretaker. As quick as she started, she found him examining the books on one of the tall wall-like shelves.

Sun floats over to him on her cloud. "Mr. Knight?"

"*Mysteries Unknown to Humans?* The Forgotten Planets of the Solar System? What are these?" the Caretaker wished to know, still sounding tipsy from the Eden Effect.

"Exactly what they say, *I intervene as I walk next to the intoxicated human.* Life is like a book. There is a beginning, middle and end. That's what these are. The stories of all life that has ever existed, with room for future Books of Life. From what you humans know of to what you still wish to know. This is the passion of the Knowledge Gods: learning and knowing. And all of it is here before you. The history of everything, *I openly admire at my Godhood's work to my visitors.*"

"Everythinnnnngggg?" the Caretaker tried to ask.

"Well… There are two that we were not allowed to keep…. *I sigh in disappointment.* One was about the war of the gods, the Day. Even we Knowledge Gods are forbidden to know of what happened back then. Disappointing, since it was I who recorded the three greatest battles of my faction. The other… I am unsure. Both were written by our branch's founder, Odin."

"Hail the All Father! The smartest of all gods!" Ratatoskr praised her Monarch loudly.

"How I wish to at least know what that other book is about. *I plead in disappointment as a Knowledge God, not knowing something.*"

"You know, I may not be a Knowledge God, but I'm seen as the *Wise* Handsome Monkey King!" Sun boasted about herself.

"It must be nice to give yourself titles like that, *I jest as I, what the humans say, roast the arrogant guest.*"

"Hey!"

"Ha!" Ratatoskr laughed. "That's what you get! You and your fat titties!"

"Ignore Ratatoskr, her kindness is like her chest. Nonexistent, *I say, feeling on a roll today.*"

"Go to Hell, bird!" Ratatoskr shouted, a tear trying to leave her eye.

Sun reached an arm toward her dazed Caretaker and pulled him close to her as she eyed the Egyptian god. "W-well, Mr. Knight is smart! Smarter than me!"

"He is smart, for what he knows. As it normally is for humans. They throw around the word *intellectual* because they have had a taste of knowledge, or think they know more than others. Compared to us, however, that's merely basic knowledge. True Knowledge is when you can know everything about a particular subject simply by looking at it, *I explain as I discuss the art that is knowledge.*"

"Just by looking at them? What does that mean?"

Thoth's beak-like mask aimed toward the cane the Caretaker held. "That cane was made by you. The original was destroyed by the Celtic monster, the Nuckelavee. It took you about thirty minutes to put the whole thing together. Your fur got caught many times in the duct tape. *I turn my gaze over to the plastic bags hanging from her staff, the Jingu Bang.* You picked up milk which will expire on the 14th, beef-flavored ramen, chicken nuggets, oranges, apples, and peaches. Those last three are especially for you, them being your favorite fruits. However, you will still eat the ramen since it is only an artificial flavor, not real meat at all, *I explain, much to her surprise.*"

The Monkey King watched on in astonishment at how much detail the Knowledge God went into simply by observing their possessions. Even her intoxicated Caretaker seemed surprised.

"W-well... It isn't! So, I can eat it!" the Monkey King uttered in a fluster.

"This is the type of knowledge only beings of my Godhood can achieve. The knowledge in these books cannot be read by those of low intelligence, *I tell the two while boasting about my own intelligence.*"

The Monkey King watched the Knowledge God in annoyance at how he talked down to her and her Caretaker. While said Caretaker had already zoned out from what the Bird-Masked God was talking about, focusing instead on the book titled *Mysteries Unknown to Humans.* He reached for the book, ignoring what the Masked God had said.

"W-wait, Mr. Knight! You shouldn't-"

As he did to Thoth, the dazed Caretaker ignored his god and opened the book. His eyes widened at what he viewed, surprised by its contents.

"Oh my god… I can't read this…"

Confused by his words, Sun looked into the book he had opened. The title of the book was written in the Divine Tongue. A single language that can be understood and read by all. Inside however, was something truly unreadable.

Words in constant flux. Warping, disappearing, and reappearing from page to page. Shifting from English, to Chinese, to Russian, to languages and text that no longer exist in the mortal world.

"As I said, only beings of my Godhood can read these books, because our brains are the only ones that can comprehend them. We understand every language known, unknown, and potentially will be known to man. Our brains and eyes are able to keep up with the moving and warping text. The books where made specifically for beings of our calibre to read and no one else, *I point out after their revelation of what is inside these books.*"

Sun and her drunken Caretaker scratched their heads, trying to make sense of the mishmashed text.

"I think I saw the name Henry… I think…"

"Oh! Mr. Knight, look! I see the word Templar! What's that mean?"

"Not the best state of mind to answer that Sun…"

"And you are ignoring me. *I sigh in disappointment at the lack of respect my guests show me…*"

The Caretaker leaned over to whisper into the ear of his god. "I just noticed he is talking like a book…"

"Oh, you're right!" the Monkey King proclaimed, sounding surprised at this notion.

"Can we please get her signed up!" Ratatoskr shouted, gaining the attention of the distract duo and the disappointed masked god. "I have other places I need to be for the All Father's sake!"

"Ratatoskr is correct, *I tell them in a more positive manner.* I guess there is always a first for everything, *I jokingly end my remark, giving her what is called a thumbs up.*"

"Kiss my fluffy ass!"

Thoth reached into the right pocket of his white coat. Pulled from his wardrobe was a piece of paper. From the opposite side, he pulled out a long feathered pen.

With pen and paper ready, Thoth walked up to Sun, the beaked mask nearly touching her face. The awkward encounter widened Sun's eyes as the bird face stared into her eyes.

The scribbling sound of paper being scratched by a pen was heard under the beak of the Knowledge God.

"Names: Sun Wukong. Monkey King, or simply Monkey. The Victorious Fighting Buddha. The Great Sage Equal to Heaven, which is only a self-made title, *I point out this fact.*"

The Monkey King's eyebrows scrunched in anger at the remark. "Hey! I hold that title with pride!"

"You are two-thousand years old, not including the few months you've been reborn. You are a double Godhood of Animal and Demigod. Though, with your personality you're a borderline Trickster. Even your fighting style shows this. But, since you use trickery as a tool for battle or self-gain, and not for hellacious acts, you do not fall under that Godhood. Your preferred weapon is the Ruyi Jingu Bang, which means Compliant Golden-Hooped Rod. You enjoy fruit and spending time with your Caretaker, Vergil Knight, who you wish to marry and have two children with."

The Monkey King nods her head yes. "Yep! That's right!"

Ratatoskr nearly jumped in surprise at Sun's answer. *That open about it?!* she thought.

"You debate on whether you should be called Sun Knight, or he Vergil Wukong. Seeing that you are a king, he should take your name. Yet, at the same time, you are leaning more towards the previous, because it sounds, how the humans say, cool, *I continue my writing of the information I continue to read out loud.*"

"Well, isn't it? It would be a great title to add to the list! Right?"

"Like many gods, you care not for modesty. You particularly enjoy the flustered expression your Caretaker gives you when seeing your bare body. Though, you do not like it when he yells at you for such. *My pen captures my every word before I even speak it.*"

"I-I can't help it. I-it's that cute face he makes…"

"Is any of this important?!" Ratatoskr shouted "Do you need to write every little detail to register her?!"

"No, but it is fun, *I joke.*"

Scratching the back of her own head. A flustered face forms on Sun Wukong. "Well, it is kind of embarrassing to get it all out like this. R-right Mr. Knight?"

Sun turned to find Vergil looking back into the book from before, no longer trying to make out what the moving text read. Now he and his intoxicated mind was simply watching the warping words, mesmerized by the show before him.

"Whooooaa…"

"I believe he was not listening, *I speak with a shrug of my shoulders.*"

"He is *really* out of it," Ratatoskr pointed out.

The red blushing cheeks of the Monkey King puffed out, pouting at the fact that her desires were spoken out-loud, only for her Caretaker to ignore it all, even with the knowledge of him not being right of mind at the moment.

"All stories must have a joke here and there, but we must cut this bit short, *I tell them as I turn the intoxicated human towards me.* Now, it is your turn."

"Wait, what?!" the Monkey King asked, surprised by this news.

Ratatoskr crossed her arms in a huff. "What, did your brains all go down to your tits? Both gods and their caretakers have to be registered!"

This news brings nothing but concern for the Monkey King. "H-how much will you need to know for this?"

"The registration mostly needs his name, age, and what qualifies him to be a caretaker. But of course, I will know everything about him as I gaze upon his intoxicated face, *I clarify.*"

"E-everything?"

"Worry not, if it is embarrassing, I won't share… Unless you want me to, *I joke to my worried guest.*"

"O-of course not! Heh heh…" The Monkey King nervously chuckled.

That scenario was not something she had thought of as a possibility. One of the rules of being a caretaker to a god was to be perfectly healthy, something of which her Caretaker was clearly not.

Having lied his way through much of his paperwork, the Caretaker by the name of Vergil Knight had hid the fact that he is a hemophiliac.

Sun knows of the disorder he suffered from. It was one of the reasons she was overprotective of him. She also knew that if Thoth found out, she may be taken away from him or even worse, he'd be punished for lying.

The Victorious Fighting Buddha was perfectly willing to go to war with the Monarchs and all the gods that served them to stay by her Caretaker's side. Still, she would rather not have him be dragged into such a squabble.

Thoth locked eyes with the dazed Caretaker as he prepared to write what he saw in him. For some reason, he halted his penwork as the calm human grabbed the beak of his mask.

"Is this covering a real beak?"

"Can you let go please? This is quite awkward, *I query nicely while hiding my annoyance at this awkward scenario.*"

"Ooooohhhh…" the Caretaker said as he slowly let go of the mask of the Egyptian god.

"Name: Vergil Terrance Knight. Age: Twenty-four. Status: Mythologist, *I write down what I speak as I have done with the Monkey King.*"

Sun leapt in between the two while displaying a frantic expression. "Well, I guess that's all you need, r-right?"

"Hmmmm? *I hum in fascination at a discovery.*"

"A-A Discovery? You mean how awesome Mr. Knight is? I couldn't agree more!" she awkwardly uttered.

"Your bodily functions are odd compared to the other humans that have come here, *I say as I try to examine the* human more. It is difficult to see due to his strange-acting god."

"W-what are you talking about? Mr. Knight is as healthy as one of those stupid hooved things!"

"You mean a horse?" Ratatoskr asked.

"He is indeed healthy. As healthy as a resurrected man can be. *I reveal what I have learned in a surprised manner that fits the discovery*."

"Hold up!" Ratatoskr shouted. The fur on her tail spiked up in surprise by the news. "You mean by mortal methods, right? Like, they restarted his heart or something?"

"No, *I correct the wrong Squirrel once again*. By divine means… The Life Cider…"

"W-what?! No way!"

"Life Cider?" Sun spoke in a loss.

"Ciiiiderrrrr… Oh!" the drunken Caretaker stepped in. "Apple Juice!"

"Ah! The stuff Loki poured on you! The juice he said he got from the Gods' Wrath tournaments!"

"He had the Life Cider flowing through his body? *I ask, intrigued by this news*. Fascinating, *I can't seem to peer past this information. I can't see any other facts about his body or mind. My eyes are drawn back to this one detail! Such a twist for a modern human!*"

"I-is it really that interesting?"

"A human resurrection hasn't happened since the days of old, *I clarify*. Tell me, has there been any issues with your Caretaker? *I continue to question*."

"Like what?"

"Hmmm, *I think loudly*. After being resurrected and seeing the damage the Nuckelavee caused... Did he show, what is called *sympathy* for those who were harmed?"

With a brow raised, the Monkey King prepared to answer the inquiring Knowledge God. "Why would he?" she says, in a suspicious tone as she crosses her arms over her bust. "From what I heard, they threatened Mr. Knight and left him behind to be attacked by that thing. Why would he care about them dying? I know if I got there sooner, they wouldn't have gotten off as easy." Her threat was spoken in a tone that matched her intent.

Hearing this sent shivers down the tail of Ratatoskr, as she nervously stepped back further away. All the while, the Caretaker looked around him with a blank stare as he was still affected by the Divine Tree around him.

"That is reasonable. Not even the most kindhearted beings would care of the fate of those who would commit such heinous crimes, *I agree with her reason*. But still, he saw much that night, *I point out*. His fellow humans skinned alive, crawling on the ground as nothing but a mass of bones and muscle tissue. All begging for the bliss of my and Anubis's judgement. Surely, that must have caused some sort of trauma?"

This information brings back memories of that night to Sun. The memory of her, the Caretaker, and the Shinto god who helped them at the last minute, walking under the rising sun. To hear her Caretaker explain how he mentally felt fine by what he saw, as if it were simply a nightmare.

"T-that Shinto god told us it was just a side effect... I-is it serious?"

"Maybe not, *I agree as I roll up my scroll*. As long as that was the only time. Unless, of course, he has shown any other issues?"

With her hands in fists and her chest puffed out, confidence formed on the Monkey King's face. "Of course not! Mr. Knight has been perfectly fine since then!"

"You mean, excluding now?" Ratatoskr jumped in as the drunken Caretaker tried to reach for her tail.

"So soft...."

"I thank you for dealing with my curiosity. It's simply in our nature as Knowledge Gods, *I kindly speak*. Congratulations, you are officially in the Tryout finals in place of Susanoo-no-Mikoto! *I announce, theatrically of course.*"

With excitement on her face, Sun Wukong giggled gleefully at the news. She grabbed hold of her dear Caretaker, hugging him with one arm. "I'm in, Mr. Knight!"

"In what again?" he asked, still out of it.

"Yay. Woo-hoo." Ratatoskr sarcastically cheered. "Can we please go now, for the All Father's sake!"

"Ratatoskr has a point, *I say in shock, realizing how unusual that is*. It is perhaps best to get him home and away from the divine energy afflicting him."

"Oh, probably a good idea! Come on, Mr. Knight! Let's get you and our food home!" Sun told her Caretaker as she picked up her fallen staff.

"Where are we again?"

"Come on you two! We have to get going!" Ratatoskr shouted.

Unsure if he would be able to walk alone, Sun grabbed hold of her Caretaker's hand as they both followed behind Ratatoskr, all while being watched from behind by the Knowledge God, Thoth.

Like for any being of his Godhood, so many thoughts went through his head. One in particular persisted. That day five years ago, when the Christian god opened his eyes for the world.

Thoth has learned that the Great Sage was overprotective and worrisome toward her Caretaker. Yet, it seemed that the Caretaker was not having the same problems as many of those humans did five years ago. "This is an interesting twist…"

CHAPTER SIX: WHISPERS OF RAVENS

Huginn and Muninn, are the eyes and ears of the All Father, Odin. Going unnoticed, even by other gods, these ravens watch from the shadows.

Now, Huginn returned to his master and his fellow Monarchs, while his brother continued to watch their target from afar.

Odin listened to the jet-black bird as it whispered in his ear, nodding to everything it told him. Meanwhile, his wolves watch in curiosity as the other two Monarchs wait for what the creature has learned.

"Hmm. Interesting," the elder god muttered as he stroked his beard.

"What is it, All Father?" Geri asked.

"Tell us!" Freki joined.

Joe leaned forward on the table. "Has he learned anything important?"

"Well, she is officially in the Tryouts now," the All Father said, still bothered by this change. "But something has occurred."

The two Monarchs watched on at what Odin had to speak of.

"What is it, my friend?" Vishnu spoke kindly.

Odin leaned forward with his fingers locked together, his face displaying concern with the news. "Her Caretaker, the human, Vergil Knight. It seems the Celtic monster caused him more damage than we thought."

Joe and Vishnu glanced at one another, at a complete and total loss for words.

"What do you mean?" asked the hooded Christian god.

"Nemesis mentioned in her report that Loki used the Life Cider on the Caretaker of Sun Wukong only to heal his injuries. However, it seems he wasn't healed," the one-eyed Monarch says with a slight growl in his voice. "He died before the Cider made contact."

The news brought shock to the Monarchs and their Enforcers. Joe stood from his seat and quickly slammed his hands on the table.

"A human resurrection!" he shouted, his uncontrolled voice shaking the building they occupied.

Alongside the booming voice of the Christian god, another roar was heard: the screams of death.

"Aaaaahhhh!"

NAMES: AZRAEL, ANGEL OF DEATH, PALE HORSEMEN OF DEATH.

FACTION: CHRISTIAN. GODHOOD: DEATH.

The Death God roared, enraged by his father, despising the words and what they meant to a bringer of death.

Swinging his large scythe, the skeletal angel threw a fit of rage. "Aaaahhhh!"

"Azrael, calm down!" Joe shouted once more, continuing his shaking of the building.

"Perhaps you should follow suit," Vishnu calmly requested the Christian Monarch.

With several deep breaths, Joe began to do so and slowly sat back down in his throne.

"Y-your right. I apologize…"

Vishnu looked back toward Odin as Joe calmed down. "Why do you think your Trickster resurrected a human?"

"Why does Loki do anything? He's a Trickster!" Odin growled furiously at the mere thought of the Liesmith. "But for the life of me, I can't see why he'd do this? It doesn't match his sick sense of humor."

"Father, can we allow a resurrected human to walk freely?" Michael asked. "What if he suffers the same fate as those from before?"

"Aaaah!" Azrael screamed.

"Perhaps you're right, my child. That may be for the best."

"Stop!" Odin shouted with his hand in the air. Huginn continued to whisper in his ear. "That may not be an option from the sounds of it."

"Explain…" spoke Joe.

"It seems our main concern is closer to this human than expected."

Joe sighed loudly at the news. "You don't mean what I think you mean, do you?"

"Yes, he is closer to Wukong than normal Caretakers are to their gods," Odin spoke in a displeased manner. "So, it seems if you want us to continue to be seen fondly by the Monkey King, perhaps we should not take away what she cherishes."

"Father, can we actually let this go?!" Michael inquired, still bothered by this revelation.

Joe lowered his head in thought. "This is quite the quagmire indeed."

"Did you hear of any issues with this human after the incident?" asked Vishnu.

Odin listened to the whispers of his raven once more. "Hmmm. It sounds like he is normal. Though, he was apparently affected by the Eden Effect."

"Ah, that's right. His God Slayer was said to have been destroyed during the Nuckelavee attack," Vishnu brought up. "But if this is true, then it may be best to leave him be for now. We do not want to enrage the Monkey King, now do we?"

Dashavatara nodded in agreement with his Monarch's words.

With a stroke of his beard, Odin nodded to the Hindu god's idea. "You may be right. At least for now."

"We agreed that we would not allow these modern humans to be exposed to that much divine power again ever since the incident five years ago," Joe mentioned. "But at the same time, if he is not showing the same issues as many of those humans did, then we will let him be. Thus, keeping the Great Sage from becoming our enemy."

"Aaaaahhhh!" Azrael screamed at the news, hitting his fist onto the table where the Monarchs sat. His touch causes it to rot under his hand. "No… Human resurrections…"

"Azrael!" Michael growled at his sibling.

"You *cough* dare act this way to the Monarchssss?" Abaddon joined in the scolding.

"Aaaahhh!" Azrael continued to thrash his fist onto the table in a fit. "No! Human! Resurrections!" he shouted with each bang.

Geri and Freki hid behind the chair of their Monarch, fearing the tantrum-throwing Death God and whimpering at his screams.

"Can you calm him down?" Odin shouted as the panicked flapping wings of Huginn slapped his face.

"Metatron!"

Hearing his name spoken by his father, the heavenly looking Avatar approached the Death God, grabbing hold of his hand before it hit the table once more.

The skeleton-like god struggled in the grip of the voiceless angel. "Aaaaahhhh!"

Metatron glared at the bringer of Death, and caused the ghostly horsemen to return the intimidation with an angry hum whispering through his exposed teeth.

With a raise of his free hand, the Metatron pointed toward Azrael. "Peace…" a whisper echoed from the covered face of the Christian Avatar.

The words alone caused the Death God to calm his body. His shoulders and arms rested as Metatron freed him from his grip. Azrael lowered his head as if he was disappointed with himself.

Azrael fell to his boney knees in a pleading position before the table he was beating. "Forgiveness..."

Hearing these words, Metatron placed a gentle hand on the shoulder of the begging angel, while his other hand began to restore the damaged table.

"Your Death God seems to only get more malicious as time goes on," Vishnu crossed his many arms at the subject.

"He's fine. You know how Death Gods act when it involves human resurrections," Joe defended his child. "Still, the whole thing with this Caretaker may potentially cause issues. If he does not show any signs now, that doesn't mean he won't later. Then, there's the fact he was exposed to more divine energy through the Librarians' domain."

"Hmm, that is true," Odin nodded. "A normal human of this era can become intoxicated and numb through the secondhand divinity the tree gives off. That is why so many of their elderly and sick moved closer to them. However, this human had Divine essence flowing through him already. Even if it is gone by now, It could reform in his unprotected body from too much exposure to the Divine Tree."

"Then, what do you recommend?" Joe asked the All Father.

"Muninn is keeping an eye on the two. If something comes up, we will know of it."

"So, we continue watching? Very well. That's the best option anyway," the Christian god agreed. "What of Ratatoskr? Perhaps we should ask if she noticed anything from the two?"

Odin shook his head with his muscular arms crossed. "I doubt it, the only times she interacted with them she was either yelling at the drunken Caretaker or whining about the chest of the Monkey King."

Joe tilted his head, befuddled by the news. "Her… chest?"

Odin batted his hand in the air. "Besides, she has one more message to deliver," The one-eyed Monarch spoke. "After all, she should know that her last opponent has changed, correct?"

"Ah yes!" Vishnu eagerly agreed. "Perhaps we should let the viewers know of these changes as well?"

The hooded god bowed his head. "Agreed. This is also a chance to take our minds off of all these issues, for now at least."

"I wonder how she'll take it?" Vishnu asked in curiosity.

Odin let out a hardy laugh. "She's a War Goddess! As long as she has someone to fight, she'll be fine! Truth be told, I'm quite excited to see who will win between these two."

"It could also be a good way to learn how powerful Wukong currently is as well," Joe added.

"You're always so serious, boy!" Odin laughed.

"Perhaps you're right. Still…" Joe lowered his head in thought. "We should have special measures, just in case something pops up during the event."

The Christian God turned back toward his four horsemen. Metatron, Michael, and Abaddon join the bowing Azrael, each understanding the serious matter their father spoke of.

"If something happens, there will be hell to pay…" Michael promised.

CHAPTER SEVEN: BELLONA, GODDESS OF WAR

A large white mansion, with decor inspired by Greek and Roman ruins. It was the home of Leonardo Russo, one of the wealthiest humans in America, head of the Warriors of Enyo Veteran's Charity, and the Caretaker to the Olympian Bellona.

Inside, the elderly 73-year-old man was dusting and cleaning shelves. His hair, mustache, and beard were done up in a style befitting a person his age. His eyes were two different colors, the left being brown and the right blue, highlighted with a small cut over his right eyebrow. The outfit he wore was relatively casual, consisting of a white button-up shirt, green coat, and dress pants.

With his cleaning cloth, the senior citizen moved the frames that decorated his shelves to dust under them. These frames contained pictures of a young soldier, happily smiling alongside his fellow troopers and proudly wearing his medals of valor and a purple heart, all of which belonged to the owner of this house, Leonardo Russo.

The dusting hands of the elderly gentlemen halted as the doorbell echoed down the hall of the mansion.

His focus shifted toward the front door with a quizzical expression. "Got past the front gate, huh?"

The man opened the large doors to the mansion. He was only met with the Olympian-style statues and a fountain that laid in the center of the house's front garden.

"Hello!" the voice of a young girl shouted.

He looked down toward the voice. His brown eye focuseed on the short guest while his blue eye stayed in place. He then saw who was talking. It was the Messenger for the Gods' Wrath tournament, Ratatoskr.

"Ah, Miss Ratatoskr, welcome," the old man kindly lowered himself to be at eye level with her. "I shall tell Lady Bellona you're here."

Hearing this caused the Squirrel to shiver in fear. Her red fur stuck up to what she perceived as a threat.

"N-no, that's fine! Really!" the young girl nervously voiced. "I-I'm just here to pass on the news of a big change in her next match." Ratatoskr pulled an envelope from her dress coat.

The gentleman took it from her small hand. He stood back up as he examined the note. "A change you say? I will hand it to her, gladly. Though, are you sure you do not wish to come in? My lady is enjoying her dinner. I am certain she would enjoy your company."

"N-no! I-I'm fine! Please give it to her!" Ratatoskr uttered.

"Of course. Do take care," the old man saluted to the young girl.

Saying their goodbyes, Ratatoskr happily leapt down the steps of the large mansion, down to her gateway at the bottom.

I swear, he was gonna make me her dinner! she nervously thought, with an expression that displayed the terror she felt, despite her joyful skipping.

With the note in hand, the elder approached the dining hall. On the walls laid ancient paintings and a bust of the War Goddess the homeowner was the Caretaker to.

However, each portrait and stone carving had one blemish that each of them shared. The left side of the goddess's face was either burnt off or shattered.

These changes were not of the owner of the home. These were from a god who chose to "fix" the inaccurate depictions.

Approaching the dining room, the sound of meat being torn from bone was heard, sounding as though a wild creature was feasting. Though it was no animal, it was a beast all the same.

At the head of the table, with many plates full of a fortune's worth of meat, fruit, and soup, a woman of muscular stature and short green hair devoured her meal.

Wearing nothing but a robe, a young woman, with her sharp shark-like teeth, tore into a large fowl leg like a feral animal devouring its prey.

Witnessing such a sight would scare a normal man, or even a divine squirrel in Ratatoskr's case, but not the old man. He spent many hours a day preparing every meal for the goddess.

The elder stood next to the binge-eating lady with a kind face, catching the ravenous woman's attention.

Like her teeth, her right eye gave off a sinister, rage-fueled expression. As for her left, it was completely blind due to a large scar that nearly covered the left side of her face.

"Have you polished my armor?" the woman asked as she wiped her mouth with her arm.

"I have. I also sharpened your sword, shield, and spear as well," the old man saluted her.

"Get me wine…"

"Of course, Lady Bellona."

NAMES: BELLONA, ENYO. FACTION: OLYMPUS.

GODHOOD: WAR. HUMAN NATIONALITY: ITALIAN.

The Olympian goddess of war, and one of the top contenders in the Tryouts, Bellona was one match away from entering the Valhalla Royale and the Gods' Wrath tournaments.

From her first match against the Babylonian crop god, Ninurta, to the Christian strongman, Samson, a week prior, Bellona had fought and happily killed her way to where she was now.

As a goddess born for war, she became a bit frustrated and easily bored when not in battle. She mostly spent her downtime either training or eating as her weapons and armor are cleansed of her victim's blood.

"Here you are. I hope you enjoy it. It is one of the best nonalcoholic wines, so I am told," the kind gentleman stated as he poured the red wine into a bronze chalice, resting in the palm of the War Goddess.

With a sip of the drink, Bellona peered at it, unimpressed, leading to disappointment for the butler-like Caretaker.

"Who was at the door?" Bellona asked in a bored manner.

"Ah, yes. The Messenger stopped by."

"Merc- Hermes?" Bellona sighed.

"No, Ratatoskr."

"Hmm?" The news was surprising to Bellona, knowing the Asgardian messenger only dealt with tournament-related news. "Is something happening in the Tryouts?"

The man pulled out the envelope, removing the G-shaped crest to open it. With the note in hand, the butler's brown eye moved as he read the note.

"Oh?" he reacted, sounding surprised. "It appears the Shinto god you were going to slay next has dropped out."

"Really?" Bellona sighed, annoyed by this news. "I was truly hoping to kill the child of a heathen Monarch. I guess that means I am in the Royale, correct?"

"Not quite"

This news stupefied the bored War Goddess. "What do you mean? That Shinto whore dropped out, right?"

"She did, but her spot was taken. Essentially, she gave it to another god."

A loud bang rang in the large dining hall as Bellona hit her fist onto the table, nearly shattering its legs and bouncing the many plates that held her banquet.

"What?!" she yelled, her temper beginning to show. Her good eye burst into blue flames as smoke seeped from the other. "What sort of joke is this?! I was hoping a Shinto would have some sort of honor! Not only does she give up before facing me, she gets someone *else* to do it!? What of the Monarchs? Are they allowing this?"

"Yes, it seems a favor was owed."

"A favor?" The blue flame of war burned out as the goddess began to calm herself. "Who is this god that one of the children of Izanami and the Monarchs would find worthy enough to enter the finals?"

The Caretaker looked up from the note. Both of his eyes pointed in the same direction, toward the goddess.

"Sun Wukong," the name left his lips.

Her eyes widened to the name. Her shocked reaction quickly turned into a smile, as the war flames burst from her eyes again. "Heh heh heh…" a calm chuckle left her mouth, slowly evolving into a mad woman's laugh.

The butler observed her, unsure of her response. "Do you know of Sun Wukong?"

"Know of him?!" Her personality changed from boredom to rage, to insane joy. "Not in the old days, but I had heard the stories after being reborn. A god who fought two factions and nearly brought them to their knees!" Bellona wraped her arms around her body and begins to caress herself sensually. "Forget the Disgraced Serpent Killer! This battle will be truly exciting!" she licked her sharp teeth as she laughed.

"So, this is a good thing I suppose?"

Bellona threw her hands in the air, victoriously. "Of course! This battle will be the perfect victory for my entrance into the Gods' Wrath tournament! Winning one war and moving into another in glory!" She lowered her hands and looked over to her Caretaker, and personal servant. Her sadistically perverse expression turned to disappointment as her flames deplete once more. "However, I guess a failure such as *you* wouldn't understand that?" she expressed cruelly.

He chuckled at her remark. "I may have lost my war, but I shall be by your side through all of yours, Lady Bellona. I, your Bellonarii who has owed you his life, Leonardo Russo, swear it."

CHAPTER EIGHT: KNOW THE ENEMY

It's been three days since Sun and I were registered into the Gods' Wrath Tryouts in Susanoo's place.

I still hardly remember anything after entering Ratatoskr's portal. Between then and coming back with serious pain in my leg, all I remember is this numbing feeling and a birdman with books around him.

Sun told me that was Thoth, the Egyptian god of Knowledge and Writing. I can't believe I got to meet such a pinnacle god inside of the Divine Tree, a place full of books about *literally* everything and I don't remember any of it!

Sun also mentioned that he had this ability to read anything like a book, knowing every little detail. That news scared me a bit. I swore Sun was about to tell me that Thoth learned I was hemophilic.

Apparently, he was more focused on the fact I was brought back to life after the Nuckelavee incident.

That is intriguing from a human perspective, even though I don't feel any different as a result of the Life Cider. I suppose for a god, coming back to life would seem like nothing, right? I can only guess I was the first human resurrection in quite some time.

Still, I'm glad I wasn't found out and Sun wasn't taken away. Though, she seemed upset because I didn't remember some of the things she said back there. She pouted for a while after that and still refuses to tell me what she said.

Though, that was then. Now we are three days away from Sun's first and final fight before the Valhalla Royale. This fight will take place at Dogma Stadium, inside the city. The same one Susanoo fought in before we met her and Momoko.

Speaking of which, the tipsy Storm Goddess and her scared little Caretaker decided to come over to congratulate us for successfully taking their place. Strange, I know.

Of course, hearing this, Ell decided to come over as well, which I'm happy about, to be fair. However, I'm not sure if she wanted to come over to celebrate or to get what she is owed from Momoko and Susanoo earlier than planned.

I'm assuming some sort of combination of the two since she offered to prepare food and is now taking Momoko's measurements.

"Please stop shaking. It will make this easier," Ell prepares to rap her measuring tool around Momoko's shaking hips.

"I-I don't want to know what this is for!" Momoko nervously cries out.

"I warned you not to bet with Ell," I remind her in the comfort of my lawn chair.

We decided to have this *party*, I guess you can call it, outside, since Susanoo offered to train Sun. Don't know why Sun agreed to this, knowing who she's up against, but from the looks of it, Susanoo is taking this sort of seriously.

Obviously, we couldn't let them use their divine weapons, so I gave them some old pipes laying around they could use to spar with.

Sun swings her long metal tube as if it was the Jingu Bang. With drunken ease, Susanoo knocks each swing away with her shorter pipe.

"Ya know, I was hopin' us playin' with long tubes would be more fun and sweat-breakin'. Ha ha!"

When I said Susanoo is taking this sort of seriously, the keywords were 'sort of'.

"You seem like you don't even know where you are. How do you keep this up?" Sun yells, sounding out of breath. "I don't see why you dropped out if you're this strong and fast."

"I-I asked the same thing…" mutters a depressed Momoko.

"If you keep moving, a naughty priestess will be fed to Orochi," Ell chuckles as she continues her measuring of the young shrine girl.

"Gah!" Momoko screams as her body freezes perfectly in a T-pose. "I-Is this fine?!" she fearfully asks.

"Ell, stop using the girl's fear against her."

"Why? I use your fear of nuns whenever possible."

"You're the reason I'm scared of nuns," I abruptly whisper to her, embarrassed of the fact.

I won against her once and thought I'd give her a taste of her own medicine. She didn't like said taste and now I have this weird phobia because of that.

Moral of the story, even in defeat, Ell wins, and she knows this.

"Ow!" I hear Sun shout after a loud thud.

I see her gripping her head in pain after being hit by Susanoo.

Susanoo rests her replacement weapon on her shoulders. "If that was a sword, hammer, ax, or whatever, you'd be dead now. Got it, Bouncy Monkey?"

"Grrr!" Sun growls as she stares at the Storm Goddess with rageful eyes. "I know that! I was focusing more on hitting you! If this fight was for real, I would have easily dodged it! Remember, I learned from the best from both the Buddhist and Taoist factions!"

Susanoo picks her ear, appearing uninterested in Sun's resume. "And I laid a killin' blow on ya with no trainin' what so fuckin' ever…"

Dropping her training weapon, Sun crosses her arms in a huff. "Again, why drop out if you're so great?" she mentions in a snarky manner.

Despite her attitude, Susanoo never explained why she offered up her spot if Sun beat her. I mean, it's the finals. After that, the Valhalla Royale. You don't even have to win the Royale to be a fighter in the tournaments. That event mainly assigns your ranking for future fights.

"Why?" Susanoo scratches her chin, nonchalantly. "Frankly, I didn't wanna fight that Olympian bitch…"

Olympian bitch? That doesn't narrow it down a whole lot. I also haven't been following the Tryouts since I lost five-hundred bucks on the first match between Ninurta and- wait…

"Oh right!" jumps Ell into the conversation, rolling up her measuring tape. "Your last opponent was going to be Bellona correct? Ares was quite interested in the news of her addition to the Tryouts."

Hearing that name nearly causes me to jump from my seat. Remembering how brutal that fight was, I can't help but yell in shock. "Bellona?!"

"Who's that, Mr. Knight?" an innocent Sun asks.

"An Olympian War Goddess and your opponent!" I loudly panic.

"Really? Awesome!" she responds enthusiastically.

"No, Sun! Not awesome!"

Of all types of gods in the Tryouts, Sun's first fight is with an Olympian War Goddess! My heart can't stop thrashing about in my chest!

"My dear Broken Knight, have you not looked into who your first match was with?" Ell asks.

I was so distracted by the simple fact that we are even in the Tryouts, I never even bothered to have checked who Sun would be fighting!

"Hey! Mr. Knight went through a lot to even register us!" Sun defends my honor. "He got all loopy, weird, and even danced his way through the exit when we left!"

"Sun, please stop…"

I don't care if she mentions the loopy part, it's the dancing that breaks my heart here.

"Oh my, how I would've loved to see that. Heh heh," Ell covers her chuckling lips with her hand.

I grab hold of my patchwork cane and lift myself from my seat. Sun walks over to help me. Now on both my feet, I confront her.

"You can't go up against Bellona, Sun! I've seen her fight with Ninurta! She is not a merciful god!"

"My, you obviously have not seen her more recent fights," Ell proclaims as she pulls her phone from her pocket. "She has gotten far more violent."

Ell raises her phone to me and Sun. Showing clips from Bellona's last four fights. She's right, they have gotten worse.

We witness clips of her tearing off flesh with her teeth, beating her enemies with their own limbs, and grinning as their blood pours onto her face.

Then, there's the vibe she gives off. A wide, fiendish expression caused by the violence she commits. It's a expression of bloodthirsty ecstasy.

"What's wrong with her?" I bring up.

"Simple. She's feeding," Ell answers. "War Gods have always asked for blood in return from those who worshipped them. They become stronger when they spill blood or if it's spilled in their name. These Tryouts have been nothing more than five-course meals for them. Still, she's not as powerful as Ares yet, as you can tell by her flames. A War god's flames will burn brighter the more powerful they become, hers are still blue."

Hearing Ell tell us this is even more terrifying than the footage on her phone. Bellona's not only fighting in this tournament, she's getting stronger and from the looks of it, far more aggressive than when she started. And Sun's her next target...

"And Don't forget darlings, the more brutal the kill, the more power is given to them! Ohohohohoh!" a familiar bombastic laugh bursts from behind us.

Sun and I leap in surprise at the familiar voice. We turn to see the androgynous figure of one of Ell's two gods.

"Loki!" Sun and I shout at once. Though, Sun is angrier at the sight of the Trickster compared to my shock.

Ever since the incident, Sun has gained a bit of animosity towards Loki. Can't blame her, but I feel hating him just makes it all the better for him.

Our shouting scares Momoko. She nearly falls over, still in her T-pose.

"Aaaaahhh!"

Susanoo walks up to Momoko, placing her hand on her Caretaker's forehead. Preventing her from falling.

"Hey, he-she! What's up?" Susanoo greets Loki in a more serene manner than Sun and I did.

With a smile on his face, the Trickster waves his long-sleeved hand happily. "Just here to bring comedy into the tragedy that is your everyday lives! Ohohohoh!" he laughs. "But as for that Olympian with the gore fetish, what would you expect from the wife, and sister, of my dear partner!"

That's right. Bellona is the bride and sibling of Ares. It was believed her bloodlust rivaled Ares's. After seeing those clips, I can believe that. If what Loki said is true, then she's mainly doing it to get stronger. Still, not a good reason to rip someone's limbs off, but then again, I'm not a War god.

"So, Loki, does that mean you've met Bellona before? Or, maybe Ares has talked about her?"

I haven't known Loki for long, but I do know that he would have responded by making some kind of comedic remark. Maybe, somehow, he'd make it an insult. Instead, he is ignoring me.

Loki is instead staring over his shoulder. His smiling face is aiming toward a tree for some reason. Focusing on it, I see a bird or something. I think it's a crow... maybe a raven? Haven't seen a bird like that around here.

The closed-eyed god aims his face back toward me. "Apologies, darling, but I can't ignore this chance!" he bows theatrically. "I'll be back!"

As he did when I first met him, he bursts into colorful confetti. I'm happy this time he isn't leaving me as monster food.

The popping sound he made from his exit causes poor Momoko to lose her balance again.

"Aaaahh!" she screams as she falls toward the ground. "N-noo! I don't want to be eaten!"

Susanoo crouches down to the panicking girl. "She was jokin' Momo. Calm down."

Turning my attention away from those two, I turn to Ell, hoping she'll give me an answer.

"Have you met Bellona, Ell? Maybe at least her Caretaker?"

Since Ares and Loki were announced to be the guest fighters in the Valhalla Royale, Ell has been watching the Tryout matches, going all over the country to see many of them firsthand. Her coming back to Calibur City and Paradise Grove was because of one of Susanoo's matches.

"I can't say I have, my Broken Knight," Ell responds kindly. "Though I do know of her Caretaker and you might have heard of him as well. Leonardo Russo."

Susanoo approaches us. Clinging to her back, Momoko hides, sticking her head out shyly. "Wh-who is that?"

"You've never heard of Leonardo Russo? Oh, that's right. You're new to the States. Still, I thought you would know of him through the Tryouts."

Momoko quickly shakes her head in a panic. "N-no! I-I don't really like talking to people," she nervously speaks. I guess that makes us two of a kind.

Susanoo leans her head in a bored manner. "He important or somethin'?"

Important would be an understatement. Leonardo Russo is one of the richest men in the country who runs a charity for war vets. Grandpa, being a war vet, had met him through said charity.

His real claim to fame is the fact that he was a war hero in Vietnam, defeating ten enemy soldiers so his two injured allies could escape.

He was also willing to risk his own life. I heard how he planned to blow himself up with the enemy.

With an enormous amount of luck, he was tossed from the explosion, only losing an eye and his left leg.

He wasn't found until a day later. He would have bled out if it wasn't for the flames from the explosion sealing his wound shut. He's both a miracle and a war hero.

That's how I explained it to Susanoo and Momoko.

"So, he's an old rich Italian war gimp? Neat…" Susanoo says, clearly unimpressed. I guess that isn't so astonishing when you're a god.

"H-he blew up!?" Momoko nearly cries in shock from the story. Gripping tightly onto Susanoo's *gi*.

Still, even though Bellona is a War Goddess, I don't think being a soldier qualifies for a caretaker. Only those high up in a religious position or a mythologist can be one.

"How did he become a Caretaker? I doubt he bribed his way there."

Ell looks at me, bewildered by my remark. "Oh my, do you not know? The Russo's come from a long line of worshipers of both Enyo and Bellona. Many of them held onto this belief through the last couple of generations, Leonardo being the last of them. As far as the Caretaker Program is concerned, he is the modern, and only, Bellonarii."

"Really?"

"His charity is called the *Warriors of Enyo*."

"It is?" Grandpa never told me the name of the charity, only what it did.

"My my, you truly are a Broken Knight in body and mind, now aren't you?" Ell chuckles.

"Hey!" Sun jumps between us, confronting Ell. "Did you just call Mr. Knight dumb?! Take that back!" her voice snarls in anger.

Sun is still not fond of Ell.

"It's alright, I was only teasing, but what a good little monkey you are, protecting your master," Ell lets out another well-pleased chuckle. Sun growls at her more in retaliation.

Thanks to the Gods' Wrath tournaments, long-forgotten beliefs have started to rise again as modern religions. Though, they are more like fan clubs than actual religions. From Ell shared, it sounds like Leonardo Russo has always worshipped Bellona.

I guess that's not too uncommon. I remember a ton of people in my college claiming to be Pagan worshippers, but I think a majority of them did so to be trendy.

"How serious of a *Bellonarii* could he be if he's recognized as an actual one?"

Ell scrolls through her phone again and shows it to Sun and I. "Perhaps this will give you an idea."

The picture shows Bellona. When she's not fighting, she still gives off an aggressive demeanor, but she also appears sort of bored. Yet, what surprises me is one thing.

"She's really short!" Sun points out what I was thinking.

Height wise, I can only assume she's about as tall as Momoko. I never noticed that until now. I guess I was too busy worried about losing my bet in her first fight.

It's sort of sickening to see such a young girl with a huge scar like that, but what else do you expect from a god of war. Especially one that is also considered the god of blood and conquest.

"It may be best not to say that when you meet her..." Ell informs us.

As for the man next to her, I recognize him from the pictures he took with my grandpa and his old war buddies: Leonardo Russo.

He seems like a kind, gentle old man, but how he stands there and salutes in this picture, that's not just a soldier. That's a man devoted to his beliefs, which means he is a man loyal to his god.

"Mr. Knight, is that how the wealthy of this country tend to look?"

His outfit is pretty casual. Not what you'd expect from a rich man.

"Maybe, he prefers this style."

"From what I've seen, the old man has become more of a butler to Bellona, taking his faith in her to the next level. I even hear he spends a fortune feeding her from his own pocket, turning away the cash that was meant to do so," Ell sounds intrigued by this.

Sun turns her head to look back at me. "How much do War Gods actually eat?"

"Enough to bankrupt a person," Ell answers, annoying Sun in the process. "At least from what I've seen with Ares. After each fight, he eats enough food to feed nine villages. It truly is a disgusting sight to see. Makes me glad I had gotten that God Card."

Ell has a ton of money. She's the richest person I know, and she loves to show it off. So, hearing her talk about how she's grateful to spend other people's money on something must truly mean it's a lot of cash to spend.

"I can't even spend my own money on a quarter of Sun's appetite…" I joke.

Sun rests her arm over my shoulder with a joyful expression. "Don't worry, Mr. Knight! Once I beat this Olympian, we'll make a ton of money in the Valhalla Royale and the tournaments beyond!"

Hearing her say this scares me. "You're still planning to fight her?!" I yell, horrified by this news.

She stares at me, at a loss as to why I'm so worried. "Why not? We signed up for it didn't we?"

"Sun! She's an Olympian war god! Those two things do not make for a good first opponent!"

The Olympians are pretty much the college fraternity of all mythologies. Well, throw in a bit of homicidal egotism for good measure.

They killed who or what they wanted when they wanted, and most often over the stupidest of reasons. They treated humans as nothing more than toys or slaves, both of which tended to be used for sex.

Ell wraps her arms around my free arm, holding it close. Even with her vest and dress shirt, I'm feeling two great things currently.

I can hear Sun growling as her grip on my shoulders tightens because of this. She wraps her other arm around my chest, pulling me closer to her.

"Don't fret my Broken Knight, I'm sure your little Helper Monkey will do fine," Ell sounds like she wants Sun to fight. "Besides, Olympians are not too bad. They're just stupid."

At any other time, I'd be loving the position that I'm in. If it wasn't for the fact they're trying to convince me to let Sun fight a godly butcher, I'd be loving this!

"Hey Cripple, wanna trade places?" Susanoo jokes.

Momoko looks from behind Susanoo. Her face is red by the sight of us. "*H-hentai…*"

I've heard that word somewhere before. Don't know what it means off the top of my head though.

To make this scene more exciting, a cloud of color confetti pops before us, forcing Momoko to scream again and curl up on the ground.

"I apologize for the short intermission, darlings, but my Mistress is correct!" Loki says as he walks from the cloud of paper. "They are stupid… Also, dangerously aggressive, both brutally and sexually to the point that my dear Caretaker makes me keep Ares miles away from her. Not out of fear for her safety, simply out of disgust for him. Ohohohoh!"

I'd be bothered if Ell does do that to Ares, but seeing all of his and Loki's fights, I'm glad she does. In all honesty, I worry for Ell, being around that war machine and this Norse hellion.

"You really picked the worst time…" Ell tells him in frustration.

126

Loki points his face toward Ell. "Ah! My apologies Mistress! I did not know you wanted to play Olympian with your boy toy," His head turns over toward Sun as she's also gripping on me. He places his long sleeves over his lips in shock. "Well, Mistress, you dirty girl! Ohohohohoh!"

Ell lets go of my arm and crosses her arms like a disappointed parent. "Where did you go off to this time?"

With a wide tooth-filled smirk, Loki raises the black bird from the tree he was ogling at. It's wrapped in pink thread and appears to be wearing makeup. Other than that, it seems fine.

"Seriously?" Ell sighs, placing her hand on her head as if she has a migraine.

"Why the fuck did ya do that?" Susanoo asks.

Loki begins to swing the bird on a thread like it's a yo-yo. "It's a bit of an inside joke! It's an Asgardian thing, you wouldn't get it! Ohohohoh!"

I free myself from Sun's grip to stand in front of her. "Enough! Sun, we're dropping out!"

Sun gasps with disappointment. "But, Mr. Knight! You said you were fine with me fighting!"

"She's the Goddess of Blood and Conquest, Sun! She will kill you!"

"So? They'll just bring me back like they do with all the other fighters!"

She makes it sound like that makes it better somehow. That's a god for you. Still, I can't let her go through with this.

"Will ya both shut the fuck up!" The tipsy voice of the Summer Storm Goddess shouts. "Seriously? Ya treatin' the sexy, big tittied Monkey King who fought Pantheons and Unfollowed from two different factions like this? The same sexy big tittied Monkey

King that scared the Jade Emperor so much, he had to call for help from another faction? Fuck, ya ain't only a Cripple. Well, you are, but mainly you're a worried little *puss* ain't ya?"

"Big talk coming from the one who dropped out in the first place," I retort.

"I admit, I did it for selfish, maybe even stupid, reasons. You're the prick whose actin' like he's all high and mighty, doing the supposed right thing, though."

"You better stop talking to Mr. Knight like that!" Sun yells in my defense, even though Susanoo was speaking for her.

Susanoo places her pipe in her mouth. "You're actin' like she's a weak, dumb human girl, while also actin' like you're fully capable of defending her if needed." With the pipe removed from her mouth, smoke leaves her cruel lips. "Stop actin' like you're more than what ya are and that she's less than what she is…"

I've heard a similar speech before. From Sun, after the Nuckelavee attack. Except hers was passion-filled. This one is simply cruel. Sadly, they are both right.

Even after seeing her fight the Nuckelavee, I still don't view Sun as the same Monkey King from legend. Not just because of her gender, but also because we've been together for a while now and it's hard to see that smiling face of hers be part of the same powerful figure who fought, and killed, for both noble and selfish reasons.

I glance over at Sun, still giving Susanoo the death stare for how she has been speaking to me.

"Sun, you understand why I'm scared of having you fight Bellona, right?"

She looks at me, confused for a moment, until a smile shapes on her face. "I know. You understand why I want to fight her, right?"

Sun claims she wants to obtain that Life Cider that Loki used, in case something like before happened again. She also claims she wants to win me the cash prize in many of the tournaments. Frankly, I think she mainly wants to fight again.

"To help me or fight?"

"Can't it be both?" she grins with confidence.

I can't help but laugh at her remark. Only a god would be this calm about being in a deathmatch.

"Alright… But you better win…"

"Of course, I will! You make it sound like losing is a possibility for me!" she chuckles.

"Woo…" Susanoo gives a fake cheer. "Well, that's as motivational as I'm gonna get…"

Sun walks up to the Storm Goddess. The expression on her face shows that Sun doesn't want to do what she's about to do.

"Th-thanks… I guess," Sun painfully tells her, almost devastated at doing so.

"No prob… But if ya really wanna thank me," Susanoo swiftly wraps her arms around Sun. "How about a kiss! Or maybe sit on my face?! Somethin!" She prepares her lips to try to kiss Sun.

"G-get off me!" Sun struggles to free herself. Planting her hand on Susanoo's puckered face.

The bombastic laugh of Loki echoes in my ear. "And here I thought I'd be the one to ruin this moment! Ohohohohoh!"

To be fair on Loki's remark, it was going to be a fifty-fifty shot on who would ruin it.

As I watch Susanoo trying to kiss Sun, unsure what to do about it, I feel a pair of arms wrap around me. Ell rests her chin on my shoulder.

"My, I forgot how worrisome you can act. So cute," she chuckles as she leans closer to my ear. "I guess someone with your *issue* has to be a bit of a worrywart," her voice whispers in my ear.

I didn't blush when I was being held by her and Sun, but Ell's current teasing is working like a charm.

Her arms were still wrapped around me from behind. I can feel her body pressing on my back. Add the whispering in my ear, she knows how to get to me without showing any skin, unlike Sun.

"D-do you have to do this now, Ell?"

"Of course!"

"H-hey! What are you doing to Mr. Knight?!" Sun yells, still fighting away Susanoo.

"Well, since you're doing that, I didn't want my Broken Knight to feel left out," she teases as her grip around me tightens. "Especially for making such a hard decision. I feel like he deserves an award!"

I raise an eyebrow at her comment. "Award?"

Sun pushes Susanoo back as she turns towards us in fury. "What kind of award?" she snarls.

Ell lets go of me and claps her hands twice. "Oh, Loki!"

"Yes, my Mistress?"

"I have their measurements ready. So, you will be able to get started on Ms. Hirata and Susanoo's *payment* once we return. Also, be a good little sprite and bring me the gift we brought, please."

"Of course, Madam!" the Trickster shouts as he tosses the black bird in the air, causing it to explode in confetti, with him following behind.

I don't know why Loki decided to do that to the bird. I guess Tricksters see everything as a target.

"So, Loki makes your costumes now?"

"He makes the finest silk for them," Ell turns her head toward Momoko. "You will love what we have in store for you two!"

Momoko whimpers in fear at what Ell could possibly mean.

Now I know that next time I lose a bet, I'll be wearing a catholic schoolgirl outfit made by a god, which somehow makes it worse.

Loki pops up next to me. Once again, scaring Momoko even more than she was by Ell. She crawls behind my lawn chair, making it her new hiding spot.

The Trickster bows as he presents something to me. A long gray case. The locks on the case suddenly unhinge as the top pops open. Inside is something I'm not too surprised by.

"A new cane?"

A long polished black cane with a custom silver dragon-shaped handle on the top.

"Aww! You don't sound impressed by it. Were you hoping to give me a *cane*?" she chuckles at her own innuendo.

"I don't know what that means, but I'm guessing it's something you shouldn't be saying to Mr. Knight!" Sun yells.

"P-please stop yelling lewd things!" Momoko pleads from her hiding spot.

Ell looks at me in a snarky fashion. "Well, I did tell you I was going to get him a new cane to replace that filthy homemade one. So, might as well make it a bit naughty while I was at it," Ell sticks her tongue out at Sun.

"Grrr… I *really* don't like her…"

I think I should give up on the idea of Sun and Ell ever becoming friends.

Though I knew it was coming, this cane certainly isn't cheap. The whole cane is a fine metal, at least in appearance. It's nice and smooth, nothing at all like the cheap wooden one the Nuckelavee destroyed.

I pick up the cane to examine it more. The dragon head has some nice weight to it. The detail on the scales and the eyes— are those diamonds?! God, she went all out on this! Only the best from Ell, like always.

I put down the patchwork cane I've been using and begin to walk with the new one. It feels great to move with this! I can't help but smile.

"This cane is awesome!"

"My, it's odd hearing you tell that to me and not the other way around," Ell chuckles again with her remark.

"Seriously, Ell!?"

"You make it too easy sometimes," Ell chuckles.

While I'm staring at Ell with disappointment at her joke, I hear growling from behind me. I turn to see Sun gaze straight into my eyes, upset.

"Wasn't the cane I made good?"

"It was, but this one will work better!" I defend the new cane.

Sun puffs her cheeks and turns around in a huff while crossing her arms.

"Aw come on, Sun! You can't be mad at me for this!"

"You were mad at me a second ago!"

"That was about you fighting a bloodthirsty butcher! This is about a walking cane!"

"Hmph!" Sun stomps her foot as she continues to pout.

As much as this is distracting me, I am still concerned about Sun fighting Bellona. Even if she does win, she'll then be in the Valhalla Royale fighting several gods all at once.

However, Sun and Susanoo are right. This is nothing to worry about for them. Sun fought and killed many powerful enemies in her past life. Some of which were probably way stronger than Bellona.

Still, she may have talked me into letting her do this, but that doesn't mean I will stop being anxious about it.

INTERLUDE TWO: WAR GODS.

War. It happens for many reasons. Some good, some not. In the end, it doesn't matter to those who have the Godhood for it. Not as long as blood is spilled for them.

Truly, one of the most dangerous of Godhoods, War Gods are warriors who bask in the red fluids that spew from their fallen enemies. If they were not part of a pantheon or worshipped by humans, they would simply be more Unfollowed.

Of course, this does not mean they are ungiving and resentful deities. No, the war gods have shown genuine care for those who worshipped and fought for them in the past.

As long as you won and killed in their name, you gained their protection and grace. However, failure is not accepted for these blood-crazed gods.

Almost every god has fought to some degree. Yet, unlike most deities, the War gods gain power directly from their victories.

They have what is called "The Flames of War". Like war, fire is destructive and can be unforgiving, but it is also a necessity in life. This flame grows when a War God spills the blood of their enemy.

The more it flourishes, the stronger it makes the War God. The more brutal the kill, the greater it affects the growth of the flames.

Being able to utilize these flames, a war god can increase the lethality of their physical weapons, as well as project energy from their bodies as a long-range attack.

Of course, the Flames of War are not their only tools. Their thick hide can withstand many physical attacks. The stronger the flames, the denser a War God's skin can be in battle.

War is a way of life for these gods. War can even be ecstasy to them. This often leads to more aggressive actions from this Godhood, potentially even dangerous. When pleasure comes from violence, then a War God truly reaches the borderline between a god and an Unfollowed.

"I can't wait to gut that Yellow Ape! My body is sweating by the thought of it alone!"

CHAPTER NINE: DOGMA STADIUM

Here we are, the day of the finals and Sun's first fight. Am I still concerned for her wellbeing? Of course! I hardly slept last night knowing what she'd be in for the next day. Unlike me, Sun slept like a log with a gleeful expression on her face.

Today would have been more stressful if we had to walk all the way into the city, drawing so much attention the whole time.

Since the news of Susanoo being swapped for Sun got out, we've gained a mix of more people wanting to take pictures of her, and fans of Susanoo who aren't too pleased about the last-minute change.

We got insulted a lot by them. She surprisingly has a lot of female fans, though none of them are kind. Sun almost hit a couple of them.

Luckily, Ell decided to give us a ride to the stadium. Of course, she rode a new sports car. She claims it's a rental, but I have no idea where you can find a rental car like this.

It's got a roofless, slick appearance with white leather seats, and a red paint job with a thin blue line going around the car. I think this is what Anthony's would have looked like if it wasn't crushed.

This day seemed like it was going to be a little easier on me. That was until my sister, Kat, decided to call.

"Nothing is wrong, Kat! I've just been having fun with Ell for the last couple of weeks!" Because of us riding in a convertible, I need to shout into my phone, over the wind.

"Vergil! Don't tell your sister about our fun! That's so inappropriate!" Ell shouts, jokingly.

I gesture her to quit it.

I haven't been talking much to Kat since Sun moved in with me. My sister was surely worried. I've been using Ell as my reason for not talking.

I never had the chance to call her or answer her calls, especially since there is nowhere I can speak without Sun making noise in the background. Now, I have both Sun and Loki behind me.

"Stop touching me, you little… W-whatever you are!" Sun yells from the back seat.

"First rule of sitting next to a Trickster! Do not tell a Trickster what to do! Ohohohoh!" Loki shouts back.

I can hear them roughhousing in the backseat. Sun is clearly annoyed at this.

"What is that?" Kat requests an answer on the other end of the line.

"O-oh, well Ell has to bring her nieces to an appointment. They're playing in the backseat." I tell her.

This lie can easily work. Kat hardly knows much about Ell, other than the fact she hates her.

"Oh… so, you like to spend more time with her family then your own…" Kat tries to guilt me for ignoring her calls. It's kind of working.

"No, no! It's that Ell's been helping me out a bit! You know, trying to find a job and stuff!"

"V-Vergil! Don't grab me there! The kids are in the back!" I hear from the driver's seat. Ell is joking once more in a flustered tone.

I place my hand over my phone, to avoid having Kat hear that. "Shut up, Ell!" I mouth at her, only for her to give me a light sarcastic chuckle in response.

With my phone back next to my ear. "She was joking Kat! You know that, right?"

"Uh-huh…" Kat clearly sounds like she does not believe me.

"H-hey! Stop that!" Sun yells out.

"For Asian women, you and that Shinto girl have big fun bags!" Loki jokes in wonder.

"What was that?" I hear Kat over the phone.

"J-just kids saying kids stuff!"

Ell lays out her hand next to me as she keeps her eyes on the road. "Let me talk to her."

I look at her hand in confusion as to why she would want that. Of course, I am hesitant to hand her my phone. Though, in all honesty, I don't know how much worse she can make this situation than it already is.

"Uh, Kat? Ell wants to talk to you."

As soon as those words left my lips, a loud click is heard, and the dial tone begins to ring. She hung up on me.

"Oh, no! Did she not want to talk?" Ell sarcastically wishes to know.

Not the first time Ell has done things like that before to my sister.

I should try to talk to Kat more. Maybe even go visit her. I don't know what to do about Sun, though. Like I said, my family is not too keen on the gods' return.

Sun leans up from the back seat, aggravated. "Mr. Knight, why did we have to take this metal thing? I could have flown us there much quicker!"

"How much stress do you want to put me under today?"

"I'm trying to focus on the battle and this Trickster keeps bothering me!"

"Yes, he tends to do that," Ell informs. Her shoulders shrug as her hands stay on the wheel.

The car begins to slow down, along with it the deafening roar of the wind. As the air quiets down, the yelling of people is easily heard as we begin to drive by our stop.

Once a normal location for sporting events, particularly football, it's now one of the battle arenas for the Gods' Wrath tournaments, officially called the Dogma Stadiums.

Though, the Dogma Stadiums in cities like ours are mostly used for smaller events such as the Tryouts.

This is the first time I've seen the stadium since it was converted. Calibur City only recently got accepted as a spot for one.

Sun views it with mild surprise. I'm guessing it's not as impressive as things she's seen before. Oddly enough, she seemed more amazed by the mall.

All around the front of the large arena, two crowds stand opposite from the left and right of the entrance. On the right, excited fans are waiting to get inside, along with photographers, cameramen, and interviewers.

On the left, protesters who are surrounded by police in case order is needed. Atheists are very likely the majority of the protesters, but I doubt that's it. When catching up on the Tryouts I remember watching footage of their activity during Susanoo's last match. There were a couple of guys I remembered from my college days. They only got in through a sports scholarship because they were wanted for our football and basketball teams respectively.

Unfortunately for them, the Gods' Wrath tournaments made human sports obsolete. Even the Olympics became a thing of the past in favor of the Valhalla Royale, and that's not even one of the more popular fights.

As a result of the tournaments, those poor guys who only got in for their sporting skills had nothing to fall back on. I'm pretty sure most of them never had any type of contingency plan, but I suppose it's easier to blame the gods than admit you made a mistake.

Sun pokes her head forward again with her hands covering her ears. "These people are really loud!" she shouts over the angry yelling on one side and the excited chatter on the other.

She's right. They are loud. In fact, why did we even stop here? I peer over to my left to see that Ell has parked us on the other side of the street from the stadium.

"Ell, why are we parked here?"

"Do you not want to go in from the front?" Ell asks us with a teasing grin on her face.

"Of course not!"

I can see Sun confused by my response. "Why not, Mr. Knight? Are you worried about the protesters?"

Well, that's half right. I've heard of these protests getting ugly, hence the police. I'm more worried about the cameras.

All the pictures taken of Sun around the mall were mostly her. No one wanted me to be involved in them (except Sun of course). For the Tryouts and Gods' Wrath in general, the caretakers apparently get as much attention as their gods.

Why does this bother me? Because I want Kat to learn about Sun from me and not the internet!

"Aww," Ell jokingly pities me. "Don't you want to surprise Kat?"

Of course, Ell knows why I don't want to enter through the front as well. I give her a nasty glare in retaliation. She just smirks at this like it's nothing.

"Oh, come on, Mr. Knight! It will be cool to finally have a picture of us together!"

Sun is right. We don't have any photos of us. There are plenty of pictures of her, including one of her as a kid the Daycare took to show me who I would be a caretaker to. Of course, there are plenty of me as well throughout the years, not including the ones I think Ell took after I lost our "bets". Never including *those* if they exist. But none of Sun and I together. It never really came up.

"I'd rather have a better picture than a paparazzi photo for a possible gossip article."

"Gossip article?" asks Sun.

"It's something humans read before our return, darling!" Loki jumps in. "Pretty much humans read these to get aroused by the humiliation of the successful! Of course, what humans consider humiliation, gods see them as miniscule inconveniences, or just a fun night! Basically, mortal world problems! Ohohohoh!" the Trickster holds his stomach as he explains in his own odd way what this concept is.

Sun looks back toward me. "Is that true?"

141

Well, he's not wrong. Wished he phrased it without the whole "aroused at others' humiliation" part. I nonchalantly nod my head yes as my answer.

"Oh me, oh my." Ell places her finger on her chin as she appears concerned. "Do you not want to go through the front that much?"

Me and Sun stare at Ell. Sun, of course, appears annoyed. My childhood friend sounds like she's up to something.

"If possible, yes…"

"Hmm… Well, I guess I could pull up to the back entrance. That's what we normally do with Ares… But it seems like a hassle… Unless…" Oh boy. I know where Ell is going with this. "Maybe if I had a cute little maid for a couple of days, that *may* make up for the inconvenience," Ell side eyes me with a shit-eating grin on her face.

"I'm not gonna be your maid!" Sun shouts.

I lower my head as Sun yells at Ell. I can hear the laughter of Loki as I sink lower into my seat.

"My dear Caretaker is not talking about *you*, darling," he chuckles.

I look up for a moment to see a dumbfounded Sun, unsure of what Ell and Loki mean. It clearly hits her as she sees me, acting humiliated on my behalf.

"Y-you're not going to make Mr. Knight your maid!" Sun shouts in surprise at the realization. "He uses a cane! Are you seriously asking him to clean up for you?" Kind of hypocritical for Sun to say that.

"Clean? No, of course not! It'll only be for a little show!" Ell claps her hands together at the idea.

"Show? What kind of show?"

142

"I'll do it!" I shout before Ell tells Sun. I truly don't want her to know anything about that. "Can we please just pull into the back now?"

"Oh my, you normally sound that forceful when you beg for—"

"Shut up! Let's go!"

Why does Ell want Sun to try to kill her?

Sun stares at me, unsure of what had transpired. I raise my head back up and give her an awkward, yet hopefully, reassuring face. She raises one of her furry eyebrows at this until she glances over at Ell with disdain.

Ell sticks her tongue out in a teasing manner, Sun wraps her arms around me from the back seat as she lets out a quiet growl. All the while, Loki sat in the back clapping.

"Ah! Such a show! Romance, hatred, sexual foreshadowing, and me! All of which makes such a grand scene! Ohohohoh!"

Loki's loud laughs begin to draw unwanted attention. It was only a matter of time before that happened.

"Hey! Over there!"

"Is that Loki?"

"And he's with some monkey girl?"

"Is she that last-minute fighter we heard about?"

All was being said by the reporters and cameramen on one side of the entrance. While on the other...

"False gods!"

"Monsters!"

"Humans aren't currency!"

"Science first! Mysticism never!"

The protesters shout. I wonder if the majority of them honestly care about science or are only upset that they'll never achieve fame? I theorize about seventy percent of the former and twenty of the ladder. That's how it normally is.

Of course, the protesters are not going to move from their spot. Not because of the cops around them. It's more so out of fear. Despite what they say, all humans understand that gods are powerful beings we can't fully comprehend or even dream of challenging.

The other side, however, has a bit more balls than the protesters as they try to get through the railing that's keeping them in their spot.

Seeing as they are preparing to get closer to us, and I can see the cameras pointed at us, I figure it's time to leave.

"Ell! Go! Go!" I frantically plead.

"Maid outfit?" Ell smirks.

"Yes! Just go!"

Despite not showing it on her face, I can tell Ell is excited as she begins to floor it. The wheels screech on the pavement before taking off.

Sun, despite her grip on me, was pushed back into the back seat along with Loki, whose laughter I can hear even through the rush of the wind. His hands are raised in the air as his long sleeves loudly flap.

After all the shit I said about the stress I feel when flying with Sun, I feel I owe her an apology after this!

CHAPTER TEN: CARETAKERS LOUNGE

Getting here from the back entrance on foot took a little longer than expected. According to Ell, it adds ten more minutes than it would going in through the front. At least it would be if you walked and used the elevator. However, Sun got too excited.

As soon as we walked through the back door, Sun immediately picked me up and began leaping up six rows of stairs.

I take back what I said, I won't apologize to Sun for complaining about her cloud. Now, I'll complain about this.

This saved us a bit of time, but for about six minutes Sun has been searching for our destination, not realizing one important thing.

"Sun, Ell was supposed to show us where we need to go!"

Sun left Ell and Loki behind when she decided to run off with me in tow, which I'm pretty sure was one reason why she did so.

"I know where to go!"

"No, you don't! I don't even know where to go!"

"I'm sure it's around- Ah!"

Sun jumps in surprise, with me still in her arms, as a cloud of shredded colorful paper explodes in front of us.

Ell and Loki appear before her, Ell seems frustrated as she dusts off the confetti from her shoulders.

"Please don't do that again," Ell sighs. "I hate having Loki teleport me…"

I guess Ell shares a similar pain I go through then. Though, hers seems to be annoying while mine is far more stressful.

"We don't need your help! Besides, your planning to have Mr. Knight do weird things!"

That's why she kidnapped me? Poor Sun, as happy as I am that she's saving me from humiliation, she doesn't realize it. When Ell is owed something, she'll always get it. I know better than everyone…

"Well, not here! Why would I share such a view with so many people around?" Ell crosses her arms as she stares down at me with the eyes of a predator with its prey in sight. "I prefer private showings…"

The anxiety I've been feeling for Sun's first fight and Ell's driving is nothing compared to the fear brought on by Ell's stare. It only gets more horrifying when I imagine myself wearing the outfit she'll force me in.

I grip onto Sun as my spine shivers. I gulp, attempting to swallow my fears.

"Anyway…" Ell says as she rubs her arm over her mouth, as if she's whipping away something. Was she drooling? "How about I bring you to the Caretaker Lounge?" she suggests with a cheerful smile. "That's where gods and caretakers meet one another before the fight."

Ell turns around and waves her hand, gesturing us to follow her as she begins to walk. Sun is hesitant with having to stick with Ell, but it's better than randomly running around.

"Here we are," Ell presents the door to what she claims is the Caretaker Lounge.

She opens the door revealing what's inside. It's a room with large, comfortable-looking furniture pointing out toward a large window with a view of where the fight will take place.

I think this was originally meant for sports team managers and the wealthy to sit and watch their games. Instead of pictures of football players or business owners, religious paintings adorn the walls, complemented with ancient bust statues from different mythologies.

Sun's eyes sparkle in amazement. "This place is neat, Mr. Knight!"

I got to agree. I've never been to a place this nice since those restaurants Ell used to take me to. Then again, when you have been living in a run-down R.V. for as long as I have, every new place seems like heaven. Though, with all the religious paintings and artifacts, this might as well be heaven.

"This place is nice, but Sun, I've been thinking we should discuss a battle strategy against Bellona."

Sun leans her head to the side with an unsure expression on her face. "A strategy?"

Sun's been training since she signed up, but we haven't actually talked about a game plan. Granted, I don't think Sun plans ahead. Still, I'd feel better knowing she has an idea.

"Yes! After seeing Bellona fight, she is not someone to take lightly. So, my idea is that you turn into your giant form as soon as you-"

"Giant form?" Sun asks.

"The form you took on in legend. You're supposed to turn into a three-headed, multi-armed giant or something of that sort, correct?"

"Oh! No, no, I didn't have a bunch of arms and heads or anything like that," Sun chuckles.

"Oh, but you can turn into a giant, right?"

"Yes… I think…" Sun crosses her arms as she appears to be thinking.

"Y-you *think*?" I repeat, getting a bit more nervous as I hear this.

"Yeah, I kind of remember something like what you're talking about, but I can't do it. Actually, I can't do a lot of the stuff I used to be able to do," Sun wears a thinking face. "I tried to perform some of my old abilities against that horse monster, but they didn't want to work. I'm definitely not as strong as I used to be. It's probably because of my new body."

So, my fears of Sun's power being overexaggerated by humans were proven wrong. Unfortunately, my reservations of her potentially weaker half-human body wasn't.

"S-so, everything I saw you do in the fight with the Nuckelavee, that's it?"

"Pretty much!" Sun happily acknowledges with no sense of dread on her face.

No jumping to the edge of the universe in one leap, no laser eyes, and even worse, no super battle mode. This isn't good, especially since she is going up against a little powerhouse like

Bellona. I was mainly focusing on those other abilities when I was thinking up strategies. With those, Sun would surely be able to win.

Another thing I noticed was that she said she tried to use these abilities against the Nuckelavee. I can remember the jumping, possibly an attempt at laser eyes, but I didn't see her showing any signs of trying to turn into her super form. I guess I was expecting her to scream as her power grew or something.

"Hey, Mr. Knight! How about after I win we go out to eat!" Sun proposes.

"Don't you mean *if*?"

"Nope!" Sun gives me a presumptuous grin.

Oh, I love my little Monkey King, but she can be too confident for her own good. Which frankly worries me in this fight of hers.

"Might as well eat now before your fight," Ell jumps in. "They normally have a buffet- Oh dear…" she says in disgust as she faces toward the left side of the room.

Sun and I turn toward the same direction. Against the wall is a table we saw as soon as we walked in. However, I was so focused on the room itself I didn't notice the shredded remains of food laying all over the table as if it was hit by a tornado.

My jaw drops in shock at the horrible sight. Sort of getting flashbacks of the Nuckelavee. The sight is *that* scary.

"Well, well! Here I thought my dear partner was a revolting eater. Ohohohoh!" Loki laughs at the sight of the mess. This god is easily amused.

I know it's only food, but this makes me really want to throw in the towel for Sun before the match even starts. Even when it comes to eating, Bellona treats it like a fight.

I let out a loud, stress-filled sigh. I see Sun examining the table. Unlike me though, she is more grossed out by the sight of it.

Maybe I'm over-exaggerating a table of dirty dishes and scraps. Right now, I think I should focus on something else for now.

"Hey Ell, are you and Loki allowed here?"

This room was meant for the gods fighting in the arena and their respective caretakers. Ell and Loki are simply guests.

"Well, it wouldn't be the first time I went to a place I wasn't allowed. Of course, you know that better than anyone. Hehe," Ell chuckles behind her hand as I notice an arrogant grin behind it. "Joking aside, yes. As a caretaker, I am allowed here. Even when Loki and Ares aren't fighting."

That would sound sort of weird, but there aren't that many caretakers walking around to be bothered about that.

Loki wraps his arm around my shoulder in a familiar demeanor. "This room truly is nothing special, darling! I mean, they'll let in any sort of freak show! For example," Loki points his arm over to a couch, resting under a framed picture of *The Last Supper*, presenting it to us as if it is a grand show. Which it kind of is…

On the couch are two familiar faces in *very* unfamiliar clothing. It's Susanoo and Momoko, both wearing something I assume they didn't want to wear.

Susanoo, smelling even worse of alcohol and smoke, lays her head back on the furniture as she loudly snores. She is wearing a tight white shirt and purple shorts that look even smaller than Sun's. She's also wearing a white sweatband on her head. It might be some sort of sporting outfit.

The only things she has left from her normal outfit is her pipe, resting between her fingers as she sleeps, her jug of unknown alcohol, and, of course, her sword, Kusanagi. The last two are rested on a nearby table.

Momoko's outfit is the exact same, except her long black hair is tied up in a ponytail. The top of her shirt isn't as tight as Susanoo's for obvious reasons.

She grips tightly onto her kendo as she shakes even more than normal. Her face is also bright red. I am guessing It's because of what she is wearing. I can tell she is trying not to shed a tear at the predicament she is in.

A normal person would query why they are dressed like this, but I already know the answer.

"What are they wearing?" I ask as Sun and I stare at the two in pity.

"They're both in classic Japanese high school gym uniforms," Ell explains. "Is it not obvious?"

Those are high school gym uniforms? Why aren't they allowed to wear pants?

"Really Ell?" I respond in disappointment.

"Well, I was hoping it would make you a little less stressed. But now that I'm looking at them, it's more sad than arousing, I guess. Plus, with how timid the shrine priestess is, I thought it would be as much fun to dress her up as it would you. Sadly, it doesn't feel the same. Even having her dress like this for the rest of the day is not as delicious as punishing you. I guess I enjoy how much it aggravates you since you make the cutest face when frustrated," Ell flirts. "As for the Shinto god, she was just no fun at all. She was all too willing to wear her outfit. Truly a bore for me. I miss dressing up my Broken Knight!" she says, sounding disappointed.

I shudder at Ell by how much she seems to *really* want me to dress for her.

"S-sorry. I don't want to wear... whatever it is they're wearing..." I awkwardly respond. "But did they show up like this?"

"Don't worry, they used the backdoor like we did," Ell smirks.

"You made them walk here like that?" I ask, flabbergasted by this.

"Oh no, no, no! That was all her goddess's idea. I even offered to drive them here, but she decided to turn it down. Her poor caretaker was not happy about any of that," Ell shrugs.

"Well... I guess that's alright..."

"Mr. Knight, this woman is cruel..."

"Not as cruel as I thought she was..."

Ell had me worried there for a moment. I thought she had gotten worse with her bets. I mean, of all the things she made me do, she never made me go out in public dressed in one of her outfits.

Sun leans close to my ear. "Mr. Knight, why is this woman your friend? I don't like how she treats you..." she whispers, repeating exactly what Kat said when she met Ell.

"I used to ask myself that question a lot..." I joke in response. To be fair, Ell is not as bad as everyone thinks. When people aren't around, she is honestly kind and sweet... Granted that is the same thing a person would say if they were in an abusive relationship, but I am serious!

"Seriously, Mr. Knight, she rubs me the wrong—" Sun is interrupted before she can finish her remark.

"*Snore*-Di I zust hear da love-*hiccup*- of my life sayin' somethin' about rubbin' her?" Susanoo quickly wakes herself up. Her tipsy voice is now a full-on drunken slur.

"Oh no, she's awake…" Sun mutters in a distress.

Susanoo gets up from the couch. She tries to walk, but her legs wobble under her as she approaches us.

"Hey, Bouncy Monkey! Hey, Cripple! Ha ha ha!" Susanoo lets out a drunken laugh as she waves her arm at us in a slow yet uncontrollable fashion.

I cover my nose as she smells even worse than before. Sun does the same, but uses both of her hands. The scent is probably hitting her harder than me. Susanoo's face is a bright red color. That, along with her speech and movements, it's more than enough proof that she has been drinking a lot more than she usually does.

"Yes, after our little dress up game, she decided to help herself to the wine and scotch I had stored away in my hotel vault. She drank several thousand dollars' worth of alcohol…" Ell groans, clearly aggravated by the loss.

"I could have stopped it, but it was quite the show! For the All Father's sake, never have I seen a woman chug down so much of Surtr's nectar! May I remind you, I was worshiped by Vikings!" Loki jumps in. "Even Thor himself would kneel in defeat!"

Susanoo leaps towards Sun and wraps her arms around her. "I came all 'tis way to wish ya luck with a kissh! Or if ya want, I can give ya a good-*Hiccup*- luck fuck!" she slurs with her lips puckered out near Sun's face.

"G-get off me! Dear Buddha, you smell!" Sun shouts at her through her hand as she tries to shake the Storm Goddess off her.

Momoko walks up behind Susanoo. "P-please, Susanoo. You have already caused enough trouble—" She stops once her eyes make contact with me. She slowly glances down at her new outfit as if she was reminded of what she is wearing. Momoko's eyes widen, and her face becomes a brighter red

153

that almost matches Susanoo's. "D-don't look at my shame!" she shouts as she crouches down behind Susanoo.

"I tried to warn you…"

"Though she's not you, I will admit she was fun to tease," Ell chuckles.

"You could have gone a little easier on the poor girl…"

"Aww, but Loki worked so hard on those outfits…"

"Truly, the Tangler's finest work!" Loki jumps in.

Ell leans in close to my ear. "Plus, don't act like you don't love this. After all, I did this for you." She quietly flirts in a whispering voice.

Well, I can't say I don't like how they look. Momoko is cute in her outfit, while Susanoo… is on a whole other level. That sexy gym outfit on her body is admittedly quite pleasing on the eyes. Still, seeing how upset Momoko is, it's a bit of a guilt trip.

I turn my gaze away from the sad sight and back toward Sun and Susanoo as they both abruptly stop in their comedic struggle.

I hear Sun sniffing the air loudly. Susanoo, on the other hand, seems like she's listening to something. In this rare quiet moment, I can hear a slight breeze.

Susanoo lets go of Sun as she slouches her shoulders. Looking like she's no longer interested in doing anything to Sun. "Guess-*hiccup*- she found ya didn't go through the front…" she sighs.

"She stinks more than you do…" Sun insults her molester.

"Tha'ss the smell of blood and gore for ya. That shit never goes —*hiccup*— away…"

I think I know who they're talking about, but I feel as though I should still ask. "What are you guys talking about?"

Following my words, I hear something clacking on the flooring in the hallways. That's not the only sound. It's the noise of some sort of wild animal breathing heavily, like a wolf in pursuit of its prey.

Loki leaps in front of our group, facing the door to the room as his arms are spread out theatrically.

"Finally! The only reason I even came was to personally meet one of my partner's lovers-slash-sister! You *know* she's probably into some weird shit! Ohohohoh!"

Knowing who Loki's partner is, I guess that answers my question as to what everyone is talking about, and who's coming down the hallway.

The clacking footsteps come to a complete halt. At the door to the lounge, a caramel-skinned woman in spartan armor stands in a profile. Rubbing her arm against her mouth.

She lets out a loud sigh as her lips begin to move. "You're Sun Wukong?" the scarred woman asks in a cold voice.

Sun carefully stands in front of me, which is not a good sign.

"I also go by the Great Sage Equal to Heaven! But most people call me Sun Wukong," Sun replies, trying to sound confident, but I can hear a faint hint of caution in her voice.

The Spartan rests her head back as she turns her gaze toward us. "So, you're a woman? Well, that makes no difference to me…" she claims. "I'll still claim your head as mine…" Her cold stern expression warps into something more unhinged.

A barbarous smile forms on her face as her sharp fangs are exposed. Her one good eye begins to ignite into a blue war flame as drool pours from her mouth, bubbling from the heat.

Sun steps closer back toward me, keeping her defensive demeanor. "Grrr…" she growls.

"I'm who the humans call Bellona!" she shouts like a madwoman. "I'll be the one killing you today! So, don't bore me, please! Hahahahahaha!" That insane laugh. Here I thought the Nuckelavee was what nightmares are made of.

CHAPTER ELEVEN: THE MAD GODDESS ENTERS

Continuing her mad laughter, Bellona walks into the lounge. Her movements are that of a mentally ill person as her feet drag on the floor. Her hands clutch her short hair. "I can't believe it's truly you!" Bellona screeches like a star-struck fan. "There I was thinking I was going to fight the Disgraced Shinto Whore. Then, out of nowhere, the Monarchs blessed me with the greatest news I could ever hope for in this boring tournament! You popped up at the last minute to bring a smile to my face! Ha ha ha ha ha ha!"

The insane howling of the War Goddess causes the already shaking Momoko to hide behind her deity. Normally, I'd chuckle at how easily scared she is, but I fully understand her here. I'm sure as hell not moving past Sun.

The War Goddess comes face to face with Sun… Well, that may not be entirely accurate. Bellona is as short as the pictures shown to us. She has to look up to Sun, who outsizes even me.

"Heh… You're crazy… And tiny…" Sun smacks her right fist into her left palm as she tries to intimidate and insult her enemy. Though, you can hear how disturbed she is by Bellona's presence.

"W-what did you call me, Yellow Ape?!" Bellona roars at Sun, causing her to flinch at the outburst.

"Told yooouuu," Ell sings.

"Please, pardon Lady Bellona…" a polite voice comes from the entrance. An elderly man stands there in a professional manner. "She is excited. She's been a bit dispirited with her last few battles. I do thank you for giving her her spark back."

159

"Uhh... You're welcome?" Sun's unsure how to respond to the thanks.

A groan leaves Bellona's mouth as her maddening face is cleared away by pure annoyance. "I do not need a failure like you to thank her for me, Leonardo!" she growls at him, like that of an enraged teenager.

"My apologies, Lady Bellona," the elderly man holds out his hand to me in a kind manner. "A pleasure to meet you, comrades of our enemy. I am Leonardo Charles Russo. The caretaker to the great War Goddess, Bellona."

He's also part of one of the richest families in the country and a well-known war hero, but he makes it sound like all he is is a Caretaker. He also takes the term too literally with this whole butler thing.

He even tolerated being talked down to by her just now.

"Oh my! Vergil, will you act this loyal when you play my maid?" Ell chuckles.

"Really? *Now* you mention that?!"

Sun swiftly turns her head towards Ell. "You're not going to embarrass Mr. Knight like that!"

So glad Sun thinks this would be the first time I'd be humiliated like that.

"A-are you ignoring me?" I can hear Bellona say angrily through her clenched sharp teeth.

"How is he humiliated if it brings joy!" Ell chuckles.

"Only to you!" Sun shouts at her.

"Ohh..." Bellona speaks, sounding as if she's come to some sort of realization. "So... that human you defend from being shamed, is that your servant?"

Sun quickly turns back to stare down the War Goddess. "Huh? Servant?" Sun repeats Bellona, lost at what she meant. I'm also a bit confused.

The one eye of the War Goddess examines me. She scoffs in a repulsive manner. "What sort of joke is this? How does such a scourge of divinity gain a sad excuse for a human?"

I can see Sun baring her teeth and growling in defense. "What was that?"

"He undoubtedly has no wealth. I can smell his weakness from here. And I can't see him being used as a concubine! Only something as pathetic and pacifistic as an Asian god would have such a creature as their servant!" Her face begins to warp back into that sadistic style she introduced herself with. "In the old days, we'd put mongrels like him out of their misery! Ha ha ha ha ha ha!"

I'm not sure what's worse, her malicious words, or her menacing tone. I do know one thing: this isn't actually about me.

I've been in plenty of these types of scenarios to know that she's trying to get Sun riled up and throw the first swing.

Insulting both me, who Sun cares a lot for, and throwing in salt towards her faction. This is definitely meant to start a fight.

This works as Sun removes her shrunken staff from behind her ear. With a quick twirl, she increases its size and strikes the blunt end on the ground, damaging the flooring below.

"Gaah!" Momoko screams at the impact of the staff.

"C-calm down, Sun! She's trying to provoke you!"

"I sort of figured that out, but it still pisses me off!" Sun snarls.

"Aaaahhh!" Bellona lets out a sound. Not a scream, but a sound of pure euphoria. Her arms wrap around her body as it wiggles. Her scarred face blushing violently. "Yes! Hate me! I want you to want me dead! Aaaahhh!" Another orgasmic scream leaves her mouth.

Sun leaps back, gripping her staff. "W-what is wrong with you?"

No longer angry, Sun is now obviously uncomfortable by how Bellona is acting. She's not the only one.

"Daaammmn, this girl is fuckin' freaky..." Susanoo says. Odd hearing that come from *her* of all people.

Momoko grips onto Susanoo as she looks over the Storm Goddess's shoulder, shaking in fear. "T-that was who we were going to fight?"

Susanoo pats the head of her shaking Caretaker. "Ha ha! Ya know if I stayed in the-*hiccup*- Tryouts, she'd be pointin' that creepy, yet weirdly hot, smirk at ush!"

"H-huh?" Momoko nervously shouts in response to her god.

"Ha!" Bellona lets out a mocking laugh as her focus switches to Susanoo. "I have seen how you fight, Disgraced Shinto. Particularly other women. Chasing them around in a fit of lust until they submit, to get away from you. If I wanted to fight a perverted lightning user, I would fight my father..." Her eye quickly examines Susanoo as she insults her. "And what the hell are you wearing? Is this some sort of joke?"

Susanoo rubs the back of her head "Ha ha. A lot of foreigners compare me to their dads, for some reason..."

"Are you intoxicated?" Bellona shouts, irked by Susanoo's disrespect. Makes sense, considering she's called the Disgraced Goddess.

"Fuck yeah! Ha ha ha-*hiccup*-ha ha ha!" Susanoo laughs.

"Do you *want* me to kill you?" the irritated Bellona shouts.

Momoko tearfully gestures *no* as a whimper leaves her lips. "N-n-n-no! S-she's always like this! N-no one is wanting anything!"

"I want shome fresh ramen. Thash the best when ya -*hiccup*- drunk…"

"P-please, d-don't make it worse Susanoo!" Momoko grips tighter on Susanoo's gym uniform. "W-why did we even come here?"

Susanoo scratches her ear with a carefree, drunken grin. "Ah dunno…"

Loki leaps in front of the duo, posing flamboyantly. "Well, clearly you two came for one hell of a match!" he answers as, from his long stylish sleeve, he pulls out a microphone and stand. Confetti burst around his clothes. As the colorful paper fades, his elegant robe became that of an old referee outfit.

"On the left, we have the six-pack rocking and milk bags bouncing Great Sage, Sun Wuuuuukooooong! On the right, with a face as fucked up as her mind and a temper as short as her legs, we have the sister/lover of my dear partner Ares, Belllllooooonnnnaaaaa!" As Loki shouts, both Sun and Bellona are not happy about this theatrical roasting he's giving them.

Four confetti bombs explode around Loki. From inside the color bombs, four small and cartoonish versions of him with strange spider-like features appear in his original outfit. All are clapping and cheering at the real Loki.

"Woooaaaah!"

"Bring on the laughter!"

"We want more of the announcer!"

"That announcer has quite the ass on him!"

Loki's doppelgangers cheer, somehow, ending up making it more about himself.

"Gaaahh!" Momoko screams at the slapstick abilities of Loki. Can't mock her for that. Loki gets more surreal the longer we hang around him.

Of all the fights I've seen him in, it's like watching a dark humor cartoon. It's like he could borderline bend reality.

"Hey!" Bellona shouts to gain back our attention.

As Loki looks over to her, his tiny doppelgangers explode into more colorful paper, disappearing as the original is yelled at. His microphone follows suit.

"What? Too much? If so, fear not darling! Good old Daddy Long Legs can be far worst! Ohohoh!"

"I know you! And this woman in the hat! You're both aligned with… *him*…" Bellona ends in a whisper.

The insanity that was in her eye is gone. Now, an expression of what I can only describe as shame forms on her face. Bellona's personality is all over the place.

"Oh my, how cute. The rude little mess of a god, who insulted my Broken Knight in front of me, is all flustered. Like a little schoolgirl," Ell claps her hands together with a realization. "Oh, a schoolgirl uniform would have been perfect for these two!" She declares as she eyes Momoko and Susanoo. "Well… guess I'll use a different model…" I can feel a dark aura looming over me.

"I-Is he here… Is Mar- Ares with you?" Bellona asks in a shy manner.

Is she seriously acting this way over Ares? I know she is one of his lovers, but this whole shy girl act is completely different from what we've seen.

Still, even with the scar, she has a cute face. This innocent farse she's pulling only adds to that.

"That is precious, darling! You wish to see your fuck daddy. Or brother in this case!" Loki jokes, scratching his chin. "Sadly, he likes to cause a bit of hell when he's out and about, so we normally keep him in a safe place. Away from the humans, other gods, and my dear Mistress here."

It is interesting seeing that Ares didn't even come to watch one of the mothers of his children, but if Olympians are anything like in myths, family may not be worth their time. Though, Bellona seems to be interested in the possibility.

The War Goddess's head lowers at this news. "Perhaps, that is for the best…" quickly, her head raises back up. All the cute features she had have been washed away by the madness in her eye as she looks at Sun and foaming at the mouth. "Wouldn't want the pressure on me as I slaughter you, Yellow Ape!" she shouts with her horrifyingly insane voice returning in full force.

Sun takes up a defensive pose once again in front of me, focusing on my wellbeing over hers. Momoko tightens her frightful grip onto her Storm Goddess and whimpering at the sight of the mad goddess.

The atmosphere here is tense. Only Ell and Loki aren't seemingly affected, of course. The dark tone instantly changes as a bright pink cloud bursts at the door. Miniature hearts and moons explode into pink mist.

"Excuse me!" I hear shouted in a cheerful voice from inside the fading smoke. With the pink mist gone we see a woman with sparkling pink chin-length hair, with a small ponytail on the right side of her head. Her eyes are like her hair, bright pink. On her face, she has a crescent moon tattoo under her right eye and a star tattoo under her left.

Her outfit is like a magical girl outfit you'd see in an anime, pink and white all over. In her hand, she holds a magic wand topped off with the head of a microphone.

"Hello, contestants! I am the party goddess of the Shinto faction, ready to bring a smile onto your faces as I host your fight!! Ame-no-Uzume-no-Mikoto!" The cheerful girl introduces herself, placing her hand over her eye in a peace sign.

NAMES: AME-NO-UZUME-NO-MIKOTO, GODDESS OF THE DAWN. FACTION: SHINTO.

GODHOOD: LOVE, MUSE. HUMAN NATIONALITY: JAPANESE.

Oh, I know who she is. The goddess of revelry. Seems about right for a Love Goddess. She also played a big role in the story of Amaterasu. Not as big as Susanoo's of course, but still.

In the Gods' Wrath tournaments, the host is always a Love God, beings who can get the crowd happy and excited. To be a Love God, you're often associated with lust, fertility, or a free spirit who loves to spread joy. From what I remember in the story of Amaterasu, Ame here is perfect for getting a crowd excited, to the point where it actually helped get Amaterasu out of the cave she was hiding in. So, she would be the perfect diety to be considered a Love God. Especially with what she did to excite said crowd. Having this story in mind, I am a bit embarrassed to look at her.

"Are we ready to show the fans our wrath, ladies?" the bubbly host leaps joyfully as she asks.

"Yeah! Let's get this-"

"Hello, my goddess of the striptease!" Susanoo interrupts Sun's response. She drunkenly walks over to the Love Goddess to hold her hand.

"I haven't seen you in forever! Come on, give the Summer Storm a kiss!" Susanoo leans in with her lips puckered out.

"Get the hell away from me, you damned disgrace of a god!" Ame shouts, shifting from the cheerful demeanor she had only seconds ago. "Damn it, you smell. And what the hell are you wearing?! Get away from me!" She yells as she begins to push back the far taller, and probably far stronger, Susanoo.

A face of disgust and rage forms on her, far different than the annoyed and angry expression Sun makes whenever Susanoo tries something.

Ame pushes Susanoo back and dusts herself off. "I don't know what's worse, the fact that I'll smell like you when I go out there, or the fact I was touched by such a failure!" she moans in disgust.

I doubt she is acting like this because of how Susanoo acted. This seems more personal. Ame is a Shinto god like Susanoo, and very attractive. I wouldn't doubt it if Susanoo did this to her daily. But she also uses that word that the others used. *Disgraced.*

"Oh, come on! Ya-*hiccup*- know ya love how I look in this! How about you give me the same show you gave my sister when she pouted like a baby, huh?"

"W-why would I do such a thing for a filthy disgrace like you?!" Ame shouts in a more flustered tone.

"Because I will give ya a kiss if ya do!" Susanoo promises as she puckers her lips once again.

"S-stop!" Ame shouts. "Why are you even here? I thought you dropped out!"

Having these two squabble and distracting everyone, I figure this is the perfect time to talk to Sun once more.

I grab Sun by the hand. "Huh?" she responds as I walk her a few feet away from the group.

I lean close to Sun as she does the same. "Sun, this is your last chance. Are you sure you want to do this?" I whisper to her nervously.

"Of course!" she answers kindly. "We talked about this."

I didn't forget what Susanoo said, but I still can't stop this uneasiness. Why can't I see Sun as what she is, not as someone that needs me to protect them, but a god?

"Sun, Bellona is a War Goddess of Olympus! She is one of the most powerful godhoods from one of the three top-tier factions! She is not like the Buddhist and Taoist gods you faced!" I whisper to her loudly. "Why do you feel you need to do this?"

"Like I said, Mr. Knight… I want to win that juice for you… I need to…" her voice sounds more serious.

I let out a sigh. "Thought I'd give it another try…"

"Gah!" Ame shrieks as she tosses Susanoo off her. "I thought I wouldn't have to deal with this bull after you dropped out!" She begins to clear her throat, and put back on that happy demeanor she had when she first walked in. "So, anyway are we all ready?"

"I've been ready since I heard who I was fighting! How about you, Yellow Ape? Are you ready for the deathmatch?" Bellona implores with her signature wide psychotic grin.

"Hell yeah, I am, Runt!" Sun yells enthusiastically with her fist in the air, ignoring the last part of what Bellona said. At least, I think she is.

"Let us hope the audience is as ready! … Sure, they may be pissed because this disgrace dropped out at the last second and a random god took her place… Totally not unprofessional of the Monarchs…" Ame mutters, sounding unsure and paranoid. "But as long as I am out there, I can make any odd scenario a happy occasion!" She shouts cheerfully.

"Like ya did for my sister?" Susanoo jokes.

"Shut up!" Ame shouts to her. "If I have to…" we easily hear her whisper. "Now, before we all get started, is there anything we need to know before the fight!?" she says happily.

Sun raises her hand in the air, waving it in excitement. "Oh! Oh! I have a question!" she shouts frantically. As Ame turns towards Sun, the joyful Monkey King leaps forward. "When do I get that healing apple juice?!"

Ame's head slants in confusion. "Healing… Apple juice…" she repeats in a loss for words.

"Do you mean the Life Cider?" Ell asks Sun.

"*Oh*!" Ame shouts. "Well, you do not get any of the Cider until you win the Tryouts. If you lose a body part or die in the fight, you will be given enough to heal, but you do not get your own until you're in the actual tournament… Sorry!" Ame happily explains to Sun.

"Damn…" Sun whines hearing this news. I pat Sun on the back as she lowers her head in disappointment.

"So, there goes that dream of yours of being a true immortal that I've heard of…" Bellona mocks Sun.

"Grr…" Sun growls at Bellona with bared fangs.

Before she does anything, I pull Sun to the side, away from Bellona and everyone else once more.

"If you are going to do this, you can't go jumping in swinging like you did to the Nuckelavee. Since you aren't as strong as you use to be, you need to treat Bellona like she is more of a threat than any god in the past!" I whisper into Sun's ear as she nods to my every word in agreement. "So, what are you going to do?" I whisper in enthusiasm to her.

"Well, I'm going to beat her to an inch of her life and move on to the Royale where I'll do the same there!" Sun explains proudly.

I was sort of hoping to hear an actual plan of some kind. "And how are you going to win this?"

"I just told you!" She continues to sound chipper. I look at her, dumbfounded at the fact she thinks this is an actual plan. She pats me on the back, hard, nearly knocking me over again. "Chill out, Mr. Knight! I got this!" Sun proclaims with pride as she continues to smack my back, forcing more pain with each hit I take.

I'm still not sure if I admire Sun's confidence, or fear it...

"Um... Excuse me!?" I hear Ame shout behind us. Sun and I turn toward her as she and Bellona stand next to each other in wait for the fight. She stares at us in frustration as her hands are crossed while Bellona stares at us in anger and most likely impatience. Seeing that rage-filled face is no less hair-raising. Not as much as that other expression, though. "Are we ready?" Ame questions, tapping her foot.

I look back and forth between them and Sun. "Uhh... Well-"

"Sure am!" Sun yells out in joy. The powerful monkey hugs me tightly, making me let out a loud grunt. "Wish me luck, Mr. Knight!" Sun places me back onto the ground. Free from her grip, I gasp for air. She leaps in joy next to Ame, bouncing up and down in excitement like a child being praised. Seeing her act like this still makes me wonder if Sun is more focused on the fight than the Life Cider like she claims…

"The victor shall claim me!" Susanoo remarks as she waves at the three, causing Sun, Ame, and Bellona to look on at her in annoyance.

"G-good luck…" Momoko nervously waves.

"You're shaking a lot. Maybe you should put on some pants," Ame shouts happily.

"Huh? …" Momoko slowly stares down at her outfit again. She quickly crouches down again. "I-I forgot I was even wearing this!" She shouts. I feel bad for her, but at the same time, I sort of want to laugh. "T-they don't even make these kinds of gym uniforms anymore!"

"Well, normal gym clothes would have been boring," Ell defends the outfit.

"I wanted to go with a retro pants-less style! Ohohohoh!"

Ame points up to the sky. "All right! Let's get this show started!" she shouts.

As the upbeat goddess stays in her pose, the ground below them begins to glow brightly. I look down to see what the source of the light is. It's a magic circle. Around the rim of the circle are the symbols of all the Monarchs and their factions. In the center, there is the large G that is now the New Pantheon's symbol.

The glow of the circle begins to consume all light in the room, leaving us in a dark room with only the bright circle as a light source.

Sun gazes upon the circle in wonder and surprise, while Bellona stands there with her eyes closed. It appears she is more focused on something else, most likely the battle ahead.

"Hey, Mr. Knight!" Sun yells, gaining my attention. Her face is shaded by the light below her, but I can still see her giving me that smirk. "I'd be lying if I said I wasn't excited for this fight!" She gives me a thumbs up.

I smile and give her a little chuckle. "Good luck, oh Victorious Fighting Buddha," I remark sarcastically.

Sun chuckles as she gives me a wink. The light engulfs the three and in a second, the light departs, bringing back the lights of the room.

"Come, darlings! The show is about to begin!" Loki shouts as he rushes towards the large screen window, showcasing the arena bellow. He leaps in the air and flips his body before landing gracefully on the couch. "Let us watch and bask in the glorious bloodshed and gore of the ultimate form of entertainment known as battle!"

Hearing him say those words make my spine tingle. I feel a hand rest on my shoulder. I turn my head back to see Ell, smiling at me. "You know, death means nothing to them, right?" she speaks in her assured tone.

She's right, though. Gods die all the time in these fights, and they come back the next day as if it was nothing. It's all because of the same reason Sun is here, the Life Cider. Sun wants to use it if I ever get hurt, or worse. Should I feel uneasy about using such a thing? Legends vary from people gaining great power from such an object to those with cursed, ruined lives.

I see the elderly caretaker of Bellona walk past me. I can hear him let out a sigh of relief through his nose.

He wipes his head with a handkerchief he pulled from his front coat pocket. "Lady Bellona can be stress-inducing. I do apologize…"

"Uh, don't worry about…"

"Yes! I know the trouble of dealing with a War God. It is as bad as dealing with a Trickster," Ell jokes.

Loki turns back towards us. "Are you bad mouthing me?" he yells at Ell.

"Of course!" Ell bats her hand at him.

"Good! That means I am doing my job! Ohohohoh!" Loki laughs happily.

"Are you Sun Wukong's Caretaker?" Leonardo asks me.

"Yes! My name is Vergil Knight. I am a mythologist!"

"Knight? Well, I haven't heard that name in forever. Are you perhaps- Oh that does not matter. I do apologize for the cruel things Lady Bellona said to you. Especially towards a young man I can relate too well with," he jokes as he bends over slightly.

As he knocks on his leg, I can hear the quiet sound of hard materiel through his pants leg.

"Though I don't want to brag, I may have you beat," he chuckles as he finishes showing off his false leg.

"Yeah. Again, no problem…" I'm glad he changed the subject there. Amazingly, the Knight name is still kind of remembered after all these years.

I look over to see Ell with a concerned expression. It is truly a rarity to see that on Ell. She knows how touchy this whole thing is. Don't get me wrong, she teases me for it. Like when she tells me she likes guys with daddy issues. Even then, she still knows how I feel about that.

"But a mythologist caretaker? That is quite rare to see. That does explain how a young American lad such as yourself is the caretaker to a Chinese deity," he points out to me. "Since we are introducing ourselves, my name is Leonardo Russo, and I am a Bellonarii to the great War Goddess, Bellona." He bows as he introduces himself.

"I-I know who you are. My grandfather met you before through your charity. But I didn't know you were a Bellonarii, even before the gods' return."

Even though many former religions are slowly rising back up, more as fan clubs than actual beliefs. Bellonariis are soldiers, and we live in a world without war. Why would they exist?

"Let's just say, when it comes to war, you need to worship the right god to survive." He explains as one of his eyes looks out toward the Arena. The glass one continues to watch me. Kind of freaky. "But I must say, I don't know a lot about Sun Wukong. However, I know she is strong. If you are a mythologist or have even seen any of the Tryouts, then you know how dangerous Bellona is, right?" Leonardo inquires. I nervously gulp and nod yes at him. "Luckily for you, death means nothing in these events..." he speaks, sounding as if he is making a threat to me. Hearing this firm resonance in his voice makes the hair on the back of my neck stand.

His appearance also adds to this intimidation. Even under his coat, I can see a bit of muscle definition. How does he have them at this age? Is this because he's a soldier or because he's a Bellonarii?

Susanoo wraps her arm around my shoulder. "Come on, ya cripple! Two badass ladies are about to hit each other sho hard, they'll-*hiccup*- knock each other's pantsh off! At least that's what I am hopin' for!" she slurs as she walks me to the couch. Her wobbling is making it difficult, so I have to hold her up. Not the best idea using the guy with a cane as support for your drunken body. Plus, having the bonus of her nearly exposed body rubbing against me isn't helping either. Then there's Momoko, who's still gripping her like a vice.

"S-Susanoo! Get off him you're to- *Ahhh*!" Momoko screams as a loud horn goes off out in the arena.

I can hear the crowd outside beginning to cheer in excitement. That is the first sign of this fight beginning. I free myself from Susanoo and walk toward the window to gaze down at the large arena, and the huge audience inside.

My first Gods' Wrath match… and I'm terrified…

CHAPTER TWELVE: TOUGH CROWD

The attendees roared in excitement as the horn blew through the stadium, sounding as loud as they were. Most of the audience cheered for Bellona. Many of them wore foam helmets in the style of their beloved War Goddess. Some swung foam swords in the air, while others had their faces painted to replicate Bellona's scars.

The lights went out in the arena as a glowing circle appeared in the center of the battlefield. *Boom!* An explosion of transparent pink hearts and yellow crescent moons burst from the magic circle as spotlights begin to focus on the center of the explosion, Ame-no-Uzume-no-Mikoto burst out from the wave of shapes and colors.

"How are we doing my fun-loving worshipers!" the goddess yelled cheerfully into her microphone. The audience roared louder at the appearance of the Love Goddess. She began to bask in the praise they were giving her. She turned away from them in a faux bashful way. "Oh, you're all too kind!" she said in an innocent delivery.

The idol goddess loved the praise more than she gave off. She and many other goddesses associated with love were always attention seekers. She may be a kind goddess, but Ame is no different, craving attention like a drug. Even when the Shinto faction suffered the loss of their sun goddess and were planning to gain her back, Ame's plan, which involved stripping her clothes off for the sun goddess and many others, was more about her gaining attention and less so helping her pantheon. No matter what her intentions were, she was still vital in the resurrection of Amaterasu.

"So, who do you wanna see?!" Ame yelled to the crowd.

"Bell-on-a! Bell-on-a! Bell-on-a!" the audience cheered.

Though she knew people came to see the fight, Ame still hated the fact that no one cheered her name just now. The Love Goddess detested how no one is showing her more love, or anything of such, compared to the fighters.

People cheering for that ugly, fight-hungry nut job! Ame thought to herself as she kept up her joyful appearance to the audience.

Ame presented the left side of the field. "In this corner! She is one of Olympus's most bloodthirsty deities and praised by both Greek and Roman soldiers as the goddess of conquest! Bellllllonaaaaaaa!" Ame yelled into her microphone, as another magic circle appears.

Bellona slowly rose from the circle. She showed off a mad joyful look as her arms spread out. Blue flames formed around her arms and head. As quickly as they appeared, the flames disperse, revealing her Spartan helmet.

In her hands, a spear rested in her left while a sword rested in her right. Added to her arsenal is a shield strapped to her left arm.

The crowd cheered at the sight of the Mad Warrior. Bellona stared out at the audience as she quietly basked in the praise of her new worshipers. They were not warriors, but they were still hers.

"Now, lets meet our brand new surprise fighter, specifically chosen to replace poor Susanoo by the Monarchs themselves!"

The audience went quiet for a moment from the news.

"Chosen by the Monarchs?"

"Is this god special?"

"I still wanted Susanoo…"

177

Ame was aware that Sun was not exactly "chosen" by the Monarchs, but this would easily gain more interest in the new fighter and most importantly, keep her audience entertained.

"She's the Victorious Fighting Buddha! The Great Sage Equal to Heaven! The Monkey King that fought her way through the Taoist and Buddhist factions, Sun Wukoooonnnggg!" She presented the opposite side of Bellona as another circle opened.

Sun began to rise from the circle. She looked down as her body slowly materializes from the light. An expression of awe and intrigue formed on her face as she watched.

Once she saw her feet exit the light, she surveyed the audience in the arena. The once loud and excited onlookers now watched quietly. Seeing how they were not as excited as she was hoping, Sun began to feel a bit of stage fright at the unmotivated crowd.

She was always used to crowds either cheering her name or screaming in fear. This, however, left her in an awkward position.

Due to her last-minute introduction, the Monkey King had no support from the audience. At best, the crowd had more interest in her as a new fighter, but mostly disappointed for the loss of the fan-favorite, Susanoo.

However, her predecessor mainly became a fan favorite due to how she "dealt" with her female combatants. Though, this kind of support was mainly from the male crowd.

Sun awkwardly waved her hand at the audience, holding her staff close to her chest. "H-hello…" Sun greeted them nervously.

The crowd began to mutter in confusion over the Demigod, unsure what to make of the whole thing.

"Did she say she was the Monkey King?"

"But she's a girl!"

"She reminds me of a character from that old anime."

"Why is she replacing Susanoo, again?"

"Well, she's kind of cute, if you're into that kind of thing."

Sun could hear almost everything they said with her animal-like hearing and the quietness of the arena.

As she looked back and forth, up and down, at the crowd, she saw her caretaker watching from the skybox. All the awkward feelings she had disappeared as soon as she saw him.

"Hey! Mr. Knight!" Sun yelled as she leapt in excitement and waved at him.

In the skybox, her caretaker covered his face in humiliation. Sun was also able to see the woman that he considered an old friend, the woman he called "Ell," snickering behind him. Seeing the two together caused Sun's eyebrows to scrunch together in outrage.

"Stupid rich lady. Acting all cool and close to Mr. Knight…" Sun muttered to herself.

Ame, Bellona, and the confused crowd watched on as Sun began to loudly talk to herself. Her caretaker's shame deepened as he watched the goddess he lived with, not realize that everyone could hear her. Simultaneously, the woman that Sun complained about chuckled at her friend's humiliation lightheartedly.

"Huh?" she finally realized how audible she was. "Oh… Sorry…" Sun apologized. She scratched the back of her head in embarrassment.

"A-all right… Now that we got the introductions out of the way… Let's get the Nostalgia Field ready!" As Ame yelled this, she pointed to the sky, causing the ground she stood on to

179

float. The ground around her revealed itself to be a floating podium.

From underneath the floating podium, a glowing orb with the New Pantheon's symbol slowly spun from where Ame stood. Sun watched in awe as the Love Goddess rose. Bellona snickered maniacally, excited for what came next.

The sight of the orb raised the excitement of the crowd. Ame could feel this and kept up her show.

"Gods! Take your battle stances!" As Ame yelled this, Sun smiled widely and pointed her staff toward Bellona. Bellona gave an equally eager, yet psychotic, grin at the Monkey King as she pointed her spear at Sun. Her war flames momentarily sparked. The guests' excitement grew more at the enthusiasm of the two fighters.

With the crowd feeling more energized, the glowing orb in the center began to increase in size. Turning into a dome, the outer layer began to approach the two fighters.

Sun watched it in shock as she saw the Nostalgia Field coming toward her. Bellona held her stance as the glowing dome began to envelop her. The crowd cheered loudly as the Nostalgia Field took over the arena ground below.

The two were in the divine dome. Now, all they needed was a battlefield.

CHAPTER THIRTEEN: THE NOSTALGIA FIELD

A magically infused battlefield, the Nostalgia Field was created by Odin for the Gods' Wrath tournaments. On the outside, it only appears as a glowing dome, but on the inside, it becomes a shadow of one of many godly domains from days of old.

It replicates these worlds to the core. The Field remakes the smells, textures, and even the beings who inhabited them to the point where they all seem almost real. At least, that is what the gods who fought in these arenas say. I guess it's sort of like a mystical version of virtual reality. No human has been inside of one. In fact, this is my first time seeing the outside of the Nostalgia Field in person.

I watch on in wonder at the glowing field, while also unsettled at the fact Sun disappeared into the void only moments ago. I look away as I hear snapping echoing in my ear, only to see Ell smiling at me as she snaps her fingers.

"Please, my Broken Knight. Try to come off professional. I know it is hard for you. Especially with what you're wearing," Ell teases. She does have a point. Maybe a T-shirt and jeans were not the best things to wear for the occasion. Ell points toward the couch. "Come now, let's sit back and watch."

Maybe I should do what she suggests. If I stand too long, my knee will act up anyway. I begin to walk to the couch facing the window of the skybox. I turn to sit down, still watching the glowing dome that is the Nostalgia Field.

As Ell tries to take a seat next to me, a familiar gust of wind blows in my direction. After the wind blew, Ell stops and crosses her arms. I look over to where Ell was about to sit, only to see Susanoo sitting there with her legs in a meditative style.

"Why'd ya stop?!" Susanoo whines.

"Because I do not appreciate the fact that the air grabbed my ass just now," Ell replies, sounding surprisingly frustrated.

Susanoo has some real balls on her. I mean, Sun is pretty scary when she is angry, but Ell is on a whole other level. No one has ever tried to touch Ell like this before, mostly because they were scared of what she would do. Still, this Shinto god really likes to make me envy her.

"Come on! Why don't ya sit your stylish ass right here, huh?" Susanoo says as she pats her lap, bringing back a memory of the mall from a while back. "Or you can take a seat right here!" She points to her face, not reminding me of anything at all.

"Susanoo…" Momoko whines by how her god is acting, all while gripping tightly onto her kendo stick. I can tell she wants to swing it at Susanoo.

Never heard of a priestess who enjoys hitting their goddess with blunt objects in response to their misbehavior. Normally, they let it go.

"Sorry, I'd much rather have that seat," Ell points to my face.

I think my heart suddenly skipped a beat. "Wait, what now?"

"Oh, but it seems so dirty, and look at all the hair on it. Heh heh…" Ell jokes as she rubs my facial hair.

I leer at her, frustrated. Don't know why, though. I knew she was teasing me.

Ell sits in the empty spot next to me. She crosses her legs and rests her hands on them so elegantly. "I guess I'll sit here. At least until you get rid of that rat fur on your face."

Ell has always done this to me when I haven't shaved in a while. She has never liked bearded men. She says they remind her too much of her dad.

"My Mistress can truly be so cruel! Ohohohoh!" Loki speaks as he sits next to Ell. He mimics his Caretaker's way of sitting.

Susanoo gives out a loud sigh of defeat. "Fine then... Hey, Momoko! Ya wanna take a seat?" the drunken goddess asks her caretaker as she pats her lap once again.

"W-why do you do these things!" Momoko yells at Susanoo.

"I can't help it! You look so-*hiccup*- cute in your new outfit! Don't worry! I ain't gonna use my wanderin' hands on ya!" Susanoo laughs.

Momoko raises her wooden weapon in a threatening manner. "Y-you better not!"

Seeing them like this does shows how close they are. Momoko seems to treat Susanoo more like a big sister, or a drunken uncle who needs to be smacked every so often. Joking aside, they do seem more like friends than a priest and god.

Frankly, I wish I could focus solely on their relationship and get my mind off of the fight in front of me. Even now, I am still distressed over Sun.

"Huh?" I feel something grab my hand.

I can feel Ell holding onto it. "Must I keep reminding you that she is a god and not as fragile as you?"

"Yeah, I know..." I smile. Despite what people think of her, Ell was always there for me when I had trouble. Behind that smug demeanor lays a kind, loving woman... I think.

As I continue to address Ell, I feel something poking my cheek on the opposite side of the couch.

I look over to see Susanoo poking her finger at me. "So, Cripple, I gotta know. Did you two fuck?" she speaks so casually.

"S-Susanoo! D-don't ask such things!" Momoko shouts.

"Oh my!" Ell lightly chuckles.

"Really?" I respond.

"Come on! I gotta know how she is!" Susanoo whines.

"Well, knowing my Mistress, there must have been many lewd and distasteful outfits worn!" Loki jumps in.

"Oh, nice! I didn't know ya were such a take-charge kind of guy, Cripple!" Susanoo says with joy and pride. "What sort of outfits did you make her wear-"

"Darling, I was talking about him…" Loki points to me. My face turns bright red from embarrassment. I hope Ell didn't tell him this.

The expression of joy Susanoo had on her face turns blank as she hears this news. Her jaw drops. "Huh? …"

"W-what?!" Momoko stares at me with the same expression, but with a bit more horror in her eyes. "*H-hentai*!" she shouts. I looked up what that meant before coming here, and I can't blame her after this conversation.

"Heh, heh…" Ell chuckles behind her mouth.

"Please, do silence yourselves," speaks Leonardo, who has been sitting quietly on the chair in the corner this whole time. "Lady Bellona is about to battle. I much prefer this be a quiet and respectful event if you do not mind," he kindly orders, not turning his eye away from the glowing dome.

We all stare at the old war vet, surprised at how serious he's treating this event.

He seems as though he's about to watch a movie or admiring art. He's quietly watching on unlike the crowd outside cheering as loudly as possible.

I look out the window. I see Ame on her floating podium above the glowing dome.

"Not a threatening domain, but truly a beautiful sight! Will our fighters make do with the arena that has been chosen as their battlefield?!" I hear outside the window from Ame.

I scan the monitors to see where Sun will be fighting. Seeing what it is sets my heart a little bit at ease. She is fighting in a place with no violence, chaos, or hatred in the slightest. A paradise.

CHAPTER FOURTEEN: BATTLE IN PARADISE

Looking around in the white void of nothingness, all the Monkey King could see was her opponent, Bellona, standing before her with an eager grin. The sound of her psychotic snickering echoed in the light.

Her view of the War Goddess was obscured by the sudden appearance of a giant orb that floated between the two. A picture of an Egyptian boat carrying a coffin through a river of darkness rotated in the sphere.

"Where will these femme fatales fight it out?!" Ame's voice echoed through the void.

The Monkey King searched the void for where the voice was coming from, but her attention was quickly drawn back to the orb in the center. The image inside was immediately wiped away as a blur of other images appeared, spinning.

Although she was unable to see what the images were, she recognized them to be former domains from different factions of gods. Different heavens, other hells, and various cities. This was how the Nostalgia Field picked its arena.

The blurring images began to slow down, showcasing the images more vividly. A gladiator arena, a tower that reached the heavens, a rainbow bridge. These were the last few areas to be seen spinning in the orb until it landed on the field the two gods would be fighting in.

A large garden appeared in the dome, full of animals and vegetation. What truly caught Sun's eye was the large tree in the center of the garden. Despite the garden being foreign to her, that aspect of the location felt so familiar.

"It looks like a battle in paradise, folks! These two lovely goddesses will be duking it out in the Christian faction's lost bliss, the Garden of Eden! Not a threatening domain, but a breathtaking sight! Will our fighters make do with the arena that has been chosen for them?" Ame's voice echoed once again.

A loud crack echoed from the orb. The Monkey King investigated what the cause was. Observing closely, Sun noticed that the globe was beginning to crack.

"All right, Gods!" Ame shouted once more as the orb began to suffer more damage. "Show us your Wrrrrraaaaaaath!" As her voice boomed through the white void, the orb burst open. Along with it, the grassy field of the garden flowed from the orb.

The white void above turned into a cloud-filled blue sky. Trees began to rise from the newly created soil. Water began to flow into falls and lakes, and animals started to take shape around Sun. She watched in amazement at the world manifesting around her, wondering if this was how the Monarchs felt when they created their domains.

She felt the arena forming under her feet. As she looked at Bellona, she saw that the field was pulling the two in different directions as it grew.

"I won't keep you waiting long, Yellow Ape!" Bellona mockingly shouted as she was dragged away from her opponent. Trees formed in front of her, causing the Violent Goddess to disappear.

The growing Eden came to a halt. The lost paradise of the Christian belief had been fully restored. Sun examined her new surroundings, basking in the beauty of the garden.

Amazement flowed through Sun's mind at how real the Nostalgia Field felt. The wind was blowing on her skin and fur, the warmth of the sun on her face, the sounds of shimmering trees and noisy insects ringing in her ear.

The sound of loud purring gained Sun's attention as she turned to face the sound.

Staring off in the direction of the noise, the Monkey King experienced the peacefulness of the garden firsthand. She found a large male lion licking a baby lamb. At first, Sun was thinking the lion was merely tasting the infant sheep. However, she quickly saw it for what it truly was, a predator cleaning what it would typically consider as prey, treating it as if it were its cub.

"Wow..." Sun whispered to herself. "This place is Shangri-La..."

She knew a little about Eden from her caretaker. As her new body grew, she would often want him to tell her stories. Not knowing many fairy tales or children's stories, he would tell her stories of the numerous beliefs he studied. One of them was the story of Adam and Eve. She remembered him describing this place as a garden made by Joe for the first two humans to become his worshipers.

She also remembered Thoth mentioning this place and how the Divine Tree's power affected those who lived in it. The Tree would cause all threatening thoughts and pain to be replaced by a numbing calmness.

Sun's eyes widened as she gazed at a lesser tree in the garden. Wrapping her monkey tail around the Jingu Bang, Sun crouched down and leapt onto one of its branches. Gripping onto the branch, she swung her body around before letting go and landing back on the same piece of the tree, feet first.

From this higher view, she took in more of the garden's beauty. She leapt onto another tree in front of her and continued onto the next. From tree to tree, she jumped as she did long ago.

The nostalgia she felt was exhilarating as she let her inner animal instinct out. Laughing in joy, she playfully jumped above the garden grounds.

Sadly, among these joyful memories of her past life, she was struck with a memory of melancholy, not of her old life, but of when she was reborn. It was a memory that had become a nightmare to her.

Rainy skies. Thunder roaring. Her Caretaker yelling her name. The strength of his arms pulling her away from the tree she was grasping onto as a flash of light blinded her.

When her eyes opened, then, she saw, to her horror, her Caretaker on the ground after a large branch swung into his knee cap. She remembers how she tried to shake him so he could regain consciousness, all while tears poured down her face.

It was an incident that nearly repeated itself a while ago, after that Celtic horror's attack.

She halted her leaping as these memories haunted her. She knew her Caretaker was weak, fragile, and thanks to her, slow. She knew she must do something for him. To avoid what happened with the Nuckelavee and what occurred back then from happening again, she needed to win the Life Cider.

"I promised I'll win… Then… Then we can go on our own Journeys!" she spoke to herself. "Of course I'll win! I'm the Great Sage Equal to Heaven! How can I not?!" she shouted with pride while freeing herself of the dark and sad memories.

With this thought in mind, she continued her tree hopping with more enthusiasm in her jumps.

As she landed onto the next tree, something caught her eye. It was a small cicada, humming on the branch she stood on.

Inspecting the tiny insect, more of her inner animal instincts began to kick in.

Her Caretaker always yelled at her for trying this. She was unsure if he could see her, but she felt she must do this.

She reached for the insect, grabbing it between her thumb and index fingers. As the bug struggled in her grip, she began to raise it to her open mouth. The Monkey King chomped down on the bug. However, something was off.

No crunch. No squish. No texture. Sun looked at her hand to see that the cicada was gone. Yet, she still heard its humming. She investigated the branch she stood on to see the insect lying there in the same spot.

"What the heck?"

Confused, the Monkey King gripped onto the insect once more. As she held it above her open mouth, she snaps her teeth down once more. However, like before, nothing happened, and she heard its humming coming from the same spot.

Sun simply stared down the insect in confusion and annoyance, unsure of what was going on. As she tried reaching for it again, the cicada flew away from the Monkey King. Still annoyed and confused, Sun watched it flee from her grasp.

The sound of an animal chittering was heard, along with the noise of small feet hitting bark.

She turned to where the branch was connected to the tree and saw a chipmunk climbing next to her. As it wiggled its nose at her, Sun chuckles.

"Man, everything here feels so real. Are you as fluffy as you look?" Sun asked as she reached out to pet the little woodland creature.

Seeing the large hand coming toward it, the chipmunk swiftly jumped from the side of the branch, off the tree. Sun watched on in shock. She knew the creature wasn't real, but she still felt as though she should save its life.

She flung the Jingu Bang in the air with her tail as she jumped from the tree. Now, with her tail free, she wrapped it around the branch she sat upon.

Her arms extended to grab the creature, but as she did, she found nothing there.

No falling chipmunk. No tiny corpse smashed onto the ground. Sun did'nt even hear so much as a thud.

As it fell toward her, Sun grabbed the Jingo Bang and continued to scan the grass in confusion. Until, however, she heard a familiar sound.

Sun looked up after hearing the chitter. She found the same chipmunk staring down at her as she hung upside down from the branch.

As Sun began to think of what was going on, she remembered more of what her Caretaker had told her of Eden. She recalled him telling her that the Angel of Death never entered in this garden. As a result, there is no pain nor violence. Only a world where death was never introduced.

She finally understood what was going on. The cicada, and chipmunk, being creatures of the garden, could not experience death. Figuring this out made the Monkey King wish she had heard of this garden in her search for immortality in the old days.

As interested as Sun was in the beautiful garden of immortality, she realized that in a battle where the death of your enemy is the only means of victory, the immortality rule of the garden wouldn't apply to her or Bellona.

Sun peered into the garden as she continued to hang upside down, trying to spot her opponent. Something stuck out to her.

It was the massive oak tree she saw from the image within the orb.

"Am I already that far in?" she thought to herself, remembering that it was the center point of the entire battlefield.

She began to swing her tail back and forth, slowly picking up speed. Feeling she had gained enough momentum, Sun unwrapped her tail from the branch and leapt to the next tree.

The Fighting Buddha jumped from tree to tree once again, grabbing branches with her hands, feet, and tail. Closing in, Sun landed on the ground before the giant oak.

Of all the nostalgia she had felt so far, the tree the Great Sage gazed upon was the most familiar. The colors of the tree, white leaves, and golden fruit were so identical to the peach trees the Taoist pantheon wanted her to watch over.

Oh, how Sun hated the tasks those gods gave her, making the Great Sage watch their horses and fruit. Remembering the tantrums she threw for the humiliation she had suffered.

She destroyed the horse stables only out of pure rage and a need to rebel. Though, what she did to the peaches was because of a dream. A dream to be immortal and rise to true godhood, far beyond her status as a mere Demigod. She wanted to stand alongside Monarchs. She heard people mention that the peaches could make any being who ate them immortal. Sun remembered how much of a fat lie that was. Eating all the divine peaches only made her stomach upset, no immortality to be found.

The tree within the Garden of Eden was almost exactly like those peach trees, but instead of peaches, golden apples hung from the giant plant. Yet, they still gave off the same sweet scent as the peaches.

Sun licked her lips at the sight of the apples. While she felt sick eating too many divine peaches, she had since forgotten the taste of them. Were they delicious or horrid?

The temptation for the divine fruit overwhelmed Sun as she began to approach the tree. She suddenly halted as words written in the divine tongue begin to carve themselves into the tree in a heavenly glow.

"Of all the trees I give to you, this is not one of them. If touched or harmed, damnation shall follow you out of paradise," a loud voice echoed from the text before Sun.

As she gazed at the text on the tree, she began to remember more of what her Caretaker told her. The first worshipers of Joe were told not to eat from one tree. When they did so, they were cast out of his paradise forever.

"M-maybe I should ignore this spot," Sun said to herself. Not wanting to see what would happen to her, Sun turned away from the tempting fruit.

Glancing at the surrounding garden, Sun heard two familiar sounds. The whines of loud steeds and multiple hooved feet marching onto the grassy soil. Those were the sounds of a creature she has grown a bit of a hatred for.

Creatures she was humiliated to guard over when she was tasked by heaven to do so. Beasts that where half of the monster that nearly took away her beloved caretaker not too long ago. They were horses, no doubt. Four from the sounds of it.

Sun assumed the animals were a part of the garden, like the lion, and the chipmunk. Yet, they sounded too aggressive to be part of this garden.

She saw the large oaks in the distance being knocked over by some sort of powerful force. The same direction of this destruction was also the same as where the horse calls were coming from.

"Yellow Ape!" a familiar angry voice yelled from the same direction. "I'm coming! Don't bore me! Hahahahaha!"

Bellona, on her four-horse drawn chariot, burst from the trees, charging her way at the surprised Sun. The brush of her helmet and her eye combusted at the sight of her enemy. A malicious grin formed as she charged. Such as Bellona, her horses' manes, hooves, and eyes were engulfed in blue flames. The wheels on her chariot rolled with similar fire.

The Monkey King quickly leapt into the air and blew a loud whistle, summoning her yellow cloud beneath her feet. Sun pointed her staff at Bellona as her cloud charged toward the horse-drawn chariot. Bellona held out her spear in a similar fashion with its flaming tip focused on Sun.

The two incoming divine weapons struck one another. Sun's more powerful Jingu Bang easily broke the tip of the War Goddess's spear. Bellona broke out into mad laughter as she inspected her broken weapon. She turned back at Sun as she passed her, seeing the glimpse of a hubristic face on the Monkey King.

"Hahahaha! You like it rough, I see!" Bellona's screamed in a perverse tone.

Sun made a quick turn on her cloud, back around to Bellona. She began to quickly catch up to the horse-drawn chariot, as they both passed the tree in the center of the garden. They both stared each other down as Sun kept up her Cheshire grin.

This boastful attitude of the Monkey King enraged Bellona.

The fight had hardly begun, and her enemy was already looking down at her. It didn't matter what her reputation was. The more Bellona saw her, the more she wanted to kill the Monkey King.

Bellona pulled out her sword from the sheath on her back. As soon as it was free from its binding, it was engulfed in the same flames as everything else in the Olympian's arsenal.

Bellona let go of the leash controlling her horses. Placing her foot on the side of her chariot, Bellona launched herself at Sun. The Monkey King gasped in surprise at the oncoming goddess. Bellona held her shield in front of her flying body, allowing the scarred-up Spartan to knock Sun off her floating cloud. The two began to roll on the ground as they landed.

No longer mounted by their riders, both the cloud and the horse-drawn chariot faded into mist and dissolved into blue embers.

Sun lifted her upper body and shook her head.

"Hahahahaha!" Sun heard. She looked up to see Bellona jumping toward the Demigod, with her sword raised above her head and ready to impale Sun.

Shocked, Sun backflipped off the ground as Bellona stabbed the spot she previously laid.

With a twirl of her staff, Sun pointed her Jingu Bang at Bellona. Bellona placed her shield before her, with her sword in a battle-ready position.

After a few moments, the two goddessess charged toward each other once more, this time on foot. Before they collided, Sun held her staff out longways. Both the shield and the staff smashed into one another.

As both sides tried to push one another back, Bellona raised her flaming blade and swung down at the Monkey King. However, as swiftly as the sword was coming, Sun kicked the burning edge away.

Bellona prepared another swipe of her blade. Catching this, Sun quickly leapt away from the warrior goddess.

Sun twirled her staff as she regained her battle stance. Bellona stood before her, no battle poses. All she did was give Sun the same sinister grin she always wore as she chuckled. Sun reverted back to her classic prideful fashion.

Sun released a light laugh of her own as well. "What Mr. Knight said about you Olympians is true. You guys aren't pushovers at all."

"I wish I could say the same, Buddhist, but you've already given me no sign of being worthy of having your blood stain my blade," Bellona mocked in a murderous tone. "Still, you have quite the reputation yourself, don't you, Yellow Ape?" Bellona snickered.

"Well, I'd be lying if I said I don't like to brag. Heh."

"Oh, please, go on! Tell me all your stories! Tell me how you stole what you wanted when you wanted! How you mercilessly slaughtered everyone who dared to challenge you!" Bellona's face became more warped with insanity as she went on. Observing her face and listening to her words sent shivers throughout Sun's body. "How you ate them! Hahahahaha!"

Sun's eyes widened. "W-what?"

"Hahahaha! I decided to gain more insight on you before our battle! With that kind of appetite, you might as well be an Unfollowed!" Bellona wrapped her arms around her body as she jumped toward the heavens. "I have done plenty of cruel, inhumane things in my life, but not even I have eaten humans!"

"S-shut up!" Sun snarled at Bellona, baring her teeth like a rabid animal ready to kill.

"Yes! That's the face I wanted! Come, lets kill each other! Hahahaha!" Bellona laughed loudly as her flames began to burn ever brighter.

Every cruel word the Warrior Goddess spewed from her crazed smile enraged Sun. Tightly gripping her staff, the Fighting Buddha raised her weapon. With a powerful leap of her legs, she pounced toward her enemy like a predator on the hunt.

As the Sage rushed toward the Mad Goddess, a glow emanated from Bellona's chuckling throat was easily seen. Bellona quickly aimed her face at the incoming Sun and fired a bright blast of flame from her laughing mouth.

Sun was caught off guard, unable to dodge in time before the flames engulfed her.

The might of the attack burned the trees that stood behind Sun. The heat caused them to collapse into piles of ash.

"Hahahahaha! I can't believe that actually worked!" Bellona laughed. "I knew the moment I brought *that* up, you'd lose control. Now, look at you! Burning alive! Hahahaha- huh?" Bellona stopped mid-laugh as she saw something unexpected.

From the flames, Sun walked out, covered in sweat. "Gah! It's so hot!" Sun whined.

"What?" Bellona gasped in surprise.

"Huh? I thought you knew a lot about my reputation. Is the fact I'm fireproof not interesting enough to be spread around?"

"Fireproof?" confused rage was displayed all over the War Goddess's face.

"Also lava-proof, molten metal-proof, and so on," Sun spoke in a snarky tone at her enemy. "You had me worried there. Only certain types of magical flames can hurt me. Luckily, the fire of a War God isn't one of them. Still, I can tell your flames are weaker than what you'd expect from a veteran War Goddess. Side effect to the new body I'm guessing?"

Bellona snarled at this disdainful attitude. "Indeed. The power I've gained from all my battles back then did not travel with my soul to this new body. However, through this tournament, I'll gain back that power and stand alongside *him* once again!"

Sun rested her staff on her shoulder as she listened to Bellona's speech. "I can't blame you wanting to gain back what you've lost, but it was petty of you to try to manipulate me into getting angry."

From behind the Monkey King, the dead trees began to rise and heal back into position as they once were.

Witnessing this caused Bellona's flames to burn in anger. "I don't know which I hate more. The fact I'm being criticized for manipulating by a borderline Trickster, or this so-called 'paradise'! Peace and tranquility? That's hell to a being who thrives for battle!"

Sun happily looked around the garden. "I actually like it. Can't always be fighting, right?"

"Such a cowardly thing to spew from your lips. I was expecting more from you."

As she prepared herself for battle once again, Sun snickered at her enemy. "I was thinking the same about you when you tried distracting me. Trust me, I won't let that happen again."

"Hahahaha! Then come! Let us see who the true victor shall be, Yellow Ape! Hahahahaha!" Bellona charged at Sun, flailing her sword around randomly like a child.

Sun readied herself, knowing it was going to get a lot more complicated.

CHAPTER FIFTEEN: THE HERO CARETAKER

Dear god, my heart nearly burst from my chest after seeing Bellona use her fire breath. Don't know how I forgot that Sun is fireproof. This is the same girl that once sat on my stove top while it was on, and it was gas powered!

I do wish I could hear what they were talking about. Whatever Bellona said clearly got under Sun's skin. It looked like it didn't last long. Now Sun is more ready than ever to win.

Maybe I should take how Sun walked off such an attack as a sign. Perhaps I should stop panicking about that and focus more on Loki, who's dressed as a cheerleader and waving his pom-pom's around as he dances…

"Go Wukong! Go Bellona! Let's be fair, this cheer's not for ya! Gooooo Loki!" He leaps in the air and lands back down doing the splits.

"Wahoo! Take it off!" Susanoo cheers loudly.

"I would darling, but you may be driven insane by the sight! Ohohoh!"

In Norse mythology, Loki truly didn't have a sex. He impregnated women and he himself was impregnated. That was one of the odder stories of the Norse. I guess his body and voice makes sense for a being like him.

As Loki stands back up, he holds his pom-poms close to his chest as he faces me. He chuckles as he opens one of his eyes and sticks his tongue out at me in a flirtatious winking gesture.

Seeing that of his scarred eye and his gestures, I swear my bladder almost gave out.

It appears that when he was reborn, his eyes were still affected by the snake venom that dripped into them from his final punishment in his past life.

"H-how do you see?" I nervously wish to know. "Is it like how Joe works?"

"I can see fine! Though, I can see a lot better with my hands, darling," Loki answers as his pom-poms turn into giant, blinking eyeballs. "Would you like to see?" he asks provocatively, as he moves the eyes closer to me.

"Aah!" Momoko screams along with me.

Ever since Sun went into the Nostalgia Field, I have been trying to ignore Loki. Yet, he makes sure that is an impossible task for me. I hear Tricksters are as attention hungry as Love Gods. Don't know how Ell does it. Just being around him for a few minutes is stressful.

"Loki, what have I told you?" Ell asks in a calm, yet stern tone.

Loki slouches his shoulders in disappointment. "The Caretaker is yours to tease…" He responds, sounding upset. "B-but he is so feeble and slow, I can't help myself!" He begins to wave his arms around in a tantrum, making the eyes on his hand to pour tears out.

"Aah!" Momoko reacts at the crying, giant eyes. I swear, Loki is going to make this poor girl faint.

"Ooohh!" I hear the audience groan outside. I quickly turn my gaze back out at the field.

I see that the crowd was groaning as Sun kicks Bellona in the face, knocking off her helmet. Well, that's a relief. Still, I'm not sure which is more stressful, Sun's fight or Loki.

I feel an arm laying across my shoulders. I look to the left side of me to see Ell. "Almost all gods enjoy fighting, my dear Broken Knight. You may be worried, but she is most likely having the time of her life," Ell reassures me.

A sigh of relief blows from my nostrils as the tension in my shoulders goes away. I think it's about time I listen to Ell and everyone else. Even in the worst case, Sun will end up fine.

"Are all children these days this nerve wracking?" I hear Leonardo speak. He didn't sound hostile, but his words did gain everyone's attention, including me. "Hmph, to fear for the wellbeing of your god. Never have I heard such a silly thing," he chuckles, not taking his eyes off the battle.

"I-is that wrong?" Momoko speaks up before I do.

"The need for a human to fear for their god is, for lack of a better word, a mockery. They've seen the creation of almost all forms of human civilization. In fact, some even helped build them. As a mythologist, I thought you would know this. They do not need your concern; they need offerings for what they've done for us… What they've done for me…"

I see him pull something from his chest pocket. It's some kind of small figurine.

"Forgive me for how this sounds, but that seems pretty old school. The Monarchs don't want humans worshiping gods like that," I speak up.

"They mainly wish not for radicalization in the name of the gods like in the days of old. I have not killed in years and when I did it was in the name of Lady Bellona."

"Ya actually killed for your goddess? Momo, why ain't you that cool?" Susanoo jokes.

"W-what are you asking?" the shrine priestess screams at her god.

A chuckle leaves the old man's mouth. "This was long before the gods' return. Back during a darker time." Leonardo looks at the figure in his hand. "The war was far from over. One of my allies was bleeding out and the other was a kid. He had no idea what he was doing."

"Vietnam…" I mutter, realizing what he's talking about.

"We were trapped in a run-down shack in the middle of nowhere. We could hear the Vietcong approaching us from all sides. We were running out of options. All we had were the landmines we were supposed to set up. That and this," He holds up the figure, showing to be a small statue of Bellona, at least how she was imagined back then, with a burnt mark over its eye. "My family claimed to have always been worshipers of Bellona, but that was simply attention-seeking. However, when you're in a war, you'll immediately want to pray to any god. In reality, you need to pray to the *right* god."

"So, you prayed to Bellona?"

"Unlike the Christian belief, you do not simply pray to Bellona. You offer her blood," he speaks in a serious tone. "I had the youngest soldier take the wounded and escape through the back while I distracted the enemy. I placed the landmine in the center of the shack while I poured gasoline that was stored there onto the floor. Through all this I kept repeating: *Their blood for my life, Bellona.* That was when they burst in. It was odd, they had guns and flamethrowers. Yet, instead of attacking from outside, they came in. That was the moment I wanted. Before they could do anything, I stomped as hard as I could onto the landmine."

I've heard this story before. Almost everyone has. I have always wanted to ask this vet one thing. "How bad did it hurt?"

A grin stretches across his face. "I don't know. I blacked out after my foot hit the bomb. I remember waking up in mud as rain fell from the sky. I felt fine, other than the fact I was now blind in one eye and could not feel my leg. It was more numbing then painful. Perhaps it was the adrenaline from the experience. It took them a day or so to find me. I was given a purple heart and sent home."

"My grandfather said that you were the only soldier back then to be given a hero's welcome."

"There were still those who spat at me, but I did have many cheering and thanking me upon my return. Months later this statue was returned to me. Now, I know Bellona did not actually protect me that day, but how this statue's burn mark resembles so much like hers and over the same eye, it reminds me of an old saying. Things happen for a reason."

My eyes widen. Seeing the smile on his face reminds me so much of my grandfather.

"Ugh… A happy ending…" Loki groans. "Talk more about the blown-up Asians! Those are the best war stories! Oohohoh!"

I pay no mind to him as I continue to interrogate him. "So, if you know it wasn't Bellona that protected you, why are you so loyal to her? I hear you even use your own money on her."

"Simple. It's a thank you," he says with a kind face. "Even if it wasn't her divine protection, my faith in her still got me through such horrible times and made me a hero. That alone is worth everything I have. Even if she doesn't care for any of it."

"Doesn't care?"

"Bellona is a War God. They ask for nothing more than victory. I may have won the battle, but that was America's only losing war. So, she isn't too proud of that. Frankly, she hates it."

He spends his own money and lives for a god that sees him as a failure, and he does it happily? He does this all because he feels his faith in her is why he's alive today. In a way, he does owe her everything.

"So, what are her chances on winning here?" Ell asks with a face that screams she's plotting something.

"Oh, she *will* win."

"What makes you think that?" I speak in curiosity.

"I have faith…"

"Faith, huh?"

"Oh my! Well if you have so much faith in your goddess, would you like to make a bet?" Ell interrupts me.

"D-don't do it…" Momoko nervously whispers.

I signal no to him. I don't want to know what Ell will do to this old man.

"Hmm… I've gambled with my own life. What do you offer?"

"Five-thousand sound fun to you?" Ell surprisingly gambles with money this time.

"That little? A bit of child's play, don't you think?"

"Yes, but it's all I have on me right now…"

I dislike how these two are acting like five thousand is nothing. And did Ell say she has that much in her pocket?

"I-I really want that money…" Momoko whispers. Sounding like she wants to join, but knows she'll regret it.

Leonardo scratches his chin. "Hmm… Why not… It will be fun. I'll take your challenge, young lady."

"Splendid! Five thousand for you if your insane little War Goddess wins, and five thousand for me if my Broken Knight's Helper Monkey wins!"

Leonardo nods in agreement as he looks back out at the fight. I lean in close to Ell's ear.

"What's the point of this bet?" I whisper.

"Well if I lose, then you owe me since it is *your* god who failed."

"H-how is that fair?" I fearfully ask.

"If this is the case, then your time as my maid increases and I'm changing your maid outfit to an apron… Only an apron…" Ell stares at me with the eyes of a beast.

I don't like where this is going. "A-and if Sun wins?"

"Then I will call us even and you won't need to play maid at all. I'll even have Loki make you a nice suit. You'll be heading to the Valhalla Royale after all!" Ell tugs on my shirt as she giggles. "How's that sound?"

Did I unknowingly agree to a deal with Ell?

"Tell me, Vergil Knight, do you have faith in your god?" Leonardo queries, as he focuses on the fight.

Maybe in this world of gods, I should show a little faith. At least to Sun.

I lay back into the couch and focus on the fight once again. "Guess I have to…"

CHAPTER SIXTEEN: GATES OF EDEN

The battle had been going for several minutes. The two combatants had been holding each other back with no serious damage to either of them, though the Monkey King had a bit more trouble dealing with the War Goddess.

Sun breathed heavily as her arms slouched, still gripping onto the Jingu Bang.

"Hahahaha!" Bellona leapt like a maddening child with glee while waving her flaming sword in the air. "Aren't you having fun, Yellow Ape?"

A tired smirk formed on Sun's face. "You're still this excited? No wonder you made it this far," she expressed as she pointed her staff at her enemy. "Don't think because I'm tired that I'm losing. I'm not out till I'm knocked-out or dead."

"Oh, I prefer dead!" the petite War Goddess shouted as she leapt toward Sun, swinging her flaming sword. With each swing, the Monkey King blocked the attack. Of all the strikes she had prevented, the flaming blade finally struck her in her left shoulder.

"Gaaaahhhh!!!!" Sun screamed.

She lost her grip on her staff. The Jingu Bang slammed onto the ground like ten brick houses as Sun held her shoulder and fell to her knees. Though the flames didn't harm her, the strike cut deeper into her veins as blood poured out.

"Hahahaha! I got you! Let's go again!"

Sun tried to keep her eyes on Bellona, only to be met with the sight of the burning shield of the Olympian. Sun quickly tried to stand back on her feet before the shield hit her face.

208

Trying to dodge, she was still struck by the round burning piece of metal…

With all of Bellona's might, her shield struck Sun Wukong's breasts. "Graaahhhh!" Sun screamed in pain once again.

Sun backs away, grinding her teeth, twitching her eye, and wrapping her arms around her chest. A small tear left one of her eyes.

Bellona stared at her in confusion. "What?"

"That freaking hurt!" Sun shouted through her teeth. She closed her eyes for a moment to process this new feeling.

For a moment, the cut on her shoulder wasn't as bad in comparison. She had been hurt like that before, but the pain in her chest is foreign. It was something she couldn't process. She had been hit in the chest in the past, but it never hurt like that.

"Human bodies are so weird!" she shouted through her teeth.

"Aaaahhh!!!!" Bellona screamed, taking Sun by surprise. The Demigod was met with Bellona as she attempted to thrust her blade into the Monkey King's torso.

With a boastful and cruel face, Bellona could feel her victory at hand with her next attack. When her blade pierced open the skin of the ape, she would be dead, and Bellona would stand over her body in victory, as she had done to many other gods before her. Despite the Monkey King's reputation, the outcome was inevitable to Bellona.

However, before the blade could touch her bare stomach, the red fur attached to Sun's top glowed. The light spread to the golden chain mail that made her top. The brightness began to increase the length of the armor, covering all of Sun's stomach.

Bellona's sword bounced off the divine metal. "What the hell?!" Bellona shouted as the victory she thought she had was thrown out the window.

With the chain mail reverting back to its original tank top appearance, and the pain in her chest fading, Sun grabbed Bellona's shoulders and leapt over her as if she were playing leapfrog. With all her might, she forced the War Goddess face-first into the ground.

Sun grabbed the Jingu Bang with her foot and tossed it into her hands as she landed back on the ground. She quickly turned as Bellona tried to lift herself back up. Sun swung her staff down on the roman's head, full force.

"Gah!" Bellona grunted as her head was shoved deeper into the soil.

With her face buried, Bellona dug her nails into the ground as her hands grip into a fist. She pushed herself back up as Sun kept the Jingu Bang on her skull.

"Grrraahhh!" Bellona growled. She slowly turned her head to gaze upon her enemy.

As Sun stared down her opponent, she noticed the muscles in the War Goddess's arms increasing slightly. Along with the growth in mass, Bellona's flames and strength intensified as well.

The rage building up in her body fed her Flames of War, increasing her abilities. With her surge of power, the War Goddess began to rise. Even with Wukong putting all her strength into holding down Bellona, it was nothing to the war-driven woman.

"Grah!" Bellona shouted as a burst of fire blew Sun away and left her tumbling on the floor. Bellona slouched over as her body's increased muscles and flames began to fade, reverting to its previous state. "Damn it... I used to be able to do that without getting so tired..." she complained as she tried to catch her breath.

Sun lifted herself back up. She noticed that she didn't have the Jingu Bang in her hands. Losing her grip during Bellona's attack, the magic staff must have flown from her hands.

"Oh crap!" Sun muttered loudly as she looked around for the staff.

Bellona turned around as she began to catch her second wind. She watched the Monkey King franticly searching for her weapon. Seeing this as the perfect chance, Bellona's callous smirk returned.

The War Goddess grips onto her sword and charged at the distracted enemy. She knew stabbing her in the chest wouldn't work, not as long as the Demigod wore her chainmail, but she knew she had other options.

Sun's quest for her staff was cut off by a burning, piercing sensation in her leg. The Monkey King stared down in horror at the sight of Bellona's flaming sword penetrating above her knee.

"Aaaahhhh!!!" Sun shouted in pain as the blade pierced her flesh, veins, and bone. Her resistance to flames failed her as the pain of the War Goddess's blade was more than enough to make up for that.

Sun scrunched her eyebrows in determination. Her left fist clenched as she prepared to strike down the War Goddess.

Moments before the knuckles collided with the sadistic Goddess's face, Bellona opened her mouth wide as a snake and bit down, gripping onto the fist with her teeth. With all the might in her jaw, Bellona bit down and tore off three the Monkey King's fingers.

"Graaahhh!" Sun screamed as she gripped onto her hand.

"Oh boy! Things are not looking well for our new fighter. Right folks?!" Ame shouted from outside the arena, as the audience watched and cheered loudly in response.

211

Spitting out the three fingers from her mouth, Bellona yanked her blade from Sun's leg, causing more pain to the already bloodied and wounded Demigod. Though the attack worked, Bellona despised such a tactic. It leaves the literal taste of failure and weakness in her mouth.

Bellona prepared to swing her blade at Sun's head as she suffered. Once the blade headed toward her, Sun caught sight of it at the last possible second. Trying her best to ignore the pain, she dodged.

Sun continued to bob and weave out of the sword's reach. Though she kept dodging the blade, Sun was struck by the flames, hitting the right eye of the Monkey King. Despite being fireproof, the heat brought back nothing but bad memories.

The Monkey King landed on her feet, facing Bellona. "Dang it! I don't need my eyes to go through that again!"

Bellona paused as she relished her opponent's pain. The blood of the Monkey King stained her jaw and dripped from her mad face.

Sun had a good look at Bellona's teeth with her left eye. Each one was perfectly sharpened and serrated like blades.

"Aaawww! Did it hurt?" Bellona asked as she let out a mad laugh.

"Heh… Nah, just bad memories… Though I could do without the leg stabbing and the biting off fingers part…" Sun weakly joked.

"What? But those were the best part! At least the pain was! Hahahahaha!"

Her maddening cackle became louder with each breath. Bellona stared into the skies as she laughed. "This fight is glorious! Despite all the pain I have caused, you are still smirking! You're more than I could ever want in a combatant! Hahahahaha!"

Seeing Bellona in her laughing fit as the perfect chance, Sun searched around for the Jingu Bang once again. In the corner of her one good eye, Sun saw the Jingu Bang wedged into a tree.

Sun placed the remaining thumb and index finger of her left hand in her mouth and loudly blew her whistle, summoning her cloud beneath her feet.

"Hahahahaha- What?" Bellona shouted.

Quickly, Sun flew toward the impaled tree and yanked the Jingu Bang out as she passed by it. With her staff in hand, Sun began to rise into the skies, above the trees.

"Running away? Are you quitting? I don't accept quitting, I only accept death!" Bellona shouted, nearly foaming from the mouth.

The angered War Goddess stomped her foot into the ground as hard as she could. A large blue fireball rose from where she stepped and quickly surrounded her. The sound of neighs could be heard from inside the flaming orb.

The fireball vanished, revealing Bellona's chariot and horses. The four horses began to act frantic in fury, whining loudly and snorting flames from their nostrils.

"Go!" Bellona shouted to them as she whipped the flaming rein. The horses charged.

Sun looked back down as she fled, watching Bellona make chase with her chariot. Sun smiled, thinking she was safe as long as she was in the air. Unfortunately, as soon as te thought went through the Monkey King's head, Bellona tugged at the rein upwards. Her horses' hooves lifted up off the ground.

The four flaming horses galloped into the sky, leaving a trail of fire in the air, removing the hopeful expression from Sun's face.

"Ah, come on!" Sun yelled.

"There is no fleeing from me! It is either victory or death! Those are the rules of war!" Bellona shouted at Sun.

"I get it! You're a War Goddess! Geeze…" Sun responded, annoyed at the constant reminder by Bellona. "Gah…" Sun grunted in pain at the injuries she had suffered so far. She had been stabbed, cut, and even bitten. If she were a human, she would be suffering far more pain, possibly even bleeding out. Fortunately for godly bodies, even those of reborn half-gods, can withstand such punishment from a fellow divine entity, at least for a while.

As one chases the other, both forces began to twist and turn in the air. Sun left a fluffy yellow stream from her cloud, as Bellona left a trail of fire behind her.

Sun swung her staff, forcing it to extend toward Bellona. Quickly, Bellona raised her shield in defense. The impact pushed Bellona and her chariot to the left, slightly.

In retaliation, Bellona tossed her flaming shield at Sun. Much like how the War Goddess avoided the Monkey King's strike, Sun leapt as the shield approached her. The burning piece of metal flew between her and her cloud.

As Sun landed back on her cloud, she extended her staff and swung it down at the passing shield. With all her might, she caused the shield to dent severely and fall to the garden below.

Bellona watched her shield until suddenly, the sound of something tearing through the air pulled her gaze back toward her enemy. That was when the War Goddess was met with the incoming Jingu Bang being thrust at her.

While she was distracted, Sun shortened her pole, only to elongate it once more. The heavy, pointed end of the staff struck Bellona in the face.

Proud of her attack, Sun reeled back in her weapon, only to find no blood on her staff. She looked back at her enemy still giving off that same cold-blooded look as she continued to charge at her.

"Well, I wasn't expecting it to pierce that War God hide of yours, but I was hoping it'd at least knock you over!" Sun shouted.

Sun continued to evade Bellona until she could conceive of a strategy that would defeat the Unbeatable Warrior. As she went through her dwindling options, something caught her eye. Something that had drawn her attention before… The large oak in the middle of the garden.

And like that, she began to recall the threat that was written on the tree and all that her caretaker had told her about the woman who bit one of the apples. This ended up damning both her and her lover as they were cast out of the garden. Not only were the apples important, but so was the tree itself. The tree the garden circled around.

"That tree and its fruit are important, aren't they?" Sun thought to herself as she began to form a possible plan.

Seeing this as the best time to fight dirty, she plucked two strands of hair from her head. She let loose her grip on the strands as the wind threw them towards Bellona.

"Huh?" Bellona noticed one of the odd strands. Suddenly, it disappeared in a puff of smoke, only for a copy of Sun to leap out at Bellona. "What the hell?" she shouted as the doppelgänger wrapped her arms and legs around the surprised War Goddess. Caught off guard, Bellona lost the grip on her chariot's reins. As she shook back and forth, trying to knock the copy off, the horses pulling her chariot began to go crazy.

Not having their master in control, they panicked. "G-Get the hell off me!"

A frustrated Bellona struggled more violently and the horses' agitation grew, leading the four war-driven beasts to head for a nosedive in confusion.

In her rage, Bellona's muscles began to increase in size, as her flames begin to glow brighter, preparing to let loose her explosive power once more.

Bellona let out a loud rage-filled scream as she spread her arms out of the copy's grasp. She lets loose another powerful eruption from her body. Due to her chariot and horses being a part of her, only the copy was destroyed, leaving a long thread of hair slowly disintegrating in the flames.

Her body reverted to its original mass once more and her flames temporarily turn into smoke. As the War Goddess tried to catch her breath, her attentionwais focused on the fact that her chariot was about to crash. In a panic, she yanked on the reins upward in a last-second attempt to steer the horses.

"Go up! Up! Up!" Bellona shouted as she tugged on the reins.

Though her mounts began to rise back up, she was too late. Her chariot crashed into the ground below.

Bellona leapt as her chariot was destroyed by the impact and her horses lay injured on the ground.

As Bellona rolled on the ground, she heard her chariot being shattered and her horses letting out pain-filled cries.

She raised her head to see both her injured horses and ruined chariot fade into flames. It didn't matter who she fought against, the fact that the Asian God wasn't dead yet irritated Bellona. The Armored Woman's blood boiled in rage. She ground her monstrous teeth together as if she were sharpening them.

She was the goddess of war and conquest! This battle was meant to be her victorious entry into the Valhalla Royale, her glorious reunion with her lover. It could not stand.

Her mind began to go blank as the rage began to take over the Olympian. She quickly rose to her feet. Flames exploded as she let out a hate-fueled roar. "Damn you! Damn you! Damn you! Damn you! Kill you! Kill you! Kill you! Kill yyyyooooouuuuu!" Bellona shouted incoherently at the top of her lungs. Flames flowed from her mouth and eyes as she continued to lose herself in a torrent of madness.

"Uh oh, folks! It seems like our little crowd favorite is losing it! Never have we seen her go this far! I guess our surprise fighter is really getting under her skin!" Ami's voice echoed from the inside of the dome.

"Shut uuuupppp!" Bellona shouted to the sky. "Where are you?! Where?! Where?! Wheerrrrreeee?" she yelled as she scanned her surroundings in the garden, as she hastily tried to locate her enemy. Her search came to an end when she was struck on the back of the head. "Gah!" she yelled out.

Bellona looked around to see where the attack came from. Behind her, she found Sun Wukong standing in front of the large oak in the garden.

"Heh!" Sun lightly chuckled as her staff reverted to its normal length from her sneak attack.

The impact was not a powerful blow as Bellona hardly even lost her balance. "H-heh, what was that? Getting tired?"

Sun didn't respond. She simply lowered the bottom of her eyelid as she stuck out her tongue out at her. "Nah!"

Even though she was weakened, she still didn't take Bellona seriously. A dangerous mistake to make toward the War Goddess. Bellona's good eye began to twitch as she growled deeply at her enemy. "Mongrel! You dare to act like this! Of all the gods of all the factions I faced, you are the most infuriating! You're the one I want to kill most of aaaaallllll!" Bellona shouted as she charged at Sun, her sword in the air.

As she charged at Sun, the Fighting Buddha stood her ground before the rage-filled goddess, holding out her staff at the oncoming berserker.

Bellona swung her blade rapidly, showing no signs of sanity in her movements. She laughed maniacally as she got closer to the battle-ready Sun Wukong.

Sun readied her staff as Bellona quickly approached. Sun swung the weapon at her, but her attack was stopped by Bellona's frantic swinging blade. The Jingu Bang was pushed back by the sword.

"I got yyyoooouuuuuu!" Bellona gleefully yells as she quickly swungs her flaming blade at Sun's head.

At that moment, Bellona could feel it. Her blade finally cutting through the flesh of her enemy. She could smell the burning flesh of her prey as the flame sword cut through the skin of Sun's neck, to the muscle, to the bone, and straight to the other side. Bellona had sliced the head off her enemy.

Those on the outside of the field watched on in shock. Though, no one is more shocked than Sun Wukong's Caretaker, who felt nothing but dread and regret for letting his god take part in the horror show.

However, Bellona's victory and the Caretaker's regret all instantly vanish as the decapitated head and body of the Monkey King burst into smoke. The audience watching gasped in surprise.

"Wwhhhaaaat?" Bellona shouted.

As the smoke began to fade, she saw something flowing before her. A long thread of red hair, cut in two, and slowly fading in flames.

That's when it hit Bellona. Sun plucked two pieces of hair from her head. One strand was where the first copy came from. The one she just 'killed' was the second one.

"W-what was the point of this-" Before Bellona could finish her question, a crackling sound could be heard. It sounded like burning wood.

Bellona stared at the oak that the double stood in front of, only to see a flaming cut from her sword carved into it.

Then, a loud bang came from the sky above. As thunder roared through the arena, the peaceful blue sky was covered by a blanket of black clouds. The only light from above came from lightning strikes. Roars and cries of the animals in the garden echoed throughout the field as a sign that their once-peaceful nature darkened just as the sky above.

"Uh-oh, folks! It seems like Bellona activated Eden's one and only obstacle!" Ame's shouting voice echoed through the garden.

"What?" Bellona shouted.

Bellona's flames quickly engulfed the blue oak. "What have you done!" a booming voice shouted from the tree. "I let you in here, and this is how you repay me!" A hand formed from the flames, pointing at Bellona. "You! It was you!" the voice shouted, sounding mightier and angrier as it went.

The Nostalgia Field didn't only recreate the domains of the gods, it also imitated the creatures who lived in them, the monsters that guarded them, and the traps that protected them. These were called Obstacles, and Eden only had one.

"Activate the Gates of Eden!" Ame shouted as the audience cheered once again.

The ground beneath Bellona began to shake. The Bloodthirsty Goddess could feel something rising behind her.

She turned around and saw the large, golden, angelic gates towering even the large oak behind her.

"One rule… That is all I ask of you to follow… now you shall be damned!" the voice shouted as the gate began to open.

As the gates unlocked, a powerful vacuum effect slowly sucked Bellona in.

"N-No!" Bellona quickly turned away from the gate, stomped her feet, and stuck her sword deep into the ground.

As the vacuum grew stronger, Bellona continued to plant her feet into the ground as she slowly moved away from the gate.

What sort of joke is this?! She was planning such a lowly trick against me!? This is not fighting dirty! This is cowardice! Bellona thought to herself.

"I will not lose to something this humiliating! I'd rather die in agony than lose in such a manner!" Bellona shouted as she tried to move away from the gate. "All of my victories have gotten me this far! In the name of my long-dead followers! In the name of my brother and lover! I will not-" Bellona halted her speech as she saw a figure falling from the sky and land next to the burning oak.

Sun walked past the burning tree, revealing herself to Bellona. Unlike Bellona, Sun was not being caught in the vacuum. Not even her hair or wardrobe billowed. The sight of her true enemy increased Bellona's rage. "By the River Styx, this better be the real you, Yellow Ape!" Bellona shouted.

"Yep!" Sun yelled as she rested her staff on her shoulder with her one good hand. "Don't need my doubles to win this now," gloated the Monkey King.

That annoying, overly confident attitude continued to enrage Bellona, increasing her flames once again. However, the flames that enveloped her body were getting sucked into the large gates behind her, yet she did not care. Her fury was focused on the enemy ahead. Nothing else mattered to her at that moment.

"K-kill you!" Bellona shouted as she struggled from the godly force.

With her struggling enemy nearing her, Sun launched herself at Bellona. With her uninjured hand, she griped her fingers into a fist and struck the War Goddess directly in the stomach.

"Gah!" Bellona shouted as she hunched over in pain. Spit fell from her mouth as she let out a pain-filled moan.

Even though her skin could hardly be pierced, the impact still hurt the goddess.

Quickly, Bellona straightened back up. "Graaahhh!" Bellona roared to the sky.

She tried to swing her sword downward at Sun, only to have the Monkey King easily dodge the attack thanks to her slowed movements due to the vacuum pulling on her . With her body bent over from the swing, Bellona glanced back up at Sun. Her sight was met with the image of the Monkey King's head heading right for her.

At that moment, the crown-bearing forehead of Sun Wukong collided with Bellona's unprotected head. The crescent moon on the crown dug into the skull of the war good.

"Gaaaahhh!" Bellona shouted, one hand gripping her head in pain, the other still on her sword, which was now dug into the ground again to keep her from being pulled into the gate.

She moved her hand away from her face to see her enemy once more, but something appeared to be wrong with her vision. She saw Sun Wukong, along with everything else, in red. That was when Bellona noticed some sort of stain on the tip of the moon on Sun's crown. She looked down at her hands. There she saw the cause of the aberration.

The crescent moon from her opponent's crown had broken through her nearly indestructible skin.

"H-how?" Bellona shouted at the sight of her own blood. "How did this happen?!" she screamed.

Of course, the Monkey King was also suffering from the attack. However, unlike Bellona, it was simply a massive headache.

Despite Sun's head throbbing, she ignored the pain and focused on the fight. She twirled her staff and swung it at Bellona. The Olympian placed her weapon-less arm in front of her. Flames quickly lit, reforming the damaged shield she lost, blocking the attack.

The force of the swing still pushed Bellona back slightly. Bellona moved her arm away from her head and swung her flaming sword at the Monkey King once again, only to have her attack blocked as well.

Bellona collected herself as she prepared to repeat her attack, but before she could do so, Sun swung the staff once more and knocked the sword out of the War Goddess's hand and away from the two combatants.

The blade fell, point first, into the ground, the vacuum tugging on it. The flames slowly faded as they were no longer in Bellona's grasp.

"Y-you Mongrel!" Bellona shouted at Sun, steadying herself against the vacuum pulling on her.

Bellona thrust her shield at her enemy. Sun saw the move coming and responded with another twirl of her own weapon, knocking the shield from its straps and away from Bellona.

Angered by the loss of her weapons, Bellona gripped her right hand into a fist and swung at Sun.

Sun dodged to the left, twirling her body as she avoided the assault. The moment her eyes made contact with Bellona, Sun held out the Jingu Bang and swung with every last bit of strength she had left. The retaliation, powered by the momentum of her spin, slammed against Bellona's stomach once more.

"Gah!" Bellona shouted as saliva spewed from her mouth. The force of Sun's attack launched her off the ground and toward the large heavenly gates behind her. Sun's attack was aided by the vacuum already pulling on Bellona. "Nnnooooooo!" Bellona shouted as she succumbed to the battlefield's only Obstacle.

As Bellona passed through the gate, the dark skies above disappeared, only to be replaced by a scorching sun amidst a blue sky. She rolled onto a dry dusty surface. As she came to a stop, she got up to scan her surroundings.

She saw a dry wasteland, full of nothing but death, the exact opposite of the garden she was in. She turned her head back to see the gate still open. Above the gate, the number five appeared in a glowing display.

"All right, folks! She only has to the count of five before the gates close, signaling a ring out! Will she make it? Count down with me!" Ame announced to the crowd outside.

Hearing that, Bellona got back on her feet and rushed toward the gate as fast as she could. As she ran, she heard the crowd counting down as the number above the gates changed.

"Five! … Four! … Three! …" Bellona came close to the gate, about to make it back inside before "two" could be said. Unfortunately, her chances of rejoining this fight were cut off by the Jingu Bang, extending toward Bellona once last time. The staff forcefully propeled her away from the entrance before quickly shrinking back inside the gate.

"No!" Bellona shouted.

"Two! … One!!!!" the crowd cheered.

"That's a Ring out!" Ame shouted in excitement.

"Nnnnoooooo!!!!" Bellona shouted as the dry wasteland around her began to fade in white light. "I-I… lost…" her words echoed in the light.

Inside the garden, Sun saw her surroundings also beginning to fade in the blinding light. Though her eyes were drawn to one thing. The once divine oak, burning in Bellona's flames, and the giant flaming hand extending out of it.

This site brought back those memories once again. A giant stone fist falling from the heavens from her past life. Her Caretaker, injuring himself to help her almost a year ago.

"Never again…" Sun muttered to herself as the white light took away the burning tree.

With all the garden completely faded into the white light, it too began to fade around Sun. The Nostalgia Field opened from above and revealed to Sun the cheering crowd outside the glowing dome.

"Wukong! Wukong! Wukong!" the crowd cheers for Sun.

"Folks, it seems like our surprise fighter was indeed full of surprises! She came into this fight out of nowhere and defeated the crowd favorite, Bellona! Folks, I give you our winner! The Victorious Fighting Buddha, Sun Wukong!" Ame yelled in favor of Sun.

Hearing all this praise for her brought joy to the Monkey King. She looked up to see her Caretaker, looking down at her with a smile. Sun could see it was not a look of pride for her victory. Rather, it was a sign of relief that she was all right.

She smiled back at him with joy. Joy at the fact that not only she won, but she was now one step closer to getting the one thing that will make sure she would never lose another beloved person in her life.

CHAPTER SEVENTEEN: SHOW OF FAITH

It feels as though over a thousand pounds have been lifted off my conscious at the sight of Sun's victory. I am more relieved that she is alive then I am happy to see her win. Still, I would be lying if I said those final moments of the battle didn't get me excited. It definitely allowed my inner passion for this tournament to break out. Hell, I was so into it that without even knowing it, I stood up and walked up to the window.

"S-she actually won!" Momoko shouts out in surprise.

"See! I told ya she -*hiccup*- would…" Susanoo tells her.

"How'd you know Sun would win?" I ask the drunken goddess.

"Cause I swore I'd do the winner and I'd rather fuck her then the half-sized Olympian… Though, I'd still have *her* fuck the shit out of me. Ha ha ha!" She lets out a loud hearty laugh.

Why did I even bother? I knew that would be her answer.

Ell crosses her arms in a huff. "This is a disappointment…"

"Why's that? You bet on Sun winning."

"Yes, but that means no naked apron on my dear Broken Knight," she whips away a fake tear.

"Really, Ell?" I hate it when I can't tell if she's serious or not.

Loki leaps next to her with a box of tissues. "Do not cry, my dear Mistress. We shall get him as your maid next time. Then you can play that game humans love so much nowadays. I believe it's called *Casting Couch*. Ohohoho!"

"Oh my, that does sound fun. I guess I'll take the money for now. Right, Mr. War Hero?" Ell smirks at Leonardo.

The old man continues to stare out to the field. He doesn't seem as shocked as I'd imagined. His eyes are wide open, to the point where I think his glass eye is about to roll out. He seems more surprised than disappointed.

"Hmmm… It seems as though you had more faith in your god then I did, young Mythologist," his widen eyes shut in a relaxed state. "Perhaps I jinxed myself making that bet. Faith and gambling do not go together. Or at least, that is what lady Bellona will shout at me. Or perhaps she'll claim my failure is contagious."

I look on at the veteran as he explains his toxic relationship. Even with this sort of abuse, he will always put his faith in Bellona. I'm honestly not sure how to feel about that.

Before I can say anything, the sound of Susanoo loudly chugging her drink keeps me distracted.

She lets out a loud sigh after finishing. "So ya let her talk crap about ya, even after all the shit ya do for her and how much faith ya give her? Pretty shitty god if ya ask me…"

"S-Susanoo! Don't say such rude things!"

The elderly war vet stands from his seat. He begins to take steps. At first, I thought he was going to tell off Susanoo or something, but he simply straightens his coat and turns to face the chair he sat on.

"Perhaps your goddess is right, young lady," Leonardo admits as he continues to eye the chair. "But I swore loyalty in return for my safety on that day many years ago. I will keep to my word…" A quick flash of light suddenly appears on the chair. From the light, she sits there. Bellona. "No matter what."

228

Her body is hunched over as she lays there in Leonardo's seat. It's as if she's unconscious. That's not what concerns me. It's the smell. Her odor is oddly sweet.

She's soaked in some glowing substance. That aura and this sweet smell, I've experienced it before… It's Life Cider.

"Oh my, she must be really unhappy if she's in that state," Ell giggles behind her hand.

"What do you mean?" I respond.

"Think of this as a safety feature, darling!" Loki yells. "Often gods do not enjoy the idea of losing. Because of this, if a god decides to act like a little hellion outside of the field, then they are put in this tranquil state. At least, until the target of their rage has left."

"Yep, all the goddesses I went up against ended up like this… don't know why…" Susanoo thinks loudly.

"Y-you know why, Susanoo…"

Bellona is that angry, to the point where she must be sedated? Here I was letting my guard down. At least she's not much of a threat right now.

Her caretaker lets out a loud, seemingly disappointed sigh. I'm not sure if it's due to Bellona's failure, or himself.

I stand up from the couch with my cane planted on the floor. "It was an honor to have you as our first opponent…" I feel that's all I can say at the moment. I'm not sad about what happened to Bellona, but I do sympathize with him.

"If you truly are going forward with this tournament, keep the faith you had during this fight. It's all you, as a caretaker, have," the veteran advises while keeping his sight on Bellona.

Hearing his words, I look back out to Sun, still basking in the praise of her victory.

Leonardo, Ell, and Susanoo all basically told me the same thing. Maybe faith is something I should put more of in Sun. It's certainly more helpful than me constantly panicking over her.

She'll fight the battles; I'll throw some faith her way. Who knows, this might make us an unstoppable team. Or I'm just saying this to make myself seem like I'm useful to her through all this.

INTERLUDE: ENFORCERS

The words of the Monarchs are divine law. Divine laws are strict, as are their Enforcers.

Many are loyal guardians, comrades, and even weapons to the Monarchs. Others simply deal out punishment and preserve the natural order around the world.

Innocent blood spilled for selfish reasons and going against the words of the Monarchs, both acts are punishable in the Enforcers' eyes.

The Enforcers range from various Godhoods, but four in particular are the most common.

JUSTICE: A type of god born to be an Enforcer. The most well-known of these Gods are the Olympians Nemesis and the Furies. Though they have caused confusion as to what Justice truly means, as they often mistake it for simple vengeance.

WAR: As previously discussed.

AVATAR: The former vessels of Monarchs, turned guardians.

ANIMAL: Gods with bestial powers and abilities.

They specifically deal with threats toward the new world order of the gods. Such menaces include escaped Unfollowed and reckless gods that display their dangerous abilities in public. Granted, this is simply a theory, but there have been rumors that the Enforcers do not solely go after other gods.

Whether or not this is true does not truly matter. The fact that this rumor continues to spread is enough reason to keep order. Order that stops human wars and crimes. Order through fear.

"…"

"The match is over…"

"But what happens- *cough, cough*- next?"

"Grrrhhh… Death…"

CHAPTER EIGHTEEN: FAILURE?

Ell decided to go out ahead to pull the car around for us while I went to pick up Sun. After suffering all those injuries, the showrunners ended up pouring some of the Life Cider on her as well. Cuts, burns, and even her missing fingers are all healed up. Other than being a bit dirty, it's as if she hadn't suffered anything at all.

She loudly sniffs her hand as we leave the stadium.

"Sun, stop that!"

"But my hand smells like that fruit from the garden!" she tells me. Sun shoves her hand in my face. "Smell it!"

"Bah! Stop that!" I yell as I swat her hand away. She is right, though. It does smell odd. Like I smelled after Loki poured it on me, and Bellona after she reappeared in the lounge.

Sun laughs at my frustration. "I do feel great after having that Life Cider poured on me! I feel so clean and healthy!" she loudly says in enthusiasm.

"You're doing a lot better than I did when it was poured on me." I wonder if it's because she is a god or if it is because she didn't die. She doesn't seem sore at all.

After thinking it, Sun begins to rub her head. "My head still hurts from that head butt, though…" she complains.

"Better off than your doppelganger," I joke. Though, I am amazed by that crown of Sun's. Not only did it break through Bellona's tough skin, but it also managed not to shatter or sustain any damage. I know the crown is made to be attached to Sun, but still.

233

Sun laughs at my remark. "Oh, that wouldn't be the first time I lost my head!"

"What was that?"

She continues to talk, ignoring my response. "But I got to say, Mr. Knight, those Olympians are a tough bunch. I wonder if all foreign gods are that strong?"she wonders. "Actually, those stories of Eden you told me about really helped me out! I probably couldn't have won without them!"

"Really?" I respond in surprise.

Sun liked to hear stories when she was younger. Most stories I knew were of different gods and religions, so I told her some of those. I didn't think she paid attention to most of them, but I can't believe she used what little info I gave her to win. My knowledge can't even help *me* when I'm betting on a match.

Was this because of my faith, or was it simply dumb luck that she ended up in an area she heard about from one of my stories?

"Oh!" Sun shouts as she leaps in front of me. "You didn't tell me what you thought of the fight!" she looks at me with enthusiasm on her face.

I truly don't know how to answer that. I mean, it was brutal but exciting at the same time. Maybe I only had that excitement because I knew if something happened, they would heal Sun.

Luckily before I can answer, something outside draws our attention over to the door.

"Sun Wu-kong! Sun Wu-kong!" people chant.

Before leaving, Ame-no-Uzume asked if we would go out through the front so the fans can take pictures. Of course, I protested, but Sun happily agreed. I guess the word of a god meant more than mine

We walk outside to see the protesters from before now gone and replaced by Sun's newly found fans taking up both the left and right sides of the exit, cheering her name after her victory over Bellona. They cheer even louder once they see her in person.

They most likely chased the protesters away. It happens a lot at the end of a Gods' Wrath match. The fans can get a little rough when it comes to this.

I can't help but enjoy the delight on her face at all the people taking pictures with their phones. Noticing this, Sun wraps her arm around my shoulders and pulls me close to get these pictures together.

I let out a nervous chuckle. Never was much a fan of big crowds, let alone the focus of one. While I do want people to think highly of me, what I don't want is fame. Especially this kind!

I know a lot of these people have cameras. I can hear them snapping their photos now. What if they put it online and Kat sees it? God, I'll never hear the end of it!

I don't have enough time to worry about that, though. Not with the sound of glass shattering above us, cracking louder than the camera snaps. The crowd quiets down as me and Sun look up above us. From one of the windows of the stadium, a fireball flies out. I can see Sun turning hostile as she grips onto me tighter.

The fireball lands in front of us and between the two crowds. The crowd screams, but quickly go silent once the flames disperse, revealing a filthy Bellona.

Loki said she was supposed to be knocked out until we had left the building. Did he mean that literally?!

She is completely consumed by the same fury she had during her fight as she grinds her jaws at the sight of Sun.

"You dare try to leave me after such a humiliating defeat?!" Bellona shouts. "Instead of giving me a warrior's death you simply knocked me out of the ring?!" she yells. "Treating me like a failure?"

Sun lets go of my shoulder and steps in front of me in defense. She bares her teeth at Bellona.

"I don't care if you were humiliated, and I *really* don't care if you think I treated you like a failure. All I wanted to do was win, and I did! Fair and square," Sun sternly retorts.

The crowd around us mutter to one another. Their conversations vary from excitement to panic.

"I'm the Goddess of War, Blood, and Conquest! You made me a failure!" Bellona shouts as spit flies from her mouth. "How can I face that failure of a Caretaker when I'm also a failure? How can I ever reunite with Ares now?"

This isn't good. Gods are forbidden to fight outside of the Nostalgia Field. After seeing these two fights, I can't even imagine what'll happen to me and everyone else. I already got caught up in one battle between gods, definitely not something I want to repeat.

"S-Sun, let's just walk away-"

"Stay out of this, you frail mongrel!" Bellona barks as she points her blade at me. Her eyes and sword are covered in her blue war flames once again.

With a quick twirl of the growing Jingu Bang, Sun aims her staff at Bellona. "Don't talk to Mr. Knight like that!" she growls at the War Goddess.

"Sun, please don't!" I plead, fearing what may happen if they fight here.

With her feet moving on the carpeted ground to the entrance, Bellona charges at her enemy. Sun follows her lead. I try to stop her, but she's already out of my reach.

The two let out their battle cries as they rush into another brawl. The crowd gasps in shock and excitement as the two gods' weapons are about to clash.

"Sun, stop!" I shout.

CHAPTER NINETEEN: THE FOUR HORSEMEN RIDE

As the weapons of the two gods collided, something happened around them. All color faded from the world. All movement halted in place.

That caused the two to stop their battle. The goddesses looked around to find that all the humans crowding the sides of the entrance were frozen. Even the birds in the sky stayed in a perfect unmoving state.

"W-what is going on?" Bellona shouted in confusion.

Unlike Bellona, Sun wasn't confused at all. No, she was more curious if anything, because she had already experienced this phenomenon.

"I-I think I've been here before…" Sun examined her surroundings.

"So, is this some sort of insulting trickery of yours, Yellow Ape?"

Before she could answer, Sun noticed her Caretaker, suspended like everything else. Like that, the memories of this place filled her with dread.

"Mr. Knight!" Sun shouted as she ran to him. She stood before her unmoving Caretaker in a fret. "M-Mr. Knight?" she said as she reached out to him.

Just as her hand was about to make contact, she phased through him. The Monkey King was shocked as she moved her hand inside her companion. Her heart sank as she was unable to touch him.

Bellona began to get annoyed as Sun's attention drove further away from her. "Don't ignore me, Yellow Ape! What is going on?"

Her enraged voice echoed through the soundless, colorless world around them. As her booming echo faded into the skies, something roared through the monochrome field. A sound too familiar to Bellona and something Sun had grown to hate for many reasons. It was the roar of four charging horses.

The galloping of the four beasts' hooves shook the desaturated earth horribly. Sun and Bellona struggled to even stand in the wake of the tremors.

Sun, fearing for her caretaker, tried to grab him before he could fall, but like before, she passed right through him. As she checked back on her companion, she saw that not only was he not affected by the earthquakes, but neither were any of the people in the crowd. Only Bellona and her suffered from the violent shaking. Suddenly, in an instant, the vibrations stopped.

The two goddesses investigated as the ground ceased to quake beneath them. All appeared to remain the same, unmoving and lacking color.

Loud and hot snorts were heard from horses' nostrils. The sound drew the eyes of the two confused goddesses to four armored figures standing above the crowd on the right.

Unlike the rest of the scenery, the four had color to both their armor and the horses they were mounted on. White, red, black, and green. They also showed signs of movement as the four beasts they rode bobbed their heads slightly.

Sun moved away from her petrified Caretaker to stand next to Bellona and confront the four armored men.

"I really hate horses…" Sun muttered as she eyed the beasts.

The horseman in white began to slowly lift his arms. As he did so, the crowd before the four began to split apart. The people remained still, only forced to slide to the opposite sides of the quartet.

The horses moved closer to the two goddesses, giving them a better view of their strange riders. The one in white held a golden bow and wore a halo above its head as he rode a beautiful white horse with a green mane. As it walked, newly formed plant life grew under its hooves. From grass to newly blooming flowers, they all sprang forth beneath the mighty steed's hooves.

The one next to the white horsemen was a heavily armored stranger, one with a flaming sword. Beneath him, he rode a muscle-bound and heavily armored horse with a flaming mane and burning hooves. The flames from its feet left a trail of fire behind it.

The next to the red horsemen was a sickly man in black, moldy, and mushroom-covered armor. Insects crawled all over his body. In his hand, he held the chains and bowls of scales. *Cough, cough*, the sickly man let out. He rode a thin, sickly horse with large, yellow bug-like eyes. Beneath its hooves, a trail of mold formed on the ground.

The final horseman was a dark green armored skeleton with half its face exposed beneath its helmet. In its hand, a large scythe. His mount was a completely skeletal creature such as him. Under its hooves, the hard ground began to blacken and crackle away. A trail of broken and decrepit road followed its path.

The horseman in red pointed to the white horseman. "He is the voice of our Father! He is the Christ Child! He is also the white Horseman of Righteousness, the Metatron!" the red horsemen shouted. He points to himself. "I am the archangel! The closest to my father's throne! I am also the Red Horseman of War, Michael!" He moved his hand to the horseman in black. "He is the Demon of The Pit! The Bringer of Pestilence and Sickness! He is the Black Horseman of Famine, Abaddon!" Finally, he moved his hand towards the final horseman. "He is the Reaper of Souls! The Angel of Your Last Minutes! He is the Horseman of Death, Azrael!" he shouted.

Wings sprouted from the back of each of the four knights, spreading out widely to intimidate their targets. Each set varied from each horsemen.

The wings on the white horseman were a sparkling, heavenly white. The red horseman's were a flaming gold set of wings. The black horseman's appeared almost like black-feathered moth wings. The final horseman's wings appeared as dead as him, black decaying feathers falling to the ground.

"We are the riders of the end! We are the Enforcers of the New Pantheon! We are the Four Horsemen of our Father!" the Red Horseman shouted as the four horses rose, each waving their two front hooves threateningly.

"Enforcers?" Sun muttered as she was reminded of the Greek goddess she met after facing the Nuckelavee. She said she was an Enforcer as well.

"Are you the ones who did this? What is going on?!" Bellona shouted at the Horsemen.

"The humans call this place Purgatory. A world between earth and the domains of the Monarchs. A place in-between time. Here, we are out of sight of the humans around us. We use it when there are too many of them around. Once we leave this world, everything will go back to the way it was before entering," Michael explained.

"Then why are we here?" Sun demanded.

"You broke a major rule of the Monarchs! You were about to fight against each other with your divine powers, outside of the Nostalgia Field! Are you aware of the devastation you could have inflicted upon these humans?"

"But she humiliated me! I demand a rematch!" Bellona shouted to them.

"She started it! I just wanted to keep Mr. Knigh- my caretaker safe!" Sun shouted as she pointed to the frozen man.

The four turned their heads to the still human.

"So, this is your caretaker? Vergil Knight... The messenger of Olympus said he had lost his God Slayer to the Nuckelavee. That is good, though. If he had it, he would have been brought here with us. You need some form of divinity with you to be brought to Purgatory. It would be best not to have any humans here. Where is yours, Olympian?" Michael questioned Bellona.

"I don't know. Probably still inside the building. Why should I care?" Bellona shouted.

"You should care because your caretaker is probably confused and frightened by what is happening around him right now. If he has his God Slayer with him, he is most likely brought here as well-" Michael halted as he saw Azrael fly off his horse.

The angelic skeleton landed near Sun's Caretaker and sniffed the immobile man.

"Rah!" Azrael screamed at him.

Sun feared for what the armored skeleton was doing. "Leave him alone!" Sun swung her staff, extending it toward Azrael.

"Rah!" Azrael shouted as he leapt back, away from the Monkey King.

Michael pointed his flaming sword at Sun. "Do not worsen this for yourself! Know your place, Buddhist!" he yelled in a threatening tone. He turned his head over to his fellow horseman. "Azrael, stop!"

Azrael investigated the face of the motionless caretaker. "Death..." the angel muttered.

Sun's eye widened upon hearing the angel.

"Yesss... We were told *Cough, cough* the Buddhist'sssss Caretaker was killed by the Unfollowed... But brought back by the Life Ccccciderrrrr..."

244

"So that is him?" Michael asked. "What's the human saying? *Two birds with one stone*?"

Sun bared her teeth as she listened to the red angel.

"Did someone say bird?" a voice shouted from above.

"Rrraaaahh-Huh?" Azrael turned in the direction of the voice. Out of nowhere, the Death Angel was struck in the face, interrupting his prowl.

All divine eyes were on the object that struck Azrael in the head. A wounded black raven, laying on the ground, twitching after being tossed at the horseman.

"It would have been better if I had both of his birds," a voice quiped. All of them peered up to find Loki standing perfectly on the tip of a pole looking down at them with a chipper demeanor. His long-sleeved hands waved gleefully at them. "You know, just to really play with the *two birds* thing! Ohohohohoh!"

"The Asgardian Trickster?" Bellona remarked.

"In one of my many fleshes, darling!" the Trickster bowed in a theatrical fashion.

"Why is he here?" Sun growled softly at Loki.

"Tell Odin to stop trying to ruin my punchlines with his damnable cawing tattletales. He was always impatient like that. Hehehe" Loki snickered.

"You are the one who used the Life Cider on this human, correct?" Michael interrogated.

"I knew it would ruffle that one-eyed old fuck's feathers," Loki pointed over to the twitching raven. "As you can tell, I meant that literally! Ohohoh! But it was a good choice on my part. Had I known he was my Mistress's favorite toy; I would have put a tiny amount of effort into keeping the poor boy out… I mean, a *very* small amount," he said as he held up his sleeved thumb and index finger close to each other.

"You should have let the human die, Trickster!" Michael yelled up to him. Such words displeased Sun greatly.

"What?" Sun growled at him.

"Be as angry at me all you wish Great Sage, but it would have been better had he died," Michael defended himself.

"What do you mean by that?" Sun yelled.

"Modern humans can't handle divine powers like they used to! Why do you think humanity still suffers from blights such as terminal illnesses and mutilations when beings like the Monarchs are able to bring the dead back to life? It is because the last hundred generations of humans are unable to physically handle divinity in their blood!"

The revelation filled Sun with distress. "W-what?"

"During the time of gods, when humanity had magical abilities, their bodies were able to harness divinity. Even then, there was no guarantee. Divinity to humans is like a drug. They will consume more and more until it destroys their bodies," Michael explained. "The virgins who give birth to the reborn gods are an exception to this rule due to their unborn children being half-human," Michael told her.

"B-but Thoth said they'd only act loopy if exposed to divinity…"

"Only when the divine power is airborne. However, inside their bodies, it is uncertain what could happen to them!" Michael shouted. "Your caretaker could end up as many of the humans my father aged backward."

"I-I don't understand?" Sun spoke in concern.

"Of course, you don't. Allow me to explain." Michael growled in a stern voice. "The elderly humans my father aged back all those years ago, not all of them lived happily in their regained youth. Many had dormant illnesses awaken and mutate in their bodies. Of course, that was the most minor issue. The real problems arose when many began to harm those around them. All of them lost all sympathy towards others. They hardly reacted to any horrid thing that they saw happen to other humans, or what they themselves had caused..."

Hearing this sent shivers through Sun's entire body. She remembered how her caretaker was not affected at all by the bloodshed he witnessed firsthand by the Nuckelavee. Any normal human would be mentally scarred by such trauma. Plus, he had the cider poured on him. This realization caused Sun's heart to sink.

The reason she entered this tournament was so she could gain the Life Cider to protect the one person she cared for. Unfortunately, from what Michael was saying, it is more dangerous to expose him to the substance than to keep it away. He can be brought back and healed easily, but he may end up becoming someone entirely unrecognizable.

"Oh, calm down, you holier-than-thou buzzkills!" Loki retorted. Everyone's attention focused back on him once again. "Blah blah blah- divine cancers- blah blah blah -people going crazy- blah blah- killing one another- blah blah! Seriously, even if your masters are half-glass-empty people, does that mean you must be as well? After all, he only had a little taste! Plus, he was dead! He can't possibly gain any addiction to it. His body couldn't even experience it fully!" Loki then pointed at the human. "See, he's not even moving! Clearly, the divinity that brought him back has long since left his body. He is simply a normal human."

Michael, Abaddon, and Azrael looked over to Metatron. After a moment of contemplating, the mute angel nodded very softly.

"Very well then… We will let this transgression slide… For now," Michael warned the two deities.

"Graah!" Azrael shouted in a tantrum.

"I said we will let it slide, Azrael!"

"Grrrr…" Azrael growled as he walked away from the colorless Caretaker, and flew back onto his horse.

Sun let out a sigh of relief and glanced up to the Trickster with conflicted eyes, unsure if she should let go of her grudge with the Liesmith for what he just did.

"You better not thank me, darling. Like I said, if you thank me, then that means I didn't do anything fun! Plus, if I did not do it, my Mistress would be quite angry, and I don't want *that* now do I?" Loki waved his covered hands.

The Mischief Maker exploded in a ball of confetti. As the colorful paper rained down, the Four Horsemen stared down at the two goddesses.

"Now that one issue has been dealt with, we shall move onto the task at hand," Michael announced. Michael, Abaddon, and Azrael pointed their weapons at the two. "You two broke the one rule of being a fighter in the tournaments! Had we not been here, these humans could have gotten harmed!" Michael shouted.

"Been here?" Bellona muttered to herself.

Sun wore a quizzical expression on her face at what the angel spoke.

"Are you saying you've been around this whole time?" Sun questioned them in a rage.

"If it was not our fight, then what reason do you have to be here?" Bellona asked.

"That is of no concern to either of you! All you need to know is that you shall be judged here and now!" Michael shouted at them as the other two horsemen looked over to Metatron.

The hooded angel in white slowly raised his hand. His palm faces upwards, as his fingers pointed directly toward Sun.

Sun stared at the horseman, unsure what he was about to do. Although, the question was soon answered as something began to grow in the angel's palm. A bright pink rose bloomed in his hand. From the thorns on the stem, more began to bloom.

The other three horsemen let out light gasps at what the white horseman had done.

"Really?" Michael whispered to Metatron.

The hooded angel nodded.

"Are you ssssure?" inquired Abaddon.

The hooded angel nodded once more.

"Hmmm…" Azrael lowered his head as he let out an annoyed growl.

Sun looked back and forth at the four of them in confusion as to what was going on. "Uh… What is happening?" Sun asked awkwardly.

"It seems not only your caretaker, but so are you as you only wanted to defend your human. Wanting to protect him from the two of you… However, you had no concern for the other humans. Still, no malicious intentions. You are free to go…" Michael proclaimed, sounding as though he was defeated. He faced Bellona. "But as for you, War Goddess…" He turned to Metatron once again.

The angel moved his hand toward Bellona. She reacted nervously to the angel's means of interrogation. The rose that bloomed for Sun began to slowly die in the angel's palm as it faced the War Goddess.

"Ha ha ha!" Azrael laughed hysterically.

"Heh heh *Cough, cough*…" Abaddon weakly chuckled.

Seeing that the blooming rose was a sign of innocence for Sun, Bellona realized that the rose dying could only mean the opposite.

"And like that, Olympian. You are found guilty!" Michael shouted.

"W-What?!" Bellona shouted. "Y-you can't be serious! The only reason I started this fight was due to the humiliating way this ape defeated me! *That* should be reason enough for her punishment!" she shouted to the four.

"Please, Olympian… You may appear to be a child, but you do not need to act as such…" Michael told her in a disappointed tone.

"Aren't Olympians and children the *cough, cough* same thing? Heh, heh…"

Hearing them talk down to her like disappointed parents, Bellona began to sink into her rage once more. Her eyes burst into flames.

"You dare talk down to me, Christians!" Bellona shouted. She raised her flaming sword and swung it at Michael. "Huh?" she uttered as her attack was stopped by Michael's own flaming blade.

Bellona tried to push forward toward the angel of war. She gripped onto her blade with both hands, and even then, she struggled. As for Michael, he held his blade with one hand with seemingly no effort. His war flames burned bright red, surpassing Bellona's blue blaze.

"Unlike you, Olympian, we were some of the first reborn through human virgins when the Monarchs returned. We have been here since the beginning of the New Pantheon. I had faced many of those who dared to go against our Father and the other Monarchs. In the state you are in, you cannot hope to defeat me," Michael told her as he continued to hold her blade back with ease.

"Damn you-" Bellona went quiet for a moment. "Gah!" blood spewed from her mouth. "W-what the hell? …" she uttered as she felt intense pain in her stomach.

"Ha ha ha!" Azrael laughed behind her.

She looks down at her abdomen, only to see the scythe of Azrael impaled into her. She dropped her sword as her arms fell to the side. Her one good eye began to lose all color as her head lowered. Her heart stopped. The scythe of the Death God had done its job yet again. It had taken another life.

Azrael lifted the body of the War Goddess with his scythe. He tossed her to the side, back to where she stood before the fight.

Sun watched in horror. Even though Bellona was about to fight her and possibly get her caretaker involved, Sun still pitied the War Goddess.

Looking over to the War Goddess's body, Metatron lifted his hand once more, pointing to the goddess.

"…Live…" a word finally escaped from the Avatar's mouth, echoing in the air.

Bellona loudly gasped for air as she lifted her head. Sun leapt back in surprise at the newly revived goddess. Bellona began to inspect her body, not finding any sign of damage caused by Azrael.

"Our Father and the other Monarchs wish to be seen as generous gods in the eyes of both you and the humans. So, let

251

us consider this, as the humans put it, a slap on the wrist. A mere warning. Keep that in mind if you, either of you, try anything like this again!" Michael warned them.

The four horses rose on their hind legs, flaring their front hooves as they let out loud powerful neighs. "You have been judged by the Enforcers of the Monarchs!" Michael shouted as the horses quickly stomped back onto the ground.

The four instantly vanished as color returned and the sound of glass shattering was heard around the two. People began screaming as shards of the stadium's windows rained down on them. Sun and Bellona looked around to see that not only has the sound returned, but the color and movement as well. They realized they were no longer in Purgatory.

The crowd that filled both sides of the entrance to the stadium began to run and shield their heads from the glass shards.

Sun saw her Caretaker trying to cover himself from the raining glass. The Monkey King instantly leapt to his aid. She rolled her body over his, blocking the shards. The shards simply bounced off her divine body. She didn't even flinch as the glass hit her.

As the debris began to stop, the confused man spoke up to his goddess. "Sun, did you two do that?" he asked about the falling shards.

"I-it's alright, Mr. Knight… You're safe, that's all that matters…" Sun reassured him, unwilling to tell him what had happened.

"Lady Bellona!" the Caretaker of Bellona, Leonardo, shouted as he ran out of the arena and toward his goddess. "What happened? Everything-"

"Shut up!" Bellona shouted to him. Though she was angry, the sound of defeat echoed in her voice. "Let's just leave…

I've already suffered enough." She turned and walked away from her enemy and her own human.

"Very well…" Leonardo agreed and followed her.

Sun gripped tighter as she held her Caretaker. "S-Sun, what's wrong?" He tried to hide the pain he felt in her grip.

However, she didn't respond, for she was lost in her thoughts, remembering what Michael had told her. The whole reason she joined this tournament was to gain the Life Cider for him, so he would never have to fear being injured ever again.

So she would never lose another one so close to her… but now she knew… The cider could cause more harm than good.

As she held onto him tightly, she was left to wonder one thing. "What should I do?"

CHAPTER TWENTY: A JOURNEY OF OUR OWN

So not only did she beat Bellona as a last-minute entry, she ended up becoming an instant fan favorite herself. You'd think Sun would be jumping around in excitement, swinging me back and forth like a ragdoll as she prances around, but ever since we left the arena, Sun has been quiet. That's not normal for her.

Since we got home, she has been sitting down on the couch, staring at the ground. It's as if she's deep in her thoughts.

She didn't even make a sound when Ell hugged me before she left. Sun's really out of it.

I finally decide to sit down next to her. "So, oh Great Sage Equal to Heaven, my Victorious Fighting Buddha! Want to tell me what's wrong?" I joke.

She glances over at me for about a moment then dots away, like a child who's in trouble, or simply someone who doesn't know how to express what's on their mind.

Is she worried about what my thoughts were during the fight? She did ask that, and I didn't give her an answer. Maybe she thinks I'm mad at her.

"You know, I was completely worried during your fight with Bellona. Her sword piercing through your skin, how she bit your fingers off. Then there was when she decapitated your copy. I nearly threw up and fainted! Even though I knew you would return, I still panicked over potentially losing you out there. At the same time, you looked like you belonged out there. Despite the injuries you suffered, you kept fighting with confidence. You're a god who fought her whole life and loved combat. No matter how I feel, I don't think I should pull you away from that… So, if it's my blessing you want, you got it…" I say with a smile on my face.

She stares up at me, still in her melancholic mood. She lowers her head back down as she begins to speak. "I did mean what I told you, Mr. Knight. I wanted to be in this tournament to get you the Life Cider. –"

"Look, Sun, that is sweet of you, but I don't want it," I tell her as she raises her head back up at me in stunned silence. "I didn't like how that stuff made me feel. I felt numb and sore at the same time…" I sigh. "I may be more likely to bleed out from a paper cut, but as long as I seal it, I'll be fine. As for something like the Nuckelavee, for as long as the gods have been here that was the only time I was attacked by an Unfollowed. I doubt I'll have to deal with that stuff daily. At least, I hope not," I reassure her, rubbing her head. Her tail slightly wags as I do so, like a dog being petted.

Sun gives me a slight smirk as her cheeks turn red. "I-I guess you're right, but I worry, Mr. Knight."

"And I worried about you. But I had faith in you… Maybe the faith between us can keep us safe, and heck, even victorious. Or maybe it can at least calm our nerves, hehe…"

Sun watches me with admiration. She quickly stands up, beaming with hope. "Such words of wisdom and motivation! You truly do remind me so much of Tang! Maybe the tournaments can be our own journey!" she announces excitedly.

I really can't take credit for the whole faith thing. That's all Leonardo. I chuckle at her remark. She sounds like a child wanting to go on an adventure. She is right, though. If I am going to be part of this alongside her, I guess it *is* our journey.

"All right then! Let this be the beginning of our own journey!" I jest in a powerful narrative voice.

Sun leaps up with her fist in the air. "Yes! This is so exciting, Mr. Knight! With my power and your wisdom together, we will make names for ourselves in the Gods' Wrath tournament!" she shouts as she tightly wraps her arms around me.

"GAH!" I grunt as she squeezes.

Even though it hurts like hell, it seems like I managed to fix her. Now she's acting how I expected her to. Although, she has me a bit concerned again. Mainly because if we do make names for ourselves, Kat might find out... Not excited for that. I do like the idea of my knowledge of the gods being useful for once though!

A knock on the door loudly rings through the mobile home.

Sun and I watch the entrance in confusion. It's ten at night. Who would be here this late? Maybe Ell? Wouldn't be the first time she visited this late. Though I hope she's not planning any sort of "special" visit like in the past, especially with Sun here. Though, I think that would only encourage Ell.

Besides, she said she had to go check on Ares and pick up a few things. However, she did tell me she'll still be in the area, so it might be her. Well, there goes Sun's happy and upbeat attitude.

I try to limp over to the door, but Sun stops me. The loud sounds of her nostrils sniffing the air can easily be heard. "Don't let them in..." she speaks in annoyance.

"Hey! Ya two home?" I hear a familiar voice shout. "Wukong, baby! I'm ready to spread my legs and embrace your love!"

Yeah, it's who I think it is. I can see why Sun doesn't want me to open that door.

"S-Susanoo! T-that's not something you shout when visiting so late at night!" Momoko shouts.

256

I glance back at Sun with a raised eyebrow. She knows what I am wondering, and she quickly nods no in response to my unasked question.

"They'll eventually open the door! Either that or we stay here until they do!" Susanoo shouts to Momoko.

"W-what?! B-but I don't want to be out in the open in the middle of the night!" Momoko shouts back in a panic.

"Guess my yellin' ain't puttin' ya at ease either, huh? Hahaha!"

"I-is he attracted to loud sounds?"

As the two continue to bicker, I turn back to Sun. We both eye at each other in annoyance as the two argue outside. I let out a sigh of defeat and limp over to the door. Sun follows with her arms crossed in anger.

I open the door to see Susanoo and Momoko, now back in their *normal* attire, facing each other in their banter. They stop their fighting as they see us at the open door.

"Hey! Cripple and my future love master, or occasional fuck buddy!" Susanoo greets us in her own weird way as she holds her hand above her forehead as if she's saluting us.

Her body is still wobbly, but from the sound of her voice, she isn't as intoxicated as before. Well, gods' immune systems burn through food and drinks faster than a human's. Just like how Sun can eat so much and not get a stomachache. I guess it also works with alcohol. Though, I can still smell the stuff on her.

"So, I see your out of Ell's outfits…" I point out.

"Yeah, well, we were told we could take 'em off when the sun set. Personally, I wanted to keep mine on, but Momo started complainin'," Susanoo says. "Please stop humiliatin' our shrine, blah blah…" she mimics Momoko.

"W-well, you *were*!" Momoko cries.

"What do you want?" Sun angerly speaks as she hides behind me.

"Oh nothin'! Just wanted to come and congratulate ya two on winnin' against the Olympian!" Susanoo bats her hand at us.

"W-will you please ask?"

"Sssshhhh!" Susanoo loudly shushes into Momoko's face as she places a finger over her lips.

"Ask what?" I jump in.

Susanoo glances over at me as she still faces Momoko in the hushing gesture. She quickly faces us.

"Well, we thought we'd come by and see what ya plan is for ya partners in the Royale?" she questions us, sounding as though she has something up her sleeve.

I completely forgot about Sun needing a partner for the Valhalla Royale. She has to pick a fighter that has already lost in the Tryouts. Since we were sort of thrown in very late, Sun and I haven't made any real connections with any other gods. I can't just pick a random god for her to team up with. From what I recall, there were no Taoist or Buddhist gods in this year's Tryouts, and the only god she had contact with is Bellona, and I doubt *she* would want to team up with Sun.

"Uh, we haven't thought of that yet…"

"I don't need help! I can win this myself!" Sun claims with pride.

"That's not how it works, Sun…"

"Well! Your search is over!" Susanoo shouts at us. She pulls Momoko close to her and looks at us as if she has great news. "We'll be your partners!"

"Huh?" both me and Sun utter simultaneously.

"B-but you dropped out and gave your spot to Sun."

"The rules say your partner had to have lost in the Tryouts! Quittin' is a form of losin'! So, playin' by the rules, I can be your partner!" Susanoo points out with victory in her scratchy voice.

Hearing this, something dawns on me. The end of Sun and Susanoo's fight, how she broke the one rule of the fight and used her divine powers.

"You let Sun win, didn't you?" I mention in a surprised manner.

Hearing this, Sun drops her jaw and stares at Susanoo in shock, having made the same realization. "Y-you planned this!?!" Sun shouts at her. Susanoo rubs the back of her head and chuckles.

"Wait, if that's true, then why risk the chance of Sun losing? And why did you even drop out in the first place?"

"B-because Susanoo won't pick a partner…" Momoko sadly responds.

Susanoo pulls out her pipe from her gi and places it in her mouth. A small spark forms from it and smokes. "Well, I didn't want to team up with any of the guys. Most of 'em were more monster than man and none of the ladies wanted to talk to me. If I'm gonna team up with someone, I'd rather it be someone I'd like to at least fantasize about," Susanoo holds the pipe in her mouth.

Me and Sun gawk at her, flabbergasted by her ridiculous scheme. I turn my attention to Momoko. "And you went along with this because …?" I await her answer.

"It was either this or Susanoo wouldn't fight at her fullest… I-I didn't want to take the chance of her losing…" Momoko nearly tears up.

I feel so bad for this girl. It's amazing how much she deals with being Susanoo's caretaker. Then again, she is a shrine priestess to the Shinto gods, so of course she would be this dedicated to her god.

"No! No! No! I refuse to team up with you!" Sun points to Susanoo as she continues to hide behind me. She looks over to me in a fluster. "T-Tell her Mr. Knight!" she shouts in my ear.

I don't know what to say. We were caught up in the master plan of a god we thought was just a drunk, perverted joke. Yet, here we are. She pulled off this entire stunt, all so she could have a pretty partner. The idea that we became part of it is sheer lunacy. So much so that I begin to laugh.

"There really is more to you than this drunk lesbian schtick, isn't there?!" I ask as I laugh. I begin to calm down. "A-alright… You got yourself a deal!" I tell her as I catch my breath.

"W-what?!" the stupefied Monkey King shouts.

"See! I told ya it would work, Momo!" Susanoo gloats with pride.

"Oh, th-thank goodness..." Momoko expresses with a sigh of relief.

Sun grabs me by the shoulders and flips me around, locking eyes with me in exasperation.

"I don't want her to be my partner!" Sun angrily whispers to me.

"She's not exactly my first choice either, Sun, but you have to admit she is a skilled fighter. She almost beat you without using her divine powers, and you said she scared the

Nuckelavee after showing off a fraction of her power. Plus, she can put one hell of a plan together. A plan, might I remind you, she thought up for something so simple and pointless. Just imagine the sort of strategies she could make on the field!"

"B-but what if she tries something with me?" Sun pouts in distress.

"I guess yell at her… maybe hit her… that's what Momoko seems to do…" I joke. "Besides, you need a partner, and she is a child of a Monarch. I can't think of any better god to be your partner."

Sun lowers her head as she gives up. She raises it as she inhales, then loudly exhales through her nose. She walks around me and puts on an unmistakably fake smile to Susanoo and Momoko. "It is an honor to be your partner…" Sun struggles to tell the duo.

"Th-thank you! Y-your such blessed people!" Momoko bows her head. I swear I hear a bit of joy in that frightened little voice of hers.

Susanoo pulls out her pipe and grins. "Alright! The Summer Storm and the Victorious Fighting Buddha! Like my late-night fantasies!" she shrieks in glee. She quickly wraps her arms around Sun, holding her close to the point her and Sun's cheeks rub against each other. "Let's seal this deal with a kiss and a bit of dry humpin'!" Susanoo puckers her lips, trying to kiss Sun. I can see the Storm Goddess slowly gyrating her hips against Sun.

My jaw drops, not because I am finding this attractive or anything. It's just so awkward to see such an act in person. I'm not even sure what to do to split this up.

"S-Susanoo, no! Th-they said yes! Don't ruin this!" Momoko pleads to her goddess, clearly not stopping Susanoo's attempt at *love*.

261

Sun's false smile is cleaned off her face as she bares her teeth at the perverted Storm Goddess. "Get off me!" Sun shouts as she tosses Susanoo off her. Throwing her back out the door. Sun wraps her arms around herself as she hides behind me again.

Even though Susanoo makes for a good partner for the Valhalla Royale, I'm not sure if it's okay to have her around Sun for such a long time. I'm worried, like with Ell, Sun might actually kill her. It seems like Sun might have bad luck when it comes to making friends with other women.

"Well, all the awkwardness aside, we'll see you later to talk more about the Royale, but right now, it's late. Let's talk-" As I try to get them to leave, Susanoo interrupts me.

"Yyyyyeeeaaaahhhhh… About that… We got somethin' else to ask ya…" Susanoo places her pipe back in her mouth. Sun and I look at her in concern. "Well, ya see… When I dropped out of the tournament, we only had a few days to stay at the hotel… Today was the last day and we don't got any place to go…"

Upon hearing this, I begin to investigate the two. Right next to their feet are four briefcases. Seeing those next to them, I already know what they want.

"No!"

"Aw come on, Cripple!" Susanoo whines.

"P-please! We have nowhere else to go!" Momoko cries with her hands together in a begging stance.

"You are not staying here! There is not enough room for four people!"

"I'll make it worth ya while!" A cheeky smile pops on Susanoo's face.

262

Hearing this, Sun pokes her head over my shoulder and stares down Susanoo.

"Alright, how?" I give in with morbid curiosity.

"You, me, and your Bouncy Monkey. All night, every night!" Susanoo gives us a thumb up. We all, including Momoko, are completely aghast.

"Huh?" I dare question the Summer Storm.

"Oh! We can even throw in that rich gal with the nice ass too!" Susanoo offers with glee.

Sun becomes even more enraged at Susanoo, probably because she just asked for a four-way involving her and Ell. She grips my shoulders as she pokes her head out further. "Nice try! Mr. Knight wouldn't agree to something so vulgar! He's a wise, classy guy!" she defends me as she nuzzles my cheek.

"Ssssuuurrreeee he is… Cause classy guys stare like he did when we wore those gym uniforms…" Susanoo eyes me, evidently not believing Sun.

Sun is right, though. I wasn't going to agree to the deal, but I'd be lying if I said I wasn't interested.

I feel my baggy shirt being tugged on. I look to see Momoko with her head lowered before she addresses me with terrified eyes.

"P-please, can we sleep here for at least the night… I don't want to be out in the dark… O-Orochi might come…" Momoko looks to be in near tears.

That's right, Susanoo said Momoko is super paranoid about Orochi returning. Well, I can't blame her for that. Not when we live in this new time of the gods.

In legend, Orochi did attack mainly at night, so I guess that's why she seems a little more timid than usual.

I feel bad for the poor, frightened girl. She sort of reminds me of Kat when she was younger. She was a bit of a nervous wreck, too, especially when it came to the dark. Seeing her like this, I can't say no to her. I probably can to Susanoo, but I think they are a package deal.

"Fine… you can stay with us until the Valhalla Royale…" I lower my head, beaten by a guilty conscience.

"Thank you! Thank you! Thank you!" Momoko shouts rapidly as she runs inside the R.V., nearly pushing me and Sun out of the way.

"Hey!" Sun shouts to the panicky shrine priestess. Gripping onto me so I don't fall.

"You're a pretty cool cripple! Tell me when you're interested in that four-way. Hopefully it will be in the next minute… Got a little too excited talkin' about it…" Susanoo lightly chuckles as she walks past us.

"Mr. Knight…" Sun lets out a quiet whine.

"I know Sun, but it's only until the Royale…" I reassure her.

"All right! So, I guess I'll be bunking with the monkey!" Susanoo shouts as she looks around the R.V.

"We don't have bunk beds…" Sun tells her.

"Did I say somethin' about bunk beds? Ha ha ha!" Susanoo laughs.

Sun stares at me in annoyance for what had taken place. I give her a nervous thumbs up in return, basically telling her I'm already having second thoughts on this.

"Uh, question, Susanoo! You do understand the concept of modesty, right?" I ask the Storm Goddess.

"The fuck's that?" Susanoo sounds as though she's joking.

I let out a light chuckle to her remark, but that chuckle begins to fade as I face Momoko as she nods her head no rapidly.

Great… This is going to be harder on us than I thought. Sun's most likely going to kill Susanoo if, or rather *when* in this case, she tries anything funny. I, on the other hand, am not sure if I'll be able to handle living under the same roof as both Sun and Susanoo…

Still, this little group of ours is sort of like the team Sun traveled with, Susanoo being the perverted pig in this case. I guess that means Momoko is Sandy by default. All we need is a dragon disguised as a horse and we got ourselves a remake of Sun's old friends.

I pat Sun's hand as it still grips my shoulder. I give her a hopeful smile, and after a moment of pouting, she returns it with her own.

So, I guess this is the beginning of our own journey then. In all my life, I never thought I would be part of something -I can't believe I am saying this- biblical! Looking at the face Sun is giving me, I can tell she is excited to be part of this new journey, a new story in her incredible life

CHAPTER TWENTY-ONE: THE TWO FAILURES

The large home of Leonardo Russo laid empty under the moonlit sky. Despite its size, no sound echoed through the halls at that moment. No cracks, drips, or creaks.

In an instant, that all changed as the booming sound of the large doors to the front of the house swung open. A loud crash echoed through the home.

"Damn it!" Bellona shouted as she stomped angrily into the house. "Damn it! Damn it! Damn it!" she screamed to the empty house. Her angry wails traveled far within her abode. As the reverbs halted, the petite War Goddess fell to her knees, staring straight into the reflective, clean floor. "I-I lost…"

"Yes," the kind voice of her Caretaker spoke. Bellona turned back in rage to see Leonardo standing at the opening doorway, watching her with a warm expression on his bearded face. "I guess you did."

Bellona faced back down to the floor. "Does this make you happy, Failure?"

"I am more smiling at how odd of a day I had," Leonardo chuckled. "First, I see my goddess lose in quite an intense fight. Then to top it off, time stopped! I was wandering around, trying to understand what was happening, until everything started moving again. Scared some poor children. I guess it seemed like I suddenly appeared in front of-"

"Is this a joke to you?" Bellona shouted. "I lost… Twice…"

In just one day, the goddess of conquest had been bested on two separate occasions. Once by the Buddhist Ape, and again by the

266

Christian Enforcers who talked down, not only to her, but towards her faction, like all other gods do.

Her goals of regaining her former strength and reuniting with her lover had ended in her first defeat. Now, she was left with the humiliation of failure by heathen gods.

"I bet you're loving this!" Bellona growled. "Having me, the one who has been scolding you since the day we met, as... one of you..." her voice nearly cracks, as if she were going to cry.

"You mean a failure, I'm assuming?"

"I'm a War God! I only have two things that matter in life! Victory and... him..." Bellona spoke. Leonardo saaw liquid dripping on the floor from where she laid. "I'm the goddess of conquest... Not the goddess of failure..."

The elderly caretaker sighed at the sad state he saw his young goddess in. "You act as though you have lost everything, Lady Bellona," he stroked his beard as he spoke. "I was part of a losing war, lost body parts, and was booed by many of those I fought for. Now I'm successful and help other former soldiers," Bellona looked up to him. Tears could be seen on her face. Even her scarred eye. "And to top it off, I live with and care for the goddess that helped me gain all of this," he said with a gentle expression.

Bellona wiped her face. "How many times do I need to tell you, I wasn't alive to do any of that."

Loud sniffing could be heard as she spoke to him.

"No, but my faith in you was. Even now, it still lives." For the first time since Leonardo had lived with her, Bellona stared at him through eyes of innocence. "You act as though you won't be able to join the Royale to reunite with Ares and face the Monkey King once again. I guess you forgot the rules of the event."

A surprised gasp left Bellona's lips. "They will need a partner who had lost in the Tryouts..."

"And you made it into the finals by flawlessly defeating all those who you faced up until that point. Who would not wish to have you join them?"

Bellona stood up, reverting back to her aggressive composure. "Why are you continuing to console me? If I were you, I would be reveling in my defeat."

The old man chuckled. "Seems a little hypocritical, doesn't it? After all, I'm a failure as well..."

She stared at him, surprised by his remark. Eventually, a wide smile formed on her face and a hearty laugh left her mouth. Leonardo joined in with a quieter chuckle.

"Alright! I will get into the Royale and not only see my beloved, but get payback against that Yellow Ape first!" Bellona proclaimed with pride and confidence in her voice once more.

"Heh, now you're acting like said ape."

"Want me to kill you?" she yelled.

"That's more like you..."

"Huh." Bellona stopped for a moment and crossed her arms. "So, who do you think would team up with me?"

"Actually, I found out an old friend of mine is a caretaker and he and his god are also in the finals right now," Leonardo explained. "So, we agreed that if one happens to lose, we'd have the other as our Royale partner."

"Are you saying you thought there was a chance I'd lose?" Bellona shouted in resentment.

"You did..."

For a moment, the scarred face of the War Goddess turned red. "W-whatever! How do you know if they will win their fight?"

As soon as she asked that, a ding was heard from the pocket of the old man. He pulled out his phone. Inspecting it, he smiled once more as he showed the message on the phone to his goddess with only the words '*We are in*'.

"I had faith," Leonardo chuckled.

Bellona relished this news. "Perfect! I'll get to fight that ape again!" her expression changed as a new thought went through her mind. "Wait, who am I partnering with? And who is your friend?"

"Oh, right. He's a friend I made in my youth during Vietnam. Well, it turned out he became a Catholic priest right after the war ended."

"Catholic? Then, I'm partnering with a Christian being. But the only one that made it to the Finals is…" Bellona paused as her signature grin formed once more. Her eye ignited with excitement. "Perfect! Hahahahahah!"

CHAPTER TWENTY-TWO: BLESS YOU...

Within the coast of Calibur city, on the outskirts of Paradise Grove, a warehouse stood. It was covered in holes, rubble, and police tape.

It was the warehouse that was attacked by an Unfollowed Celtic beast. The area still smelled of death and blood. However, what laid inside the building didn't mind the scent. In fact, it loved it.

The moonlight shined into the windows of the warehouse, illuminating a single figure resting in the middle of the building. He was a thin man in Spartan armor, held down by chains and a large rock on his back. The large Spartan armor and helmet nearly fell off the slender body of the man.

The large boulder that weighed him down carried talismans of different religions and in multiple languages, with one written in Chinese over the his face. Underneath his immobile body laid a glowing circle written in ancient text.

In front of the trapped man, two large swords were impaled into the ground before him. One, a golden blade that had seen many battles. The other, an oddity of a blade as the hilt was comprised of bones. Both weapons, such as his armor, were undeniably too large for the shriveled man.

Around the figure, rotting fleshless corpses laid. Time had claimed the bodies as maggots consumed their bare nerves. Their lips and eyes were completely devoured by the insects. Even still, their fear of the monster that claimed their lives still rested on their petrified skulls.

"Huh…" the man growled quietly.

The door on the side of the warehouse flung open. From the outside, Loki ran in, dressed in a pink dress with a poodle on it. His arms were covered by long silk gloves as he held a brown bag of groceries in his hands.

"Darling, I'm home!" Loki shouted happily, trying to sound as though he were a housewife from an old televised sitcom as he skipped over to the man.

"Huh…" the figure grumbled, this time in a more annoyed fashion.

"I know I've been super busy on you, but when you see the meal I have prepared for you, you'll forget all about your troubles!" Loki explained, keeping up with his domestic act.

"Huh…" the man began to shake.

"What is that dear?" Loki interrogated, leaning in closer with his hand next to his ear.

"Grah…" the Spartan grunted as he struggled to make eye contact with Loki.

The Trickster saw the talisman on his face. "Oh! That's right!" Loki snapped his fingers, leading his cloths to explode into confetti, reverting his clothes back to his normal long-sleeved robes. "Let's just get this off you…"

The Trickster yanked the mystic paper from the figures head. With the charm removed from his face, small flames ignited in both his eyes and mouth.

"Why are you here? …" the Spartan inquired in his weakened state.

"Well, our beloved Caretaker felt tired, so I told her I would come and check on you!" Loki answered happily.

"She lets the one being I hate more than her come check on me?" he groaned in disgust.

271

Loki crossed his arms as he formed a pouting expression. "That's simply cold of you, darling! After all that I have done for you! I am the one who brought the Nuckelavee here, and I am the one who let those people die in your name!" the Trickster said. "I even hid away the corpses of the last victims, so you could have someone to talk to while we were away!" Loki pouted.

"What is the point of all this bloodshed… What purpose does it serve if *I* am not the one causing it?" The flames on the man burned brighter as he shouted. "This new world… Hardly any chaos… No rape, no murder, no war… This is not a world for me to call the new Sparta… The only satisfaction I have is this damnable tournament. But to kill an enemy, only for them to return… I have truly grown tired of this whole farce…" The disheveled man sighed as he talked. "You and that wretched woman keep me trapped here like a disobedient mongrel, keeping me from reigniting the beauty in this world!" he shouted as he tried to break free from his prison

Loki crouched down to the man's level. "Aw! Boo-hoo! I'm a deity of an obsolete godhood! I must be locked away because I can't behave on my own! My dad turned into a swan and raining piss to fuck women! Wah! Wah!" Loki repeatedly mocks the frail man. "Hmmm, then again, maybe *I* should not be the one to judge that last bit, now should I?" he thought aloud. "But, if you could be more trusting, then you wouldn't have to be locked away! Should I remind you of the whole incident involving Fort Knox? Humans are not always going to believe several gas tanks went off from the inside… Well, they might if it appears like that again…" Loki chuckled to himself.

"I heard humans say it was one of the most heavily guarded places on this planet… Maybe for them, at least. I carved through those soldiers and their machines like the trash they were… Now leave me alone… I can't stand that laugh of yours…" the flaming figure muttered.

"How rude! Here I was, going to give you the greatest meal you have had in such a long time!"

"What sort of food would make me feel like that?"

"First things first!" Loki happily replied. "Do you not want to hear who won the finals?" he talked as he nearly pressed his face to the Spartan's helmet.

"I told you… I've grown bored with these bastardized death battles..." the blazing man sighed. "Let me guess… My little consort…" he whispered, sounding unsurprised.

"Nope!" Loki shouted happily, leading the Flaming Spartan to look up in surprise. "Your sister-wife lost in the finals! In fact, she lost by a ring out!" He began to laugh.

"That pathetic woman… Losing in such an idiotic manner... And to that Shinto whore no less…" the man sighed in annoyance.

"Oh yes! She did not take her loss well at all! She actually drew the attention of the Big Four! Of course, they were there for other reasons… Oh! That reminds me! She did not lose to the Shinto drunk…" Loki told him in an unruffled fashion.

"What …?" He stared at the Liesmith, lost for words.

"Weeeelllll, you see, the Monarchs owed the Demigod who defeated the Nuckelavee a favor, and the Shinto god had been smitten by the lovely curves of this scrappy little god. So, said Dmigod asked the Monarchs to be in the tournament, and the Storm Goddess dropped out so she could enter in her place!"

"A Demigod who was owed a favor by the Monarchs has now entered the Valhalla Royale, after defeating my consort? Who is this being?" The Spartan was curious.

Loki leaned over to the ear of the man. "Sun Wukong…" Loki happily whispered.

"Sun Wukong? … I've heard that name before…Sun… Wukong … Sun Wukoooonnnngggg! Ha ha ha ha ha ha ha!!!!!" The man began to laugh maniacally.

Excitement filled the trapped Spartan's body as he laughed. His thin muscles begin to increase in mass, shattering the chains that wrap around his body. The flames on his face and helmet began to ignite in a more powerful inferno. The stone on his back started to crack as the talismans burned away from the overwhelming power. He slowly stood to his feet as the stone crumbled on his back. He stomped on the magic seal on the ground beneath him, shattering it.

A cape of flames burned on the Spartan's back as his body grew into his armor. Freeing himself from his prison, his power reverted to its normal state, as did his body. His true stature was tall and muscular. His head was completely engulfed in flames. The only sign of a face was the fire that burned through his eyes and mouth.

"I have heard many tales of the Great Sage! I am truly grateful for this! Thank you, Shapeless Smile!" he shouted as he pulled his swords from the ground.

"Like I told you darling, I had a meal for you that you will love! I hope you enjoy it, Ares." Loki clapped his hands in mischievous joy.

NAMES: ARES, MARS. FACTION: OLYMPUS.

GODHOOD: WAR. HUMAN NATIONALITY: GREEK.

Ares began to walk toward one of the rotting bodies. The ground beneath him melted and boiled with each step he took, leaving a burning and bubbling footprint behind him. He stared down at the bodies below.

"Of all factions, the names of five beings strike fear in the hearts of the Monarchs. The Eater, The Father, The Star, and that damned Light! Then there is the Great Sage, who nearly killed a Monarch simply by opening its eyes!" Ares stated as he stared at the corpses. "If I can defeat her… I can defeat any Apex! Including that blasted Light! Ha ha ha ha ha ha ha!!!!!!" He laughed as he burst flames from his mouth and onto the rotten corpse on the ground.

The smell of the burning rotten flesh filled the air in the warehouse as the flames spread around the building.

"Oh dear, the Mistress is not going to be happy when she sees what you have done to this shithole…" Loki disappointedly spouted.

"When I meet the ape on the battlefield, I will tell her something I always wanted to say when I first heard of her tale … Only two words… Bless you…"

EPILOGUE ONE: TRUST AND THEORIES.

On many occasions, the Domain of the Librarians was quiet for Thoth, perfect for reading and writing at his desk in the middle of the large library. Unfortunately for him, the Knowledge God had very loud guests just as often.

Hermes placed a card on the floor. "And I win again." The name '*Ishtar*' was written at top of the card, with a depiction of a warrior woman with wings and dressed in ancient garb.

"What?!" Ratatoskr whined. "H-how could I lose this time? I had finally summoned the mighty Odinson, Thor! How could he lose to a Babylonian?"

"You know, Ishtar is both a War and Love goddess. So, she has an advantage against gods who favor women. You should have gone with Loki. He's immune to Love Gods' charms," Hermes explained.

Every so often, the two messengers came by the Librarians' estate to play a card game based on the Gods' Wrath tournaments, with each game going to Hermes.

"B-but Thor is more battle-driven than sex-driven!"

"True, but the field is the Tower of Babylon, which gives her a boost in power," Hermes explained as he began to clean his cards from the table. "Maybe you should add other factions to your deck. You're pretty limited with only Asgardians."

"How dare you?" Ratatoskr shouted in an offended tone. "The Asgardian faction has the most powerful and popular fighters of all time! Why would I sully my deck by adding other, less cool, factions?"

"Because you lost nine times in a row, and that's only today," Hermes chuckled.

"Gah! I hate you!" Ratatoskr shrieked. "Hey, bird brain! You think this is bull, right?"

"I, Thoth, the god of Knowledge, continue to look down into my book, escribing pen to paper, all in the hope that Ratatoskr sees I am busy and leaves me out of this…"

"You said all of that out loud!"

"It is at this moment I fear my plan may have failed…"

Next to the three, a large magic circle shined brightly, alerting the trio.

From the light, Joe, Odin, and Vishnu appeared, accompanied by the four horsemen.

Metatron had his hands together as a warm glow illuminated from them. As it faded, the avatar releseed the injured raven from before. It flew from his palms and back onto the shoulder of the All Father.

"Great All Father!" Ratatoskr gleefully ran toward her Monarch, wagging her fluffy tail. "It is an honor for you to grace us with your presence!"

"Apologies, Ratatoskr… This is not a visit of grace…"

Hearing the serious tone of the Asgardian Monarch, Thoth continued to sit in his chair, only confronting them with his gaze from behind his mask.

"Names: Thoth, God of Writing and Mysticism, The Self-"

"Must you do this every time we meet?" Joe questioned.

"It's a habit, *I respond nonchalantly.* Have you lost weight? *I ask the Christian Monarch, noticing the lack of body fat."*

Odin crosseed his arms intimidatingly. "Care to explain why you did not bring what you had learned from Sun Wukong and her Caretaker after your meeting?"

"That is not my job, *I explain to the confused All-Father.*"

"Hey! You can't-!" Ratatoskr's mouth was immediately hushed by Hermes, who gave her a gesture to be silent.

"What you learned about the Caretaker was more than enough reason to inform us," Vishnu spoke.

"Since we are asking questions, may I query how you know so much of our meeting? Perhaps, it was because of that raven I noticed flying through my Library? *I interrogate the Monarchs, despite obviously knowing the answer.*"

"We were watching the Monkey King, not you." Joe clarified.

"I know, *I confirm, tilting my head to them.*"

"You know the trouble she caused…" warned Vishnu.

"But the Buddhist Monarch allows her to continue existing. Both back then and in the modern-day. From what I see, even the Christian Avatar has decided she is no threat, *I remind the God Kings, putting my pen back in its rest.*"

The Metatron raises his palm as the same beautiful flower from before returns.

The Christian god places his hands in his pockets. "We could have saved a lot of time if you had simply told us whether or not she was a threat."

"If she was truly a threat, I would have dealt with her. It is my duty to always side with order and against chaos, *I clarify*."

Odin stroked his beard to the words of Thoth. "Hmm, tell us, which do you think we are?" Hearing the bearded god ask such a thing, the Horsemen began to feel uneasy. "I feel there is another reason you did not tell us…"

"I do not serve you, Asgardian. I serve none of you, not even my own faction's Monarch. I was not created by a Monarch, I created myself with the purpose of making sure that good always wins. That is why I remade myself centuries ago, to continue this…"

"You may not serve us, but are you on our side?" Vishnu interrupted.

"Perhaps, if you're willing to make a trade, *I set my plan in motion*."

The hooded Monarch stepped forward, pulling his hands from his pocket. "Perhaps we can make a trade," he agreed as many silver coins fall from Joe's hands. Each coin carries the symbols of Christianity, Asgard, and Hinduism on one side, while   random names lay on the other, the names of humans.

"I care not for your profits. Though, I do see more from the All Father and the Trimurti then from you, *I point out the Christian Monarch's lack of coins from the pile*. What I want in return is what I have always wanted…"

"You will not get the books!" Odin shouted.

"I can rebuild my body as many times as it takes, but I need my books to rebuild my memories. I need those last two books… Then I'll decide who's side you are on… *I speak threateningly*."

"It is best you do not read from those books. You do not need to be reminded of the Day nor do you need the information from the other book," Vishnu replied.

281

"Secrets and a lack of trust are truly not good signs. *I speak truths to the quiet god-kings as they continue to pester me.*"

Odin stomped his powerful foot on the ground. "Ha! You're one to talk. Did you forget I use to be a Knowledge God too? You may hide it better, but I can see you have your own secrets."

Thoth turned away from the Monarchs momentarily before facing them again. "It is about that human of Sun Wukong's, Vergil knight."

"The one resurrected? We've proven he is of no harm," Vishnu batted his hand at the subject.

The coins floated back into the hand of the Christian God. "In fact, we are letting him go for now, to avoid antagonizing Wukong."

"That's reasonable. Though, I believe there is more to his story than we think… It's only a theory though… *I let slip to gain interest in this fable.*"

Odin strokes his beard once more. "Care to tell us?"

"First, the books…"

Odin crosses his arms in frustration at Thoth's persistence. "Is this obsession with these books truly for you to determine who's side we're on or are they for your own hunger for knowledge?"

"Perhaps… But you do not trust me with the knowledge of those books, and I do not trust you with any of my findings. Trust in one another is what separates good from evil, and order from chaos."

"Perhaps we can trade something else?" the Hindu monarch recommended.

"Hmm. As said prior, I do not want any of your profits. How about a question answered for me in return for one of yours? Just to show me a sign of trust, *I propose the solution to our problems.*"

"We will not tell you what the other book is about..." Odin said.

"I figured as much. Then how about this? Along with the resurrection of the human, I was drawn to something on Wukong... What is that crown on her head? *I ask, knowing they will most likely speak the answer in one way or another.*"

The Monarchs glanced at one another.

Joe stepped up to speak. "It's meant to keep us safe. That is all you need to know... Now, what is this theory you mentioned earlier?"

Thoth turned away from the Monarchs. "You go with a cliché vague answer? Then I shall be vague as well. My theory... is one of great importance for those involved, *I respond with my own inexplicit answer.*"

"You childish bird!" Odin shouted.

Thoth immediately stood up from his desk. "I do not fear the Monarchs, nor death. So, you can stay here and bicker with me, or you can leave me to my studies..."

Ratatoskr leaned close to Hermes. "I didn't know Thoth could be so serious. He hardly even narrated," she whispered.

Joe turned back to his fellow Monarchs and the Horsemen. "Come, let us take our leave."

"I will give you a warning though. As a sign of trust on my part, *I interrupt their exit.* If my theory is correct, I would recommend you continue leaving the human alone."

"You make him sound like a threat to us," Joe looked back to Thoth.

"Not him… Possibly Wukong… Possibly another…. Possibly not… It's a theory now, so it's full of possibilities... *I jest.*"

"So, what do you recommend?"

"Stop spying on them. I and the Messengers shall keep an eye on the duo."

"What? Why us?" Ratatoskr shouted.

"Because I need something unintimidating, *I say to the loud Ratatoskr.*"

"Screw you, bird!"

The Monarchs locked eyes at one another for a moment. Joe was the first to break the stare. "You and the Messengers are free to do as you wish, but my Horsemen will continue to watch from afar. Just in case."

"Not only them, *I interrupt the hooded god.* I hear your rival has made it into the Royale as well. So, he will be close to Wukong, correct?"

"My rival has nothing to do with the business of the New Pantheon."

Thoth sat back into his chair. "Perhaps it wouldn't be a good sight to have a Monarch conspiring with a Heretic, now would it?"

"… Of course not… Don't you trust us at least that much?"

"*I begin to write into my book, looking away from the Monarchs.* More of a benefit of the doubt… You may go. *I swat my hand, gesturing them to leave.*"

The Monarchs stared down Thoth as a light formed around them once more, eventually disappearing in the brightness.

Hermes and Ratatoskr approached Thoth as he wrote.

"What exactly do you want us to do?" Hermes questioned.

"If it's odd or surprising, tell me, *I inform the small Messenger of the plan.*"

"That's it?" Ratatoskr spoke.

"That's all we can do for now. Though, I will admit there is a high possibility my theory may be false, but you can never be too safe when it comes to such a theory…"

Hermes and Ratatoskr looked at each other, confused, before turning back to Thoth as he continued to write.

"What is your theory?" asked Hermes.

Thoth halted his writing, yet continued to look at the book. "It's the first step… toward something greater."

EPILOGUE TWO: FORGETTABLE DREAMS.

The sound of a heavenly hum wakes me from my sleep. I am met with the bright blue morning sky. Am I outside?

Despite the sky's appearance, it looks as though it's snowing, but the snowflakes, they're glowing in a pink aura, like little lights. They're falling gently toward me. I can feel the warmth from them as they fall on my body.

My body feels so relaxed… Is my head on a pillow? The sound of the beautiful humming, I hear it above me.

My eyes move in the direction of the sound, not only to find out who or what is humming, but also to see what my head is resting on.

It's the lap of a beautiful woman in a black suit and white tie. She has long white hair that covers her eyes from my view. All I see is the loving smile she gives me.

She herself sits under a rotting tree. It nearly ruins the lovely sight of the pink lights and her presence.

Her hand caresses my cheek gently. Her touch also brings up a warm feeling in me.

My gaze on this mysterious woman is ruined by the distraction of a sudden tickle on my nose. I think one of the falling lights is resting on my face.

I can't move my body or even wiggle my nose to try to shake it off.

The woman halts her angelic melody to let out a chuckle as her hand moves from my cheek to my nose, plucking the light from it. She holds it in my view so I can finally see what it is. A feather. A pink glowing feather.

I gaze back toward the sky where the lights have been falling. That's when I see them. They are all feathers, falling gently down to Earth.

She holds the feather before her lips and lets out a soft quiet blow, sending the feather away, back into the air. Her hand rubs my face again as the melody begins once more.

"Fallen bird. Please, don't cry. For with tearful eyes, the ground you'll lie. My fallen bird. Please don't hate. For with that in your heart, shall seal your fate. Feathers, falling from my wings. Glowing for my precious knight. No need to fear at all. Let us finally take flight. Alone, I know that you are. But with my wings, I won't be far. From our nest, we have been thrown. But together we won't be alone. Abandon by those who cherished us dear. Done so because of fear. Together, we will always be. I don't know if its destiny. Feathers, falling from my wings. Glowing for my precious knight. No need to fear at all. Let us finally take flight. My little bird. I'll help you fly. I know it's scary, a roll of the die. But I promise, together with me. Hand in hand. We'll both be free."

Her lyrics are beautiful and relaxing. She rubs my forehead as she hums the melody once more. I continue to watch her smiling lips.

The melody stops as her lips mouth something.

"Can you hear my words yet?" I make out. My body gains a bit of movement once again simply to nod no. She frowns at this news. *"We'll get there soon,"* her mouth moves. She moves her head closer to my face. Even now I can only see her mouth. *"Until then, my blessing."*

She continues to give me that caring look as she continues to rub my head. She moves her palm as her lips come closer to my forehead, kissing me...

I wake up in surprise. Not flailing or anything, simply with a loud inhale through my nose. I glance around at my surroundings.

It's night. I'm still in my RV. Susanoo and Momoko are sleeping on the floor. I hear Sun letting out a loud yawn from her bed.

"Mr. Knight?" Sun rubs her eyes as she checks on me. "What's wrong? A bad dream?"

As soon as she spoke, the memory of that weird dream fades from my mind. I can't remember anything about it, only that it was weird. Another forgettable dream, I guess.

"I don't know, Sun... Let's just go back to bed..."

The end...

ABOUT THE WRITER

William T. Kearney is a fan of anime and mythology who has a great team of creative talent to help him make this series a reality. Also, an amateur animator on the side who produces a satirical animated series on YouTube staring his mascots, Augustine the Crookedman and Bell the Crooked Catgirl. He and his collaborators hopes the series garners as much love as they put in.

Follow on:

YouTube: Crookedlore Productions

Facebook: Crookedlore

ABOUT THE EDITORS

Andres Perez and Zach Cole are experienced in the field of writing and editing. As each have their own series they proudly make.

Andres's mech action comic series "Primal Warrior Draco Azul" has just come out with its second issue as well.

Zach's ongoing "Jeremy Walker" series is a well-received urban fantasy thriller. He is currently putting together a comic adaptation of this series.

Follow on:

YouTube: KaijuNoir

Facebook: Primal Warrior Draco Azul

Facebook: Zach Cole- Author/Artist

ABOUT THE ARTIST

As a result of Denny Roth's unavailability, Banana Takemura took over as Book Two's artist with his unique and vibrant style. We're glad to have him on board and we look forward to seeing what else he will bring to the series.

Follow on:

Facebook: Banana Takemura

Up next: Book two character designs by Banana Takemura

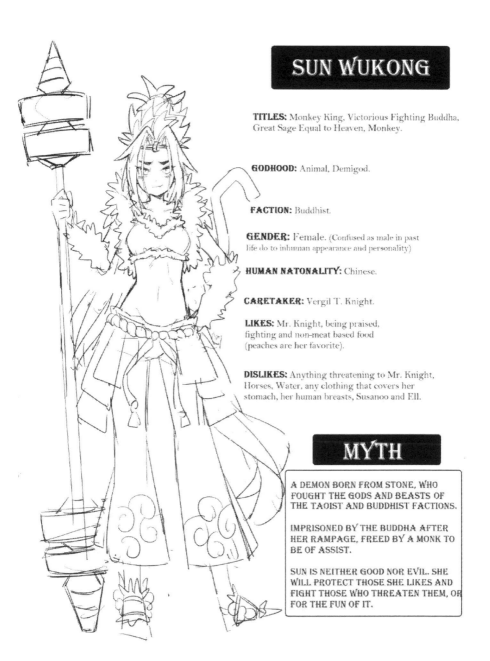

SUN WUKONG

TITLES: Monkey King, Victorious Fighting Buddha, Great Sage Equal to Heaven, Monkey.

GODHOOD: Animal, Demigod.

FACTION: Buddhist.

GENDER: Female. (Confused as male in past life do to inhuman appearance and personality)

HUMAN NATONALITY: Chinese.

CARETAKER: Vergil T. Knight.

LIKES: Mr. Knight, being praised, fighting and non-meat based food (peaches are her favorite).

DISLIKES: Anything threatening to Mr. Knight, Horses, Water, any clothing that covers her stomach, her human breasts, Susanoo and Ell.

MYTH

A DEMON BORN FROM STONE, WHO FOUGHT THE GODS AND BEASTS OF THE TAOIST AND BUDDHIST FACTIONS.

IMPRISONED BY THE BUDDHA AFTER HER RAMPAGE, FREED BY A MONK TO BE OF ASSIST.

SUN IS NEITHER GOOD NOR EVIL. SHE WILL PROTECT THOSE SHE LIKES AND FIGHT THOSE WHO THREATEN THEM, OR FOR THE FUN OF IT.

VERGIL T. KNIGHT

STATUES: Mytholoist.

NATONALITY: American.

AGE: 24.

CARETAKER FOR: Sun Wukong.

LIKES: Reading, the gods, classic films, being with Sun and Ell.

DISLIKES: The lack of modesty from Sun and Susanoo (though he secretly likes it), Sun getting injured, getting injured himself (particularly by Sun's affection), Ell forcing him into feminine outfits.

KNOWN ISSUES: Hemophilia, Injured knee.

SUSANOO   MOMOKO HIRATA

ELIZABETH "ELL" M. FALL

LOKI

LEONARDO RUSSO

BELLONA

RATATOSKR

HERMES

THOTH

JOE

VISHNU

ODIN

METATRON   MICHAEL

ABADDON

AZRAEL

Made in the USA
Middletown, DE
12 May 2022

65657827R00175